The Brotherhood

The SEAL Strike Series

Book Three

by

M. L. Strong

DEDICATION

To all the unsung heroes, to those who gave their all, their last full measure, for me, my children, and my children's children. A sacrifice in blood and pain, a sacrifice to keep us free. A sacrifice made on, and sometimes off, the battlefield.

Long Live the Brotherhood!

ISBN: 978-0-9994810-7-3

www.mlstrongauthor.com

Chapter One

The quart bottle of Maker's Mark skittered across the hardwood floor. The bottle's journey came to an abrupt end as it struck the old baseboard of the small bungalow with a loud bang. The bottle bounced a foot and slowly expended its energy, spinning slower and slower. Matthew Barrett clutched his toe, twisted a bit to the right, and then sat down hard on the old sofa. *Fucking bottle!*

He'd broken most of his toes at one time or another, but he'd never gotten used to the pain of striking one against a solid object. As he lay there rubbing the sore appendage, Matt vaguely remembered emptying the offending bottle just before passing out in the lawn chair that served as the second piece of furniture in his not-so-swanky fifteen-by-fifteen-foot living room. It was his fault for tossing the bottle onto the floor the night before, his fault for kicking it when he stood up. It was his fault. Always his fault.

He glanced at the alarm clock sitting on a makeshift end table. The construction was early hobo; he'd crafted the object by placing a piece of plywood on an upended cinder block. Functional, if not attractive. The clock told the tale. He'd forgotten to set the alarm the night before, and that meant he was going to be late for work.

Matt stood up and gingerly tested his ability to put weight on the toe. He'd survive. He limped a direct line to the closet-sized room that masqueraded as a bathroom and brushed his teeth; there was no time for a shower. Even if he got lucky maneuvering through the Key West morning traffic, he'd still be late. *Another day, another fuck up.*

He rinsed out his mouth and ran a hand through his long, blond hair. He needed a haircut; he'd needed a haircut for over two years now. The vagabond chic look fit in with the Key West vibe and gave people the impression he was an established local.

It wasn't true, but Matt didn't discourage that impression; the last thing he wanted to do was talk about his past.

It had been only two years since Matt was medically retired from the teams and set adrift. The primary purpose in his professional and personal life had been the brotherhood, an elite mix of comics, crazies, intellectuals, and ruthless critics who collectively represented the best fighters the Navy had to offer. His life had been unceremoniously destroyed with the casual stroke of a doctor's pen.

With all the hype and bullshit in the movies and on TV these days, he risked becoming a local celebrity if the word got out that he was once a SEAL. Then he'd have to move again. Matt poked at the grey streaks showing here and there on his tousled head, then reached over to the back of the toilet to retrieve his well-worn Seiko dive watch.

He was once blond and young. Younger anyway. At 37 he should be counting his blessings that he was even alive, but he knew age was a relative concept. At 35 he'd been an old man in the teams: broken, shot, and slower by a few steps than the other, much younger enlisted SEALs. Now he was… Matt placed the watch around his left wrist and checked the time again. *Why the hell haven't I sold this yet? I don't need a fucking dive watch anymore.*

The street outside his building was quiet, but he knew that wouldn't last. His Vespa fired up on the first try, a minor miracle he didn't take for granted. It was the perfect means of transportation in Key West, a bit hairy once he jumped out on Highway 1 heading north; but it got the job done and it was cheap. Matt pushed the sunglasses down from atop his head and pushed the kickstand back. One quick glance to the right and he was on his way. His boss was going to be royally pissed.

In Matt's opinion, Key West should be a candle scent. It always smelled like a mixture of rum, green living things, and the sea. His nostrils flared as he hit Highway 1 and opened the throttle. He loved this part of his day. No thinking or dwelling on the past, simply the road and the blue water on either side. The Vespa buzzed rather than roared as it tried to maintain the minimum speed, irritating the cars around him.

It took 35 minutes to travel north to the shuttle launch on Little Torch Key, and the trip was, as usual, too short. He pulled into the gravel parking lot and eased to a stop in a spot dedicated to employees. A quick check told him he was 15 minutes late. Matt limped into the unattractive building that served as the Little Palm Island reception area.

Little Palm was a resort famous for its exclusivity and fanatic adherence to a no electronics policy. Guests stayed in five-star quality tree houses that ringed the perimeter of the property, all with views of the water. Matt had never been inside one of the tree houses. His job was simple: operate the shuttle boat that took the guests to the island and return with the guests who were checking out. As Matt passed through the office space and onto the dock, he spotted his boss, Carl, glaring at him.

Carl was a tool, a grade-A dork. His father inherited the business of managing the island and the shuttle service, then put his dumb ass son in charge so the lazy shit would have an income. The island itself was privately owned and had once been the winter sanctuary of none other than President Truman. Carl was fat, stupid, and right now he was pissed.

"Where the fuck have you been? I called your cell phone and your fucking voice mail is full. Don't you realize our guests have been sitting here waiting for your dumb ass?"

Matt calmly suffered through the indignity. Carl wasn't worth losing his job. If the little shit had half a clue about who Matt was, or had been, he'd piss his pants. Matt took comfort in that thought. He turned toward Carl and grinned as nonchalantly as he could.

“I’m sorry. My scooter got a flat. Couldn’t be helped.” Matt maintained his grin, waiting for Carl’s response. Typically, Carl backed off from these routine engagements.

“Whatever, old man. I don’t want any excuses. Get your sorry ass onto the shuttle and take those people to the resort. We can talk about your future when you get back!”

Matt lowered his head a little and broke eye contact with Carl. He didn’t need to respond. He been in this situation multiple times since getting kicked out of the Navy two years earlier. He’d once been a decorated hero, an officer and a gentleman. The son of a Medal of Honor recipient, used to praise and adulation. Now he was just a guy trying to make rent. He liked this job though; he hoped Carl was only posturing.

The shuttle was a shallow draft launch that could carry ten passengers safely. It was painted a deep blue, a blue that blended aesthetically with the calm water. Matt stepped onto the narrow deck and eased painfully into the cockpit of the shuttle. He looked over his shoulder to ensure his passengers were seated, then watched as Carl and another employee tossed the lines into the boat with a wave.

He eased the throttle forward slowly, turning in a lazy arch to the right until he was clear of the other shuttle and the dock. He waved back at Carl, happy to leave the jerk behind. He’d driven all manner of vessels during his career: rubber boats, kayaks, speed boats, even mini-submarines. So being the skipper of a tourist shuttle was a piece a cake. It wasn’t fancy and it wasn’t fast, but it was elegant in its own peculiar way. Matt loved his job.

Twenty-five minutes later, Matt throttled back and goosed the engines until the shuttle, little by little, was nestled up against the long pier. Two men stood by on the pier to toss lines across the shuttle. Matt shut the engines down and took the bow line to the forward cleat and secured the line in place. One of the men on the pier jumped into the back of the shuttle and secured the stern line to the aft cleat.

Matt didn't have to say a word. A third man appeared, who greeted the guests and welcomed them to paradise. The passengers climbed up on the pier and followed their newfound friend as Matt and the other two men waited.

"We have anybody going back?" Matt asked.

"The day manager and the assistant chef are going to the mainland," one of the men answered. "It should be an hour or so before they are ready to leave."

Matt grunted to indicate he understood. He wasn't allowed on the island. The hired help might spoil the serenity of the resort if they were spotted roaming about. Matt didn't give a shit. He loved reclining on the boat, the bright sun warming his face and the gentle movement of the small vessel lulling him to sleep. He was afforded this little pleasure from time to time. Normally the return trip passengers were ready to go, so this was a treat.

Matt slipped in and out of consciousness. He never dreamed during the day. His mind remained mercifully blank, unlike the night when his dreams tormented him with replays of missions that went terribly wrong. It was always the same type of dream, even if the backdrop changed from urban fighting to combat in the desert or the jungle. The plot was consistent though: Matt's decision got a teammate killed, and he was powerless to do anything but watch. Night after night. Initially he'd thought the drinking would help. He was wrong. Drinking only turned him into a drunk; the dreams were always waiting for him.

The sound of people talking, getting closer and closer, disrupted his serenity. His passengers had arrived, and it was time to go to work. The ride back went quickly, and the two men in the boat knew better than to engage him in idle chitchat. Matt was a rough-looking character, and he still knew how to communicate by using his eyes alone. And they conveyed *leave me alone*.

Carl was gone when Matt finished tying up the shuttle, and that suited him fine. He was on call until early afternoon, so he could hang around the reception area or go somewhere else. He decided he was hungry. Funny how he never felt hungry, he just decided to eat. He walked out to the parking lot and fired up the Vespa. It was only a mile or so north to Kiki's Sandbar, a quaint little hole-in-the-wall that catered to tourists wandering far beyond the confines of Key West and travelers moving up and down Highway 1.

Kiki's was pleasant, and he casually ate a light lunch, then milked a few beers until his shift ended. Matt stopped drinking and went to the restroom to clean himself up. He looked at himself in the mirror and saw an old man staring back. He was only 37. The years of stress had aged him, but it was the booze that had done most of the damage. A two-year binge will do that.

Matt washed his face and slicked back his hair, trying to look more presentable. As he left the small eatery, he stepped down to the pavement and felt a piercing bolt of pain shoot up his right leg. He stopped mid-stride and bent over, holding his breath and gritting his teeth until the waves of pain subsided. The Taliban bullet had really messed up the nerves in that leg. The extensive debriding of the wound by the Navy doctors hadn't helped matters.

Matt wiped the involuntarily tears from his eyes as he stood up. He was a hot fucking mess. If it wasn't the leg, then it was something else. There was a time he'd yearned for combat, a chance to prove to his brother SEALs that he measured up to their standards, standards established by Navy special operations warriors going back to World War Two.

There weren't enough SEALs to go around after 9/11, and the next decade-plus of continuous war saw the few that did exist sent into combat, over and over again. Matt's naïve dream of confirming his worth had been satisfied and then some. He had thirteen combat tours of personal and professional validation, and the physical and mental scars to prove it.

The ride home took forever; and when he finally pulled in alongside his place, Matt was ready to go to bed. The cycle of his life these days was uncomplicated. No friends, no love interests. He woke up, went to work, came home, fell into a deep sleep until the early hours of the next day, and began drinking, always the drinking.

Once in awhile, when he was feeling more decisive than usual, Matt would take his 9mm handgun out from under the torn couch where he stored it and place the weapon on the table in front of him. He would stare for hours at the fine tooling, the exquisite design, marveling at the technology that had replaced knives and spears.

He never quite mustered up enough courage to use the gun; but in his heart, he knew that moment was out there, waiting for him. Someday he would do the right thing and end his miserable existence. End the pain.

Matt went up to his bungalow and kicked the pile of mail further out of the way so he could get the door to swing open. He hadn't read mail in a long time. You had to give a shit, focus on what everybody else thought was important. That was bullshit. Nothing was important anymore.

However, he deviated from his normal routine to deal with the smell that hit him as he stepped into the room. He was amazed his neighbors weren't up his ass about the stench. Matt rotated his head, first one way and then the opposite way, loosening up his neck as if preparing for a fight. Time to clean his man cave!

It took Matt two hours to clean every room, Navy style. His trash filled up and then spilled over the receptacle outside the building. *The neighbors are going to love that,* he thought, smirking. He didn't have cleaning solvent of any kind so he improvised and used hot water. The carpets were the last thing to clean before he finally finished and plopped down on the couch.

Maybe he should start looking for another job, he mused. Carl was getting more irritated each day, and he knew that eventually that asshole would summon up the courage to can him. He needed to work. The Navy disability pay was always there for him, but that was how he paid for the rent and utilities. He drank whatever was left.

He knew he had an iPad somewhere in the place, but it probably wasn't charged. He got back up and began to search the bungalow more thoroughly. He found his smart phone first, and placed it in his pocket. He kept looking until he found the iPad under his bed, wedged under a shoebox containing his military awards and various warfighter insignia. He ignored the shoebox and pulled the iPad out.

The kitchen still stank a little, but Matt's efforts to clean the refrigerator and the sink were paying off. He scanned the room until he spotted two charging lines dangling from the wall next to a toaster that he knew for a fact didn't work. Without thinking about it, he plugged in the iPad and the smart phone. He was out of Maker's Mark.

He was tired. He'd missed his usual window for napping, and he didn't feel like going the ten blocks to the liquor store to get resupplied. Matt returned to the room with the couch and sat down. It was seven in the evening. He curled up and pulled down an old afghan blanket to cover his head; it helped block out the street sounds. He'd go to the liquor store tomorrow.

Chapter Two

The screeching brakes of a delivery truck outside on the street shook Matt rudely awake from his deep sleep. He lay there for ten minutes looking at the sun's rays filtering into his bungalow and dancing across the various objects scattered about the room. He knew instinctively that something was different. Matt swung his feet out and onto the carpeted floor. One look at his dive watch spoke volumes. *Shit!* He'd handed Carl his justification to fire him.

He was twenty minutes late. Add the transit time, and he'd miss the first shuttle run to Little Palm Island completely. Matt sighed and leaned back. He was starving. First things first. Eat, get cleaned up, and check the iPad for job openings. The sound of little claws scratching across the kitchen floor nearby sent a pang of guilt through him. Steve probably didn't need to be fed by a human, but Matt had adopted the little guy as a pet. Or was it the other way around? His little companion never complained. He never judged Matt's behavior, and that was why Matt considered him more than a pet. The green iguana was Matt's only true friend.

After a quick change of clothes and a Navy shower, consisting of a splash of cold water on his face, Matt headed for the front door. The thought suddenly occurred to him that taking his iPad along would allow him to search for jobs while he ate his food. Matt turned around and went back into the kitchen to retrieve his tablet, and as he did so he noticed the smart phone laying there, now fully charged. Absentmindedly, he grabbed the phone and dropped it into the right cargo pocket of his bright yellow shorts. It was time for Momma's.

The walk was short, only six blocks. Mornings in Key West were magical. Quiet, mildly warm, and colorful. It was a special time of the day when there was just enough sunlight to splash vibrant color everywhere, but not too much. Matt felt sluggish and less alert than normal. He knew why. It was his body reminding him that he needed to swing by the liquor store on the way back.

Momma's was a local favorite. Established in 1938 by a retired Jamaican cook, the little building had seen tens of thousands of patrons pass through its rusty doors. Matt loved the place because it was simple and cozy, a place that felt to Matt like a nest or burrow. You could see everything, identify anyone who walked into the restaurant, be safe. Besides, the food was good. He pushed through the outer screen door and was happy to see that his favorite table was free.

The scooching of his chair caught the attention of the one waitress servicing the patrons. She looked back over her shoulder and smiled. "Good morning, sunshine! You're in awfully late, I see."

Rhonda was a refugee from life just like Matt. She was a bit heavy now, but Matt knew her background. A former Miss Detroit, she'd started life successful and happy. Then the party scene and bad choices pulled her down into the seedy world of drugs and, eventually, the executive escort business.

Her movie star looks and sultry body paid off, selling herself for sex provided all the money she needed and more; but the more she made, the more she spent. Snorting most of her earnings up her nose. It was inevitable that her behavior would catch up with her. Arrested three times, once for prostitution and twice for possession of narcotics, she still didn't stop the madness. So, when the court took her young daughter from her, it only made things worse.

Matt knew the story. Rhonda hit rock bottom at age 30 and then left Detroit and all the bad memories behind. For seven years since arriving in Key West, Rhonda had been clean and sober, her daughter a fading memory. Matt calculated that the girl would be 19 now. Rhonda's story was one of struggle, loss, and finally, recovery. She was a deep soul who'd found peace with the universe in her own way.

"Early is a relative concept," he tossed back.

Rhonda stopped and took a long look at her customer. "Why, Matthew Barrett, did I detect a sign of intelligence in those snarky words? You usually communicate with grunts and snorts. I may not be able to handle this new and improved version."

Before he could stop himself, Matt grunted. He felt sharper. Could one night of sobriety make that much of a difference?

"Now there's the man I know and love. The usual?"

Matt nodded and ended the conversation by rudely opening his iPad. Rhonda was used to rude people, and she turned back to yell out Matt's order to the cook.

"Four eggs, scrambled with cheddar. Two linked sausages and a side of wheat toast!"

Matt never deviated. The only real meal he usually sat down to eat was breakfast. He loved breakfast. It reminded him of his mother, Grace Barrett. She was loving and pleasant, and the thought of her made him feel warm inside, but only for a moment. The thought of her smiling face inevitably led to thoughts of his overbearing father.

Arthur Barrett had been a man's man, a United States Marine. His personality had been larger than life; it filled every room he walked into, and he was a stickler for execution. In some ways, the crucible of Matt's childhood forged the young man capable of surviving the world's toughest commando course. He was old enough now to acknowledge his father's part in that personal achievement. It hadn't always been the case.

He began his search for job openings in the Florida Keys. If he had to buy a real car to travel north further than Little Key, he'd do it; but he'd much rather use the scooter. The pickings were slim on the job boards, but this was only one resource to find employment. Everybody who lived in the Keys knew jobs were at a premium; they popped up quick and disappeared even quicker. If a position was still posted after a few days, there was invariably something wrong: low pay, shitty hours, maybe the commute. Matt cut and pasted the information for three possible opportunities and closed his iPad.

As if on cue, Rhonda placed his breakfast on the table, leaning over as she did so. Her ample breasts nearly tumbled out of her loose blouse; Matt didn't notice. His eyes were focused on the plate of food. The smell reminded him of how hungry he was. "Thanks, Rhonda. I see you had the cook add an extra sausage."

"Nothing but the best for my customers! You trolling social media for a date?" Rhonda leaned back and placed her hands on her hips.

Matt blurted out a short laugh, then stifled it. Rhonda stepped back in feigned surprise and placed her hand on her chest. "My God! I do believe that is the first time in two years I've ever heard you laugh. Are you sick or something?"

Matt had tried to cut off the response to her funny question, but the impulse to laugh was just that, an impulse. "I don't quite know, Rhonda. I ran out of booze yesterday and was too tired to go out and get some more. I guess last night was the best night's sleep I've had in a long time."

Rhonda's eyes teared up a bit as she listened. She knew enough of Matt's story to be happy for this one small thing. Matt was a bit embarrassed by her emotional reaction, so he tried to reset the mood.

"No, I'm looking for a job not a girlfriend. If you hear of anything, let me know."

Rhonda got the message. He was throwing the wall up again. "Okay, sweetie. I'll ask around discretely."

"Thanks. I appreciate it." Matt watched her walk over to a table where a couple had just sat down. He looked down at his breakfast. Next stop, Hudson's Liquor Barn.

Two days later, Matt was sunning himself on a bench. He often rode over to Naval Air Station Boca Chica to watch the planes and helicopters work their flight patterns. The incredible professionalism of the aircrews he worked with and the stimulating experiences flying in all manner of military airframes reignited a high school fantasy to become a fighter pilot, but life had taken him in a different direction.

His fleeting dream to fly was a victim of politics from a period just before he entered the Navy. In the timeframe between Bill Clinton's election in 1992 and the end of his second term in office in 2000, his administration pursued a policy that broadly decimated units of the armed forces and bit deeply into other military capabilities, too.

Nearly 400,000 infantry positions were eliminated to downsize the Army in the years leading up to 2000. Fighter wings in the Air Force and Navy were reduced in numbers; pilots were offered exit packages, as were the officers in special operations. Training dollars were cut and fuel usage curtailed, limiting training hours for the aviation crews that remained in the service.

This "Peace Dividend" policy recognized a new world order. One of peace and prosperity. One without global super power struggles and proxy wars fought between competing ideologies. Then less than two years later, the folly of this policy was clear. America was at war, and she wasn't ready for the extended nature of the struggle that lay ahead.

So, as the great war on terror began its two-decade effort to eradicate radical, religious extremism around the globe, the US military found itself relying on former servicemen and women in the role of contractors. At the same time, it was clear to military planners that there was one unit that was least affected by the late nineties draw down: US Special Operations Command.

Matt was oblivious to all the history, the causes leading to the effects. The Navy wasn't interested in adding new pilots, so he was content to push for the SEAL teams and even happier to make the cut. He, like every young SEAL, had wanted to prove his abilities and his courage where it counted--in combat. He eventually was able to achieve this goal; but as his combat tours added up, he became acutely aware of the two policy-driven consequences of the Peace Dividend.

The first consequence was an overreliance on special operations forces to execute common infantry missions. SEALs special forces, Rangers, and a whole host of other special units were deployed and employed with dizzying rapidity in Iraq, Afghanistan, the Horn of Africa, the Philippines, and in northern Syria.

This policy saved lives. Special operators were older, more experienced, more technically trained, and better equipped. They were more likely to fight and win on the battlefield than regular forces were. Fewer casualties always was politically attractive, so they kept sending the best. Wearing them down. Breaking the men and eventually entire units.

The second consequence was related to manpower. The entire special operations command was organized to support episodic missions, special tasks of limited duration. The personnel structure was designed accordingly. The groups were small: tiny woven and integrated families of specialists. SEALs were the maritime option; but since the attack happened in New York, they'd been fighting in the sandbox, right alongside their Army counterparts.

When the global war on terror began, the Pentagon realized they were 350 SEALs short of the projected demand. Recruiting kicked into high gear, millions were spent, and special preparation courses were established to get SEAL candidates ready for the crucible of BUD/S training. It didn't work. There were only so many willing volunteers; and of those that made it to the SEAL basic course, seventy-five percent quit or were dropped, consistent with historical norms.

As a result, SEALs deployed, and deployed, and deployed. After ten years, it wasn't uncommon for operators, Matt's teammates, to have more than fifteen back-to-back combat tours. Without replacements or sufficient numbers to rotate the men in a sane and compassionate manner, the SEAL operators grew older and the years added up.

By 2010, a third of the community had twenty years of service, a milestone that traditionally meant retirement. Bonuses to extend careers and emotional pleas not leave their brothers or the fight were employed by the leaders, and it worked for a time. Then the totality of the damage became too much for anyone to fix.

Large numbers of SEALs were medically discharged for multiple combat injuries and wounds. First it was a trickle, then a torrent of cases. Mental breakdowns increasingly were caused by the stress, mostly from splitting loyalty and time between family and the SEAL brotherhood. An impossible choice. Suicides, divorces, operation after operation to repair broken bodies, head trauma clinics, experimental programs to fight PTSD . . . the glamor was gone. It was America's longest time of martial conflict, and the special operators were tired and broken.

The idea of flying private or otherwise remained just that, an idea. Matt never had the time to pursue any personal, selfish goal. No hobbies, no time for a family, and no desire to watch a family disintegrate as they watched him leave over and over again, perhaps never to return.

Matt's eyes snapped open. The loud throaty roar of an F-18 Hornet signaled it was time to pay attention. A Navy reserve unit was orbiting off the shoreline, taking turns landing and taking off. They executed what was referred to as a touch and go, a simulated emergency procedure, should a pilot not be able to snag the plane's tail hook on the ship's arresting wires. Matt liked this training because it was all power and noise, a free display of naval air power.

Twenty minutes later, it was all over. Matt felt his nose burning and decided he'd had enough sun time. He hopped on his trusty Vespa and took it across town to a place called Stoney's. Stoney's was a new restaurant, and their signature sandwich was the Rueben. Matt loved Rueben sandwiches. The business seemed to be surviving. Sitting across from Sloppy Joe's, the iconic Key West bar made famous through Ernest Hemingway's patronage, provided Stoney's with lots of free exposure. The food was great, too.

Matt slapped the kickstand down with his foot and paused to look at his surroundings. He couldn't shake old habits. Situational awareness was drilled into every SEAL operator. Pay attention; the environment was communicating to you in subtle and passive ways. Safe or threat. The street was mildly chaotic. At night this place will be thriving, Matt knew. Sloppy's always pulled in the tourists and the local drinkers.

He turned and took a step toward the restaurant. The vibration in his pocket confused him for a moment until he realized that he'd brought his phone with him today. Matt had only checked off two jobs online, and he couldn't believe anyone was calling him this fast. Maybe this was good news! He pulled the smart phone out and answered.

"Hello. Barrett here."

"Hi, handsome!" Rhonda's voice was unmistakable.

"Glad you think so. What's up?" Matt felt let down.

“I put feelers out after you left this morning, and I have something that might interest you. It’s a private protection thing. My friend Judy is dating a high-tech guy who is making waves, in a good way. He’s concerned his ideas are going to be stolen. He told her he was even afraid for his life. I suggested he might need a bodyguard a few days ago. Anyway, I called her this morning, and he wants to meet you. Interested?”

Matt’s shoulders dropped. He’d expected Rhonda to have a real job for him. He had no interest in babysitting a weak, millennial, metrosexual geek with paranoid delusions.

“Thanks for thinking of me, Rhonda, but I don’t want to be a guard.”

“It pays really well. Judy said you could almost ask anything, and this guy would agree. Why not give it a shot?”

Matt didn’t want to offend Rhonda. She was being a friend and trying to help. “I’m familiar with what the job entails. It’s a 24/7 gig, less security protection than personal assistant. Laundry pickup, fuel the car, buy a gift for their wife, and so on. You’re a good friend and I appreciate the thought, but I’m not their guy. I’ve gotta go.”

Matt hung up and walked into Stoney’s. The waitresses all knew him by sight. No menus were needed; he never deviated from his special lunch. He placed his smart phone on the table, and just before the screen dimmed out, he noted he had five text messages. Odd.

He let the phone go black and spent the next few minutes studying the cast of characters sharing the space with him. Six patrons total: two by the front and four in the back. One empty seat meant someone in the party was using the restroom. Once comfortable, he relaxed and looked at his phone again. Who the hell would be texting him?

Chapter Three

The Rueben smelled incredible, like all the smells of everything good combined into one overstuffed stack of edible pleasure. He ate in silence, enjoying the moment. The thought this might be the last time he could afford to eat in a restaurant flashed through his mind. *Fuck it! Job or no job, I can survive on ramen noodles and Maker's Mark.*

He hesitated, just for a moment, before swallowing the last bite. Why should a sandwich make life feel so tolerable, good even? Matt swallowed and followed it up with a long drink of water. He wiped his hands to remove the grease and stared at his phone.

The caller ID identified the persistent offender as Tom Burnell. Matt knew that name, but it didn't make sense. He hadn't worked with Tom since 2015, right before Tom lost his leg in an IED explosion near Kandahar, Afghanistan. They'd been in the same joint task unit together, but Matt was the operations officer and Tom was an operator in a SEAL troop. Their paths crossed from time to time in the old dusty building, used to store supplies and miscellaneous shit, that the team guys used as a gym.

Like most SEALs, Tom was a driven warrior type. Less cerebral than most, kind of a rowdy, loose-cannon personality. He was plenty smart. He just enjoyed projecting the cowboy persona, the sort of guy who wore T-shirts with sayings like, Ride for the Brand, and Cowboy Up. The IED had killed two Rangers and maimed a total of six operators. Tom's injuries also caused paralysis, affecting the use of his remaining leg.

As he sat there ignoring the bill laying near his right hand, Matt remembered the event in excruciating detail. The frantic radio calls from the predator operations officer who'd witnessed the explosion in real time. Updates filled with emotion and weak on facts. It was the man's first time in-country and it showed.

Then the calm, steady voice of the troop commander calling the special operations combat center on the SAT radio. Details, names, injuries, and a request for casualty evacuation assistance for six WIAs and recovery of two KIAs. His voice was monotone, his pace professional. A veteran.

The chain of events followed standard operating procedures. SOPs practicing all too frequently in the sandbox. The wounded were flown back to Kandahar to be patched up or stabilized for the long trip to Landstuhl, Germany, where the serious cases were taken. That's where Tom went along with two other wounded men.

Matt had lost track of Tom's progress a year or so after the incident. His time in Afghanistan ended three months later; and by then Tom was in Bethesda, Maryland, recovering from double amputation surgery. He had a family, but Matt didn't recall if he'd had kids. *Tom Burnell, why are you reaching out to me?*

Matt struggled. If he read the messages, he knew what would happen. The floodgates might fly open, releasing memories. Memories he'd tried to forget and repress, mostly through sheer force of will and a bottle of Maker's. It's why he stayed isolated from his past; it wasn't worth the pain.

Tom pulled a twenty out of his pocket and put it on top of the bill. It was the last of his cash, and he'd been afraid to go to the ATM to get more. If he didn't see the balance, he could go on pretending he was doing all right. He stood up, grabbed the smart phone, and stuffed it into his board shorts. As he left, he gave a second thought to the idea of being an executive protection guy.

If he didn't find a job, he'd be forced to compromise his dislike for that type of work.

Steve had a nasty habit of jumping up on the coffee table. He was there now, one eye staring at Matt and the other eye watching the kitchen. The square glass of Maker's Mark was sitting untouched within inches of the green iguana. Matt had been lost in thought for over an hour, pondering his life, his fate, and now Steve.

Steve didn't judge Matt's behavior night after night; he was simply an observer. A guardian angel or a demon, unwilling to intervene, but more than happy to watch the shit show that was his life. He couldn't stop coming back around to Tom Burnell. The texts were so random, as bizarre as if they'd been from a tribal chief in Kenya: *Hey Matt, how's it hanging*?

He'd left his smart phone in the bedroom, hadn't yet read the messages. Every time he mustered up the nerve to walk in there and discover the meaning of the mystery, his courage failed him and he sank back into the abyss. Oddly, the ordeal hadn't yet compelled him to drink. The square glass sat where he'd placed it two hours earlier, untouched.

The Maker's Mark began to speak to him. It was lonely, it missed him. Why had he ignored his nighttime pal? He knew the square glass was right. He knew where the comfort of oblivion could be found. For two years, it hadn't let him down, not once. Matt bent forward and reached for the drink. Steve backed up a few steps then turned and leaped off the table and onto the floor. He wiggled his way at unusual speed into Matt's bedroom. The phone.

If Steve was a demon or an angel, the message was clear: follow me. Matt dropped his arm and stood up. This was going to rattle around in his head until he found out what Tom wanted. Then he could return to his routine. He walked across the room and flicked on the light as he entered his small nine-by-nine-foot bedroom. He ran his hands through his grey-blond hair and let the air bleed out through pursed lips.

"Fuck it!" he said out loud. Steve bobbed his head up and down. He agreed. Fuck it!

Matt went to the stool at the side of his bed that served as a nightstand and picked up the smart phone. There were two more messages. Matt's gut told him something must be very wrong in Tom's world, unless this wasn't about Tom. Had one of Matt's old teammates died? Oby or Boone? He scrolled down the texts to the first one, dated five days earlier, and began to read.

It was all about Tom. He was living in Grosse Pointe, Michigan, in his parent's original home. They'd passed away in a car crash in 2016 and left their home to their only son. He'd been married, Matt remembered that much, but the whole thing went sideways after his return from Afghanistan. He went on to say it was as much his fault as hers, Barbara was her name. She couldn't handle Tom as a victim, an empty soul. They separated and then divorced.

Matt was two texts into the narrative and still didn't know why he was the beneficiary of this tale. He hesitated. Was there bad news coming? He took a deep breath and continued reading. Tom and Barbara had one thing in common; they both adored their daughter, Victoria. Vicky was smart, athletic, and focused. *A chip off the old block,* Matt thought to himself. Tall for her age at five foot eight with raven black hair, usually worn in a pony tail. Easy to spot in a crowd. *Where is he going with this?*

By text four, Matt finally learned the reason behind the outreach. Vicky was vacationing with her mom in Hawaii four weeks ago, and Barbara lost her. One minute, Vicky left her mom at the hotel and went to Waikiki's International Market Place alone to shop; the next she was gone. It was nighttime; and the two were enjoying the market's jungle feel, tree limbs interwoven overhead, tiki lights, and fun music everywhere. Vicky went to the public restroom while her mom waited outside, focused on a pretty string of puka shells. That was the last time Vicky was seen by anyone.

Matt stopped reading. It didn't make sense; but then again, his instincts were screaming foul play. If this teenager was as smart as Tom said she was, she wouldn't get lost; or if she had, she would've gone straight to a cop for help. Tom's last three texts explained how he'd attempted to get the Honolulu police to find his daughter and their theory.

Matt read this part twice. The police believed Vicky was snatched against her will by human traffickers. People looking for girls her age with her look, first to hold and then to sell on the local or international black market set up for such things. Matt was engaged despite his desire to remain detached.

Tom was unable to travel to Hawaii. He was pleading for Matt's help. The police said the window to find Vicky on the island was small, a mere two weeks at most before she would be removed, likely by boat, and transported to somewhere else in the Pacific. She would be sold there or moved again to the more lucrative markets in Asia and or the middle east, and there she would be sold as a sex slave.

Matt reread all the texts again, looking for anything he might have missed. He wasn't in shape for this shit. It had been two years since he'd been squared away enough to do anything. Tom was barking up the wrong tree. He couldn't help.

Matt lay back on his bed and closed his eyes. The texts swirled around in his head, words and meaning jumbling together then reorganizing into the dramatic story and request for help over and over again. Matt's breathing became heavy and he drifted off to sleep. Steve watched over his friend for a while then wiggled back into the living room on his way to the kitchen. The square glass full of Maker's Mark sat alone on the coffee table.

The sunlight poured into the living room as Matt shuffled through and into the kitchen. If he didn't get a job soon, he'd be forced to draw down his savings. He cranked up the coffee maker and listened, rubbing his eyes as the machine made industrial sounds, the noisy process of creating his second favorite drink.

He wasn't worried about money; he'd been living small for two years. His retirement and disability payments kept coming; and since they were directly deposited into his account, he had no idea how much had piled up. His decision to move to Key West wasn't thought out too well, but he knew a warm place would be cheaper.

He loved the water and thought he'd become a SCUBA instructor, work doing something he loved. But he was fired from one and then two dive shops after coming into work reeking of booze. The word spread quickly in the small tight-knit community; the role of SCUBA instructor was no longer an option.

That led to the boating industry. He was at home most places he worked. Boat crews were a transient lot, and like him, most had a story to tell. A few were drifters, others on the run from something or someone. A few were even vets like him. It felt like a dysfunctional family to Matt. The gig at Little Palm Island was his third boat company job. *I don't want to be a fucking guard!*

He sat down with his cup of coffee and tried to keep the text messages away from his conscious mind, pushing them back into a special place where he kept his old life safely tucked away in a nook. As long as it stayed dormant, hidden, he wouldn't have to face the stark contrast between the two Matts, one a hero-warrior and the other a boat-driving drunk.

It wasn't working. He decided to give into the pressure and think about Tom Burnell and his young teenage daughter, Vicky. Without the personal experience of being a father, Matt could only guess at the anguish his fellow frogman was enduring.

He instinctively realized the worst part for Tom would be the inability to strike out, to act on his own physically, to find and save his child. But why did he choose Matt? Did all his other friends, family, and former teammates say no? Was Matt his last hope? He was sure that was the case. The scuttlebutt in the community would be cruel yet accurate. *Matt Barrett, Mr. Navy Cross, is a loser. Don't count on that guy; he's a washed-up has-been, a drunk.*

His self-loathing aside, even if he was Tom's last choice, he couldn't ignore the plea for help. At a minimum he could call him, hear the details. Maybe Matt could offer sage advice or connect him with a professional who was better equipped to assist Tom.

Matt stood up and went to the kitchen counter. He disconnected the smart phone and found the second text, the one with Tom's contact number. He lived in Michigan. What was the time difference? Matt was suddenly hungry. After breakfast, he'd make the call and see what he could do.

He took the time to shave and take a shower, a rare cleanup exercise that he did unconsciously. He rummaged through his drawers trying to find something that was clean and not terribly wrinkled. *Why do I suddenly give a shit about the way I look?*

It was Rhonda's day off, and Matt was glad. He felt guilty turning down her job lead. He knew she wouldn't care and certainly wouldn't hold a grudge, but it still felt rude of him to say no. Matt finished his breakfast and walked outside. He felt the phone in his pocket. Not now, not yet.

The Vespa sputtered to life, and he rolled away from the restaurant. A coastal ride might be just the thing. He was delaying the act of calling Tom, and he was painfully aware he was losing confidence. His drive to remain disconnected for so long was struggling with a deeper sense of responsibility. He wasn't sure which would win out, so he procrastinated.

Six miles north of Key West, there was a scenic parking spot. Matt pulled into this and shut off the scooter. He looked around and saw nothing but beautiful clear water. The occasional car or truck zipped by, but he didn't pay attention.

Matt pulled the smart phone out and stared at it for a full five minutes. He was taking a big step backward, into his past. Did he want another SEAL relying on his judgment again? He pressed the phone number and the hyperlink dialed the call immediately.

The phone was answered and there was a long pause. "Hello. Who is this?"

Matt felt like throwing up. He fought the impulse to toss the phone over the guard railing and into the ocean. “Tom, it’s me. Matt Barrett.”

Chapter Four

Matt realized he was shaking. It was a panic attack, or at least he thought it might be. He'd never experienced one before. He took a deep breath, inhaling through his nose and then exhaling slowly through his mouth. He relaxed his grip on the smart phone.

"Tom, are you there?"

"Didn't think you were getting my texts," the voice answered back. "Where the fuck are you?"

Matt relaxed a little bit more. Tom's voice was barely recognizable, but the smart-ass team guy tone was like music to his ears.

"I ran away to Key West. Quit life and hid down here so I could eat fish and drink myself to sleep every night without being hassled by stupid people." There was a long pause. Did Tom regret reaching out to a washed-up old drunk? How reliable could Matt possibly be?

"Yeah, I did that for a while, too. Hid in plain sight. Drove my friends and my family away so they couldn't stop me from destroying myself. Happy to hear there are no stupid people down in Key West. I don't remember you as much of a drinker though. New habit?"

Matt grunted. "Yeah, two years now. I didn't have any family to run away from, except my mom, but she isn't a problem. I just don't want her to …"

"See what you've become?" Tom finished the sentence.

Matt's jaws tightened and then relaxed. "Yeah, something like that."

Tom got to the point. "Matt, I need help. My daughter, she …"

Matt thought he heard what sounded like muffled sobbing on the other end of the phone. There was a long pause, and Matt wasn't sure what to say. Deep inside he was feeling something, an old urge to fight, to help his teammate. In that moment, he was pretty sure knew what he was going to do.

"Tom, send me your address. I'm in between jobs right now, so it'll be easy to break away and fly up there. I'll help you as much as I can, but I'm a little rusty. Sound like a plan?"

The sobbing subsided and Matt again waited a respectful period of time before Tom responded. "Thanks, Matt. That's more than I expected, but having you here will be a big help. Thanks."

"What are brothers for?" Matt ended the call. He needed to get some shit together.

Grosse Pointe, Michigan, was a sanctuary of wealth and privilege floating in a sea of low-income housing built in the mid-1960s as a government solution for poverty. All the gesture did was create a worse form of poverty. Drugs, violence, and decay culminated in race riots, fire, destruction, and in the end, permanent hopelessness.

Matt watched the new normal flash by as his Uber driver wove in and out of traffic. Tom lived on the southwest corner of Grosse Pointe. He'd explained that his home, his parents' home, wasn't a mini-mansion and certainly wasn't as grandiose as the homes lining Lake Drive, homes built by men who helped change the world, men like Ford and Dodge.

Matt saw the trees, oddly green and full after so much grey since leaving the airport. A right turn, past a small gas station, and fifteen houses later, he arrived. Matt watched the Uber drive away, then studied his surroundings. Tom had been accurate in his description.

The one-story brick home in front of him was tidy, moderate, and not unremarkable. The homes behind him though, were an impressive collection of 4,000- to 6,000-square-foot buildings. Not the mini-mansions coveted by so many baby boomers over the years; these homes were stately works of early twentieth century architecture.

Tom had instructed Matt to go around to the back of the L-shaped house, and he'd be waiting. The driveway led straight back, opening to a large concrete pad tucked inside the ninety-degree angle formed by the two sections of the home. Matt noticed the yard was trim and neat. He'd expected something different for some reason, perhaps a Michigan version of his unkempt bungalow.

A pole to the right of the pad rose up from the edge where concrete met grass, a basketball rim and backboard reminded Matt of fun, laughter, taunts of friends, and hours of lonely practice. There had been a similar setup in his backyard.

"I was pretty good, you know."

Matt glanced to his left. The big door to the two-car garage was open. Tom's voice had emanated from the darkness within. He heard the chair before he saw it, and Tom emerged into the light at the edge of the opening.

"Yeah, me too. Brings back great memories. Funny how we could spend so much time focusing on a game."

Tom looked up at the net then back to Matt. "I still come out here once and a while, try my skill. But I get frustrated trying to retrieve the fucking ball, so I give up. That used to be my standard operating procedure: start then give up."

Matt wasn't sure how to respond, so he just stood there looking at the backboard. After a minute of awkward silence, Matt turned and walked over to his former teammate. He extended his hand and thought he caught a flicker of sadness in Tom's eyes.

"What, no bro hug?"

Matt instantly connected the fleeting look with the words. He corrected his mistake by leaning down. Tom took his offered hand as Matt gave him a hug, slapping him on the back with his left hand.

"Sorry," Matt said, standing back up. "Been a long time since I touched, let alone hugged, anyone."

Matt peered over Tom's head and into the garage. It was oddly configured as a large living space. Apparently, Tom had an issue with the concept of walls and corners. Out here, his chair had no limitations.

"Nice digs!"

Tom looked over his shoulder. "Yeah, I decided to stay out here. With my parents gone, I couldn't stand the silence. It used to be a home filled with noise and the sound of feet scampering everywhere. Not anymore."

Unconsciously, Matt looked up to gauge the position of the sun in the sky. Tom saw this and knew Matt was determining the time of day.

"Thanks for coming all the way up here. It's past lunchtime. Did you eat?"

Matt nodded. "Grabbed some chow in the airport. I'm good to go."

"GTG, good to go. You were always GTG, as I recall. Is it okay if I call you Matt instead of sir?" Tom's face broke into a grin.

Matt smiled back. Team guys constantly found fault with each other in humorous ways. Being fucked with by a teammate meant you were an accepted member of the warrior brotherhood; but like all brotherly relationships, there was room for laughter and loving criticism.

"Sure, you can call me anything you want." Matt was feeling edgy. He wasn't used to traveling, and he certainly wasn't quick witted enough to mentally spar with Tom.

"You got anything to drink around here?" Matt asked, searching the converted garage.

Tom saw the look in Matt's face and gritted his teeth. He'd hoped Matt could sprinkle some of his smart officer fairy dust on his personal problem and help him get his daughter back.

"If you mean alcohol, the answer is no. After I lost the leg in 2014, I hit the Kool-Aid pretty hard myself. It took losing my wife and daughter to wake me up. Haven't had a drop in this house in over eighteen months."

Matt stopped looking when he heard the hard tone in Tom's voice. He was thirsty; but it wasn't time to hit the rack, so he didn't need a sleep aid. There wasn't a single good reason to drink, except fear. The fear of failing a fellow SEAL, who desperately needed his help.

"On second thought, fuck that drink. Water will do just fine, that is unless you have a sob story about water, too."

Tom smiled. "One bottle of water coming right up!"

Matt took the water and finished it off in less than two minutes. He was always dehydrated and rarely did anything about it. This time he felt something click in the back of his mind. Hydrating was critical to mission success. Stress increased the likelihood someone would focus on the challenge to the detriment of their biological needs; a biological organism could not function at peek proficiency unless maintained. Water was smart.

Matt would do his best. His best hadn't been much to write home about lately; but Tom deserved to find his daughter, and he couldn't do that without a lot of help. He walked over to the tall plastic trash can and tossed in the empty bottle.

"From the beginning, tell me what you know. Everything. Don't leave out a single detail. By the way, can I borrow some paper and a pen?"

Matt took the pen and the spiral notebook Tom handed him and opened it. The first twenty pages or so were filled with poetry and sketches.

"Your handiwork?"

Tom shook his head. "No, that was Vicky's school notebook from when she was about eleven years old. I don't have any new notebooks."

Matt saw Tom's eyes well up a little, and he decided to get on with the interview. He needed to hear the story; then he'd figure out what, if anything, could be done.

"She's a good artist. I'll just start on this clean page." Matt flipped the notebook open and set his pen to paper. "Okay, from the beginning, start with this trip to Hawaii. Who knew about it beforehand?"

Tom looked startled. "What do you mean? You think it's someone we know here? Someone who followed her?"

Matt raised his hand. "Whoa there, calm down. We need to look at every possibility. I'm not a professional detective, but I've been involved in enough NCIS and JAG drills in my time to know they look for facts first, then sort them to discover clues that lead to multiple theories. Each theory is run down, and eventually, if successful, they figure it all out. The worst thing we can do is jump to what appear to be logical conclusions. That might leapfrog right over something important."

"See, this is the thinking I knew you'd bring to this shit show. Okay, let's get started!"

Matt spent the next two hours probing every aspect of the planned trip to Hawaii. Most of Tom's knowledge came from texts and phone conversations with Vicky leading up to the much-anticipated vacation. He kept Tom on topic, but allowed him to vent every so often about his ex-wife, Barbara. His vitriol wasn't convincing. He was still in love with her and felt betrayed and abandoned.

They took a quick bathroom break and went back to it for a few more hours until Matt could see Tom's energy dropping. He was on various pain meds for the leg, so staying alert enough to sustain a serious dialogue was sapping his energy. Matt put the spiral notebook aside and laid the pen atop the scribbled markings.

“I think that’s enough for today, Tom. Why don’t you do whatever it is you normally do, and I’ll order us some pizza. Sound good?”

Tom rubbed his eyes and nodded. “I like pizza, but no cake though. I know how you officer types love your fucking cake.” He smiled weakly at his own joke.

Matt laughed. “I may have been a cake eater, but at least I can spell and read. Leave me alone so I can call the pizza place. Oh yeah, where do you get your pizza from?”

Thirty minutes later, they were both eating pizza and trying to top each other’s stories. Tom told Matt about the night he lost his leg. The surgeons had to remove it all the way up to just below his right hip. No fiber carbon option for him; you needed a knee for that robot shit, he pointed out. Matt saw Tom become more alive when he told his team guy stories. They were funny, well most of them.

Like Tom, Matt rarely shared tales of daring-do, all heroism and dash. No fuckups and no mistakes. Those missions happened, of course; they made up the majority of the combat operations SEALs participated in, regardless of the theater of war. SEALs would just rather hear about the time it all went sideways. Much more entertaining and everyone could learn something from the telling.

Matt checked the time. “I have very few contacts, Tom. We’re going to need more people involved in this if we’re going to be successful. The one contact I do have, though, is a good one. Steve Auger. He was the troop chief at SDV Team Two when I first saw combat, and I had the privilege of pulling his ass out of Colombia a few years later.”

Tom nodded. "I remember both of those ops. Didn't know that you led a rescue to get your old chief, though. That sounds like he owes you more than a case of beer. Maybe beer for life or something close to that."

They both laughed and Matt continued, "Steve got out after catching one too many bullets. He joined a K and R company, kidnap and recovery. The company is called the Bollinger Group. It was started by an ex-FBI agent, Jackson Bollinger. They specialize in finding and recovering everything from runaways to people kidnapped by terrorists. They're good; and if Steve's still with them, he'd respond to my reaching out to him."

"Holy shit, Matt! That's a great asset."

Matt looked around the garage. "All I need is a computer with Internet access. You still paying your bills?" Matt smiled.

Tom pointed out a short table in the back corner of the garage, and Matt walked over to check it out. Tom had a fairly new laptop and mouse sitting on a four-foot-high table with coasters. The coasters allowed Tom to roll the table anywhere he wanted. Matt took advantage of this and pulled the rig back toward the front of the garage where Tom sat in his wheelchair.

It took a few minutes to find the Bollinger Group corporate website; but once there, Matt quickly found and clicked on the "About Us" tab. Steve's name was right under Jackson Bollinger's; he'd risen to Chief Operating Officer or COO.

"Good for you, Steve!" Matt clicked on the hyperlink, and in a second he was looking at an older version of his friend and mentor. Steve had aged, but getting shot at and occasionally letting the bullets hit you would do that to a guy. Matt read the biography and then clicked the contact link.

Tom watched quietly as Matt typed his message into the form and, after a quick proofread, hit send. "Well, that's it then," he exclaimed. "If I know Steve, he'll respond by calling me within twenty-four hours. You got a bed I can use? I suddenly am very tired."

"Absolutely. You can sleep in my old room inside. It's got a king-sized bed and it's hardly been used. I sleep out here." Tom jerked his head in the direction of a two-foot-high pallet made up of a box spring and mattress lying on the garage floor.

"That will be fine, Tom. Why don't we both get some rest. If Steve contacts us, things will start to move fast."

As Matt lay his head down on the pillow, he played the day through his mind like a movie of someone else's life. He had spent almost two days clean and sober. His brain was firing in a way he thought was gone forever. He also felt hope, not for himself, but for Tom. Steve was the right guy to fix this problem. Tomorrow, things would start happening.

Chapter Five

Matt woke to complete silence. He'd been dreaming, but not bad dreams. Dreams of his time in the teams. Faces of brothers lost and brothers still fighting the good fight had filled his night with a rare positive feeling of belonging. *Was it the booze?* His routine had been disrupted in many ways these last couple of days, and he wasn't unhappy his nightmares were a victim of that disruption.

Matt rolled over and turned on the lamp. He checked his phone; it was six in the morning. *Damn!* He felt well-rested, but there was a strange, lingering headache he'd felt the day before, too. He played the last few days through his mind and realized he hadn't been truly shitfaced in a week, ever since seeing Tom's texts.

The smart phone indicated he had an email message and a voicemail. He decided to read the message first; it was from Steve. *Great to see that you're still alive, heard rumors you were attempting to kill yourself one bottle at a time. I'll call in a few minutes, but I'm sure I can help – Steve.*

The message came in right after Matt went to bed the night before. He listened to the voicemail, same message. It was good to hear Steve's voice. He'd wait until 8:00 to call him back. Until then, he was pretty sure there were a few slices of pizza left.

Steve Auger woke up every day at the same time, 4:30 AM. His routine was straightforward: shave, cold shower, work out, warm shower, groom his mostly long, dark brown hair, get dressed, and consume a green power protein shake with two raw eggs blended into the mix. At 5'9" and 200 pounds, his lean muscular frame still gave people the impression of power rather than speed. But Steve's appearance was deceiving. He was a fitness fanatic and ignored the aches and pains associated with his various training injuries, combat wounds, and advancing age. He'd retained his hand-to-eye coordination and wicked hand speed through daily discipline. It rarely came in handy these days; but he wasn't willing to slow down, not yet anyway.

Matt Barrett's email had taken him by surprise. Nobody had seen the former SEAL officer in years, and everything he'd heard about Matt since he'd retired was either bullshit or just plain bad news. The email was professional, direct, and urgent. It didn't appear to be the work of a man on his last leg. Steve decided to flush the rumors and deal with Matt the way he remembered him, a combat leader of the highest caliber.

Winner of the Navy Cross, the Silver Star, and multiple other awards for bravery under fire, Steve remembered Matt as a thoughtful leader, an officer who earned the respect of his men both on and off the battlefield. Steve owed this man his life, and he would do whatever Matt needed him to do. He was sure of that fact.

Things at the Bollinger Group were moving along nicely. The business started by "Jax" was in its mature stage. Lots of referral work, and the cash flow was significant. Jax had a smart business model. He used contracted experts for his assignments. Little to no overhead outside of the work, which was covered by the healthy fees he charged his clients. Things were so smooth that Steve was getting a bit bored with it all. Matt's email sounded like just the challenge he needed.

Steve checked his watch. 7:15. Just enough time to hit the bag and then a shower. He had a conference call at 8:30, so there was plenty of time.

Matt finished off two slices of pizza and then went into the master bathroom to get cleaned up. The warm water was invigorating, and he didn't want the shower to end. Tom's voice resonated through the walls.

"Hey! You want to save some water for the rest of us?"

Matt shut off the flow and toweled off. He rummaged through his bag and found a shirt and pants. The shower in another bathroom kicked on, and then he heard Tom singing. Whatever it was the man went through, he seemed to be all right now. How ironic that once he'd defeated his inner demons, this crisis was thrust upon him. Matt strapped on his wristwatch and shoved the freshly charged smart phone into his pocket. It was 7:55.

The backyard was pleasant. Grosse Pointe came off as a utopian environment, mostly because of the stately trees and expensive landscaping that defined everything within eyesight. Tom's backyard felt like a private garden, and the sounds of the wildlife waking up made the experience even more cathartic. At exactly eight o'clock, Matt dialed Steve's number.

"Hello. Steve Auger here."

Matt felt a rise of emotion he hadn't anticipated. "Steve, this is Matt. How the fuck are you, man?"

The voice on the other end of the call softened a bit. "Holy shit, sir. I thought you were dead or nearly dead. I'm doing great. How the fuck are *you?"*

Matt heard the tone in Steve's voice. The question wasn't random. Steve had tried to keep tabs on his former troop leader, and he was concerned.

"Better than normal, and normal hasn't been that great," Matt answered. "You look prosperous. A little greyer than I remember, but prosperous nonetheless."

Steve chuckled. "Yeah, well, it was a ball buster for a while. Jax, that's Jackson Bollinger, brought me onboard near the beginning. We had some rough times, tapped the savings accounts, and all that start-up nonsense. We're solid now. Three years into it, and we are doing well. So, what's the deal with Tom's situation?"

Matt spent a few minutes running down the basics. Steve asked a lot of questions, good ones. Matt was happy to respond until he started running out of answers.

"I'm tapped out, Steve. I've told you everything I know from what Tom has told me. Thoughts?"

Steve paused for a moment before answering. "We need to get to Hawaii. The rest of the information is there. I can be on a plane by seven o'clock tonight. What about you?"

Matt wasn't ready to fly to Hawaii. He didn't have a lot of money, and Tom had explained that he was just making the house payments. He felt embarrassed to have to explain, but it was the truth.

"I'm free to travel anywhere, but I have an issue with funding. Tom can't bankroll this project, and I can barely scrape up enough to ensure I can get to Hawaii and back home."

Steve laughed. "Fuck that noise, sir! Haven't you been listening? Jax made me an equity partner. I'm well off, certainly capable of flying your lame ass to Honolulu. Are you with me?"

Matt's eyes began to tear up involuntarily. He knew Steve felt he owed Matt for the rescue in Colombia, but that was business. Just a mission and part of the job. He didn't have to carry Matt. On the other hand, he couldn't help Tom if he went back to Key West. He was at a decision point in his life. Was he ready to commit everything for someone else, yet one more time?

He took a deep breath and let it out. "Okay, I'm in. For Tom's sake. Thank you. He'll be overwhelmed with gratitude."

"Don't start taking bows just yet. The kidnapping business is tough. Fifty percent of these girls are never ransomed and therefore rarely found. We have our work cut out for us in Hawaii. I've got a few contacts there, so we will get some local help. But no promises. Okay?"

Matt agreed and then gave Steve all his personal information to facilitate the ticketing. They would meet at the Royal Hawaiian Hotel. The big pink complex on Waikiki beach was impossible to miss. The said their goodbyes and hung up.

Matt felt that tingling again. His adrenaline was kicking in, the old pre-mission jolt of energy. He'd believed the feeling would never come back, that it was gone forever, but here it was. He needed to brief Tom on their plan. Getting to Hawaii was the easy part. The hard work would be finding anybody with real insight into what happened to Vicky.

The deep blue water was incredibly beautiful. The final approach to the Honolulu airport was slow and low, providing Matt with a spectacular view of the reefs and long lines of surf. The little dots scattered across the near shore indicated the waves were good enough today for the locals to come out and play.

He waited nervously for the plane to land and taxi up to the ramp. Steve might not be happy with what he saw walking off the plane. He looked much older than his 37 years, and he hadn't executed so much as one push-up since leaving the Navy.

Matt exited the concourse and scanned the crowd, looking for Steve. A sign caught his eye, FNG. He'd found Steve. Steve saw the reaction in Matt's face, so he lowered the sign and stepped forward. The two men embraced in a standard bro hug and leaned back to size each other up.

"Just sayin'." Steve's assessment was short and to the point.

"Yeah, I know. I've been on the Maker's Mark diet for about two years now. Ever heard of it?"

Steve laughed. "No, must be one of those Veteran's Administration things. They all turn out badly. How the hell are ya, sir?"

The two former special operators walked together to the baggage claim, exchanging tidbits of their lives and musing over the fate of SEALs they'd both known.

"Oby is still in; he's a Master Chief now. In fact, I believe he's the command senior enlisted man at SEAL Team Three," Steve noted. "I always liked him. Straightforward and calm under any kind of stress."

Matt nodded. "He was a pleasure to be around and to work with. The kind of guy you'd go have a beer with and want by your side in combat. A good combination."

Steve agreed. Both men knew that being a great guy to hang around with wasn't an indication of how somebody would perform operationally. There were the classic team guy profiles: great operator but an asshole, the asshole who couldn't shoot straight, the great guy who sucked when it came down to executing tactics, and the great guy who was also a great operator. Oby was easy to like and to respect.

"What's the plan, sir?" Steve Auger was comfortable deferring to Matt as always.

Matt rubbed his jaw. "I figure we start with the mother. Barbara is supposedly still in Honolulu. Tom thinks she's still at the same hotel near the Ala Moana shopping center. I suggest we go there and see if we can find her."

The two former SEALs jumped out of the car and said goodbye to the Uber driver. The ride from the airport had been productive. The driver's brother was in Five-0, the famous Honolulu police department. He was full of information about the local gangs, the international gangs, and even the sex trade.

It was his opinion, based mostly on listening to his brother rant on the subject, that most of the kids snatched off the streets in Hawaii ended up in a commercial ship within an hour or two of being kidnapped. If the ship was under a foreign flag, it would be very difficult for Five-0 to follow up leads quickly.

The red tape might take long enough to allow the ship to depart, taking its secret cargo with it. This made it near impossible to recover the victims. From first report of a possible abduction to departure from the commercial pier might be a matter of only hours, not days.

Steve had grabbed the driver's business card just in case they wanted to follow up with the man's brother. Matt and Steve walked into the lobby of the Outrigger Waikiki and went to the front desk. Barbara was staying in the hotel, so they were in luck. Matt called her room using the courtesy phone, but no one picked up. They left an urgent message for her at the desk and decided to check in themselves.

While Matt was in his room unpacking, his smart phone buzzed. He picked it up and scanned the text from Steve. Barbara was back and had called him. She was willing to meet them for dinner in the hotel restaurant. Matt looked at the time; he had three hours. A strange thought crossed his mind. He waited for it to go away, but it was persistent. An urging deep inside he couldn't ignore. He sent a text to Steve and finished unpacking.

Thirty-two. He could only do thirty-two fucking push-ups. Matt sat up and stared at the old man in the gym mirror. He was more of a mess than he'd realized. After the initial positive motivation to work out for the first time in over two years, the reality of his physical condition had quickly destroyed the rush he felt walking into the fitness center.

As he kneeled there looking at the floor, another darker but more familiar urge pushed its way into his conscious thoughts. He wasn't supposed to meet Steve until 4:30. They were going to discuss the game plan, how to question Barbara, and what to do if she stonewalled them or became too emotional to be useful. Matt stood up and grabbed his room key from off the bench. He had time for one or two drinks.

Steve had heard the rumors and frankly had a hard time believing any of them. The Matthew Barrett he once knew was arrow straight, always calm, poised, and in control. He couldn't remember seeing the man drink, let alone get drunk. But the man he saw sitting at the hotel bar was more than drunk; he was wasted.

He checked his watch. There wasn't enough time to change plans. He'd have to get Matt back up to his room, then interview Vicky's mom by himself. What the hell had happened to Matt that could have pushed him this far down the rabbit hole?

Matt didn't see Steve sit down next to him, but he felt a presence to his right and glanced in that direction. "Just warming up for the big meeting." Matt's words were slurred and his eyelids drooped down, blocking half his vision.

"No big meeting for you, I'm afraid." Steve placed his hand on Matt's shoulder. "You're in no condition to sit down and talk to a mother looking for her kidnapped daughter. I'll take the meeting, and we'll regroup in the morning."

Matt's eyes opened wide and he began to protest, but something in the way Steve looked at him stopped the words from coming out. He saw the disappointment, a look he'd never seen on the Senior Chief's face. The look pierced him, straight through to his soul.

This is why he'd stayed away from the teams. The guilt of the brotherhood, the shame of not measuring up when everyone around you was counting on you, depending on you. Always heroic and always disciplined. Matt wasn't that guy anymore and now Steve knew it, too.

Chapter Six

Barbara Burnell was a ten by anyone's standards. Steve watched her glide into the restaurant dressed in skin-tight white shorts and a flimsy blouse that hugged her curves with every step. Steve knew she was divorced, but it didn't feel right to hit on Tom's ex-wife. And of course there was the whole kidnapping thing.

Barbara looked around the room before sitting where the waiter indicated. She adjusted her long black hair and slowly crossed her long shapely legs. Steve realized she was completely aware of who he was and where he was, and this was just a show. She was obviously conscious of the effect she had on men. Barbara casually looked around the room and acted surprised when she spotted Steve. He gave her a little wave and walked over to her table.

"Team guys are hard to hide once you know what you're looking for," she said reaching out her hand. Steve shook it before sitting down.

"I've heard that before," he said, smiling. "My name is Steve, Steve Auger."

"I thought there were two of you. Someone named Matt, I believe? Tom emailed me that you were both coming to Hawaii to help."

Steve thought about Matt for a second. He hoped he was alright. The two of them were going to have a heart-to-heart in the morning. If Matt couldn't get his shit together, he'd cut him loose. Tom's daughter was in trouble; and regardless of his respect for Matt, or the man Matt was, he wasn't going to fuck this mission up.

Barbara's eyes showed the deep strain she was under; but she was attracted to Steve, and he could read that in her eyes, too. "Matt, Matt Barrett. He was an officer in the teams, big hero and all that. More importantly, he was tactically one of the smartest men I ever worked with. A natural leader, too. He'll be available tomorrow. I'll be able to handle this part of the process without him. I work for …"

"Yes, I know. The Bollinger Group. Your company focuses on finding and recovering kidnap victims. Your clients are usually corporations or high-net-worth families. Your company charges quite a sum for these services. How am I going to pay for your involvement? I'm neither a corporation nor rich."

Steve was impressed. The team guy in him had an answer ready to go. The classic "*Oh I'm sure we can work something out"* line. He immediately felt guilty for letting his dick think for him. She may be gorgeous and charming, even smart; but he was a professional, and he was here to help a brother, not get laid.

"Tom is our friend, our brother. We will do whatever we can to figure this out, and if possible, find and bring Vicky back to you."

He saw the flirty attitude dissolve and the distressed mother come through. Barbara started crying. Not loud or crazy, just a stream of tears running down her face. Steve didn't know what to do from his side of the table, so he unrolled his dinner napkin and handed to her. She took it and dabbed her wet cheeks.

"Thank you."

Steve waited another few minutes to allow Barbara to regain her composure. She must be exhausted, he thought to himself. Once he felt it was the right time, he began to speak.

"Have you decided what you would like? A drink to start with perhaps?"

Steve closed his mouth and looked at the waiter a bit too harshly. A drink might be a good idea. "Barbara?"

The waiter left with their drink orders, and Steve got down to business. He explained that Matt had interviewed Tom extensively, but most if not all of that information came from Barbara. He asked her to be patient as he went through the timelines, the police reaction, and activity since the kidnapping. Then he probed to find any memory she might have prior to the abduction that might point to a suspect or suspects.

She got better, stronger, as the questioning continued. The margaritas were helping the process, too. Steve matched her drink for drink; and when he realized there were no more questions to ask, he stopped. Her eyes looked sad, tired. She was taking this hard.

"That's it, I guess. I have your number and your email address. From this point on, Matt and I will run down leads here on Oahu. Speak to the police and a few other people I know, who have a grip on the underground activity here on the island. You've been great. I can't promise anything, but we'll pull out all the stops to find Vicky."

Barbara listened, and as she did, she leaned forward ever so slightly. Steve couldn't help noticing she'd unbuttoned the top two buttons of her blouse while in the restroom. She had classy breasts. Round and not too big, just enough to peak out of the blouse and taunt Steve. He hadn't been with a woman in six months. Too much work, too much traveling. The invitation was clear.

"I need a good night's sleep," Barbara stated with a slight slurring of the word *sleep.* "I need you to sleep with me, hold me until I fall asleep. This may not be part of your mission, but it would be a kindness. I need the warmth of another human being tonight."

Steve wasn't going to meet up with Matt until breakfast at nine in the morning. There was nothing stopping him from saying yes. He ran through the list of pros and cons. She was vulnerable and in a mild state of shock. Her emotions were hidden but that was a coping mechanism, Steve knew. He could walk away and let her deal with the night alone or…

Matt finished his third set of push-ups. He was sweating profusely and shaking, too. He rolled onto his back and placed his shoes on a bench. After two deep breaths, he started a slow set of crunches, his second set. He was dreading the arrival of nine o'clock. He'd woken up to the vision of Steve's face the night before. That, after a reoccurring dream about his father.

In the dream, his father was lecturing him about duty and responsibility. Matt apparently had failed in some cleaning task at home, and to his father this was an intolerable act. Matt didn't remember living through the conversation, so it must be a construction, a fabrication in his mind. The dream started a year earlier. Somebody was trying to get him to see the light.

"Hey buddy, are you done with this bench?"

Matt looked up at the older hotel guest and nodded. He rolled to his right and stood up on wobbly legs. The week or so of sobriety had lowered his resistance to alcohol. After only five drinks the night before, he found himself drunk and sick at the same time. While getting dressed to work out, he'd made a promise to himself. No drinking until after the mission was completed. Then he could go back to only true friend, the iguana, and … SHIT!

Steve was up at five, showered, and dressed for the day by 5:45. He kissed Barbara good-bye, and she only smiled. She'd gotten what she needed: a few minutes of lovemaking and six hours and counting of sleep. He scanned the room to make sure he had everything and then quietly closed the door behind him.

Back in his room, Steve pulled out the card the Uber driver had given to him. He'd wait until eight to make the call. He needed to reach out to Jackson's point of contact also. Steve changed his clothes and watched the news for an hour before grabbing his wallet and cell phone and leaving the room.

The hotel lobby was empty, but the concierge had his stack of complimentary papers ready and waiting. Steve grabbed a copy of the *Wall Street Journal* and tucked it under his arm. A nice walk down the beach of Waikiki was in order.

He felt better than he had in a long time. A different sort of good, not the kind of afterglow when a mission or a rescue was successful. Maybe he should consider dating again when he returned home.

At nine Matt walked out of the elevator and immediately spied Steve sitting in a lobby lounge chair. "I see you're up bright and early!" he tossed out as he closed the distance.

"You feeling okay this morning?" The concern in Steve's voice was genuine, and it made Matt feel less like a loser and more like a friend who'd fucked up.

Matt stood over his old teammate and put his hands on his hips. He stared out through the open entry to the street beyond. Then he looked down to face the music.

"I'm sorry. I've been a drunk for two years now. Nobody counts on me, except a buddy of mine; he's sort of a roommate. He depends on me for food, and, well I forgot to make arrangements."

"Is he paralyzed or something? Why would you have to feed your roommate?"

Matt looked down at the floor before answering. "Because he's a lizard. A big ass green lizard. That's why."

Steve laughed. "If you say so. I'll stay out of your twisted personal life. By the way, we have shit to do."

Matt looked up and nodded. "I want to find Vicky and will do whatever it takes to make that happen. I swear to you right now, on my trident, I will not touch a drop until we have her back safe."

Steve was surprised by the sudden change in mood, but he appreciated the words. He stood up and gave Matt a hug. "A simple, *I feel fine, let's eat breakfast,* would have sufficed for an answer, *sir.*" Steve said the word *sir* in a way Matt remembered all too well. It was a drawn-out pronunciation. A subtle enlisted man's way of communicating that they thought an officer was full of bullshit. In this case, Steve was just joking. Or at least Matt hoped he was joking.

Matt smiled and stayed silent. He'd made his pledge, and Steve wasn't making an issue of his behavior the night before. They were good to go. The two men walked into the hotel restaurant and were seated near a large open window looking out toward Diamond Head.

“What did Vicky’s mom have to say?” Matt asked, waving the waitress over to their table.

“She was very helpful, especially with the police interaction. Tom conveyed her understanding of the details accurately.”

“So, what’s the next move?” Matt thanked the waitress for the coffee she’d placed in front of him and poured a little cream into the blackness.

“I called the cop; you know the Uber driver’s brother. He gave me the low-down on the local boys playing with the sex trade. They tend to keep their victims close, move them to the north shore, and hide them with relatives until the heat dies down. Then they drug ’em up and sell them to executive escort companies working the hotel and cruise line industry. When I described Vicky in some detail, he changed tack, thinks it’s also probable she was snatched for a higher level of buyer.”

“So, she’s still here?” Matt pointed to the pastrami omelet and handed the waitress his menu. He waited until Steve was finished ordering before asking again. “Is she still on the island?”

Steve took a sip of his coffee and replaced it on the saucer. “Maybe, but only if the local grabbed her and not a headhunting team working for big money. They would’ve whisked her off the streets and into a commercial cargo hold within hours. By now she’d be halfway to the east Asia market. By the way, what’s this about a lizard friend named Steve? He’s your roommate?”

Matt smiled. “Something like that. A big green iguana that decided he wanted to live in my place. He’s harmless and a good listener. I had to call this morning to ask a friend to go over and feed him. With all this shit happening, I'd completely forgot."

"So, you do have somebody counting on you!" Steve broke out laughing.

"Okay, smart ass, you still haven't answered my question. What's our next move?

The flight to Kauai was short and scenic. Matt could see why so many people visited the islands and why many of them decided to live there. Steve stood up and grabbed his bag from the overhead compartment; and Matt, who was traveling without a bag, followed Steve to the stairway and down to the hot runway below.

The taxi ride out to the ranch took forty minutes; winding roads and farm traffic made it slow going. Their destination was a place known as Hope Ranch, but officially it was called the Kellogg Ranch. The Kelloggs had settled on the island right after World War Two, when nobody gave Kauai a second thought.

They purchased a thousand acres on the western side of the island and began trying to grow everything from grapes to pineapples. Eventually they made a fortune in agriculture and reinvested that money into a boat service, which eventually became the first tourist cruise line running between Maui, Oahu, and Kauai. Kellogg Cruises was still in operation today.

In 1995, the old patriarch of the family died. He left the ranch to his granddaughter, Beatrice Kellogg. They were on their way to see her, because she was something of an expert in the Pacific sex trade.

Her ranch had been a recovery center ever since she had inherited the property. She used horses as part of a method known as equine therapy to help victims of abuse, people with severe post-traumatic stress syndrome, and often, young girls and boys rescued from sex traffickers.

The taxi pulled up to the gate, and Steve punched in the numbers provided to him by Beatrice over the phone. Jackson's local boy back in Honolulu wasn't up on the sex trade, but he did know people who might be helpful. Beatrice was his suggestion.

The taxi stopped in front of a plantation-style building, single-story but huge. The building must be over seven thousand square feet, Matt estimated as he exited the car. Steve paid the driver, and in seconds the two of them were standing alone on the first step of the porch.

"Gentlemen, welcome to my home."

The voice was warm and inviting. A musical quality made the sound interesting. Beatrice was standing back, inside the large double doors, open to let the breeze into the house.

"You must be Beatrice," Steve said, stepping up onto the broad wraparound porch.

"Well, if I'm not, I don't know who could be!" The woman stepped out into the light, and Matt instantly liked her. Her face was angelic, reminding Matt of every mom in every commercial he'd ever watched. Steve stepped forward and shook her hand.

"Thank you for taking the time to speak with us. We have a problem, and maybe you can help."

Matt stepped up and also shook her hand. "Yes, we have a friend …"

Beatrice raised her hand. "I'm aware of your friend and his daughter's abduction. In my line of business, you get to know people who know things. I had the story before your plane took off from Honolulu. Now come on, we don't have much time!"

Beatrice spun around and disappeared into the house. Matt looked at Steve and shrugged. "I guess we should follow the oracle and see what she knows." Steve chuckled at Matt's reference to the movie, *The Matrix*.

As he followed Beatrice, Matt was too concerned to laugh at his own quip. He could only hope she truly was a supernatural guide. In his heart, he was less and less sure Vicky would ever be seen again.

Chapter Seven

The back of the plantation home opened up to reveal a large paddock filled with five ponies. Matt had never learned to ride, but he could appreciate their beauty. Horses have a pride of self that can resonate with people. They were serene and noble. He was beginning to see why they might be effective therapy animals, but he'd prefer a dog any day over a horse.

Beatrice led them to the back porch and indicated they should sit on the large wicker couch looking out over the paddock. Steve and Matt sat down, and she sat opposite them on a comfortable glider suspended from the ceiling.

"The person you're looking for is Roger Maddox. He's South African by birth, tall, thin, and self-conscious of his face, which was pockmarked by a bout of severe acne as a teenager. He received a better than average education, studying finance at the London School of Economics."

Matt pulled out his notebook and began jotting down details while Steve started the interview process. "Beatrice, how could you know who took Vicky? There could be hundreds of potential kidnappers from what our sources are telling us."

Beatrice sat tight-lipped, clearly unhappy at being interrupted. Rather than answer the question, she paused, then resumed her lecture on Roger Maddox.

"His lavish lifestyle as a youth was supported and made possible by his aunt, a reclusive but nurturing influence in his early life. He evolved over time from stockbroker to banker and then landed in the import-export business. At age 46, he's become a global broker in anything valuable: currency, drugs, rare art, and, of course, people. Specifically, children between the ages of 9 and 15. It's his specialty."

Matt raised his hand to politely pause the flow, and Beatrice stopped. She nodded, allowing Matt permission to ask his question. "This sounds personal. I mean you look angry when you speak of this man. Has he hurt you or someone close to you?"

Matt watched the emotions flicker across her face, but only for a second before her mask of control was reestablished. Matt got the distinct impression that this kind, warm lady would be comfortable hurting anyone she believed was evil.

"Over the years I've had at least 100 children and young adults pass through this place, Mr. Barrett. Every one of them had a story, a nightmare to tell. The evil had different names but always the same intent: the exercise of pure power over the weak and defenseless. Roger Maddox is responsible for untold misery. So, yes, it's personal for me, Mr. Barrett."

Steve watched the exchange and waited patiently for Matt to finish. He wanted to get more information about this man, Roger Maddox. "Beatrice, is there a reason you think he might be behind this particular case?"

"Roger Maddox is a predator, and I know he has hunters operating in the Hawaiian Islands. He funds, manages, and sometimes directs the higher end of his human trafficking business. But he never gets his hands dirty directly, at least not in the acquisition of young girls and boys."

"Who are his clients?" Matt asked.

"His business clientele is the wealthy and powerful. Elected officials, corporate leaders, despots, Americans, Asians, Europeans, anyone willing to pay top dollar for what they want. This scum orders children from him as if they were ordering food for a catered event. Of course, from time to time he sets aside product for his own pleasure."

Steve and Matt took it all in and waited for her to continue, but Beatrice was finished. Matt heard the sound of laughing voices from somewhere in the house, and it reminded him that Vicky wasn't a special case. She was a statistic. One of far too many kids who fell victim to men like Roger Maddox.

Matt saw her glance at her watch and she noticed. "I'm sorry, gentlemen. I do have a schedule, and I'm afraid I only have a few minutes left before I must end our chat. Is there anything else I can help you with?"

Steve cleared his throat. "We've been told the offshore market uses commercial ships to transport the abductees. If Vicky has run afoul of someone like this Maddox character, where would his people take her?"

"Go to Thailand, Mr. Auger. You'll have to spread some money around to get information; but his operation is based there, and someone may be able to direct you down the right path. If you do find him, can you do me a favor?"

Matt nodded as he put his notebook away. "Sure, Beatrice. What's the favor?"

Beatrice stood up and smoothed out the wrinkles in her bright green skirt. "If you find him, don't have him arrested. Kill the son of a bitch. Erase his evil from this earth."

The flight back to Oahu was uneventful, but just long enough for Matt to dwell on Beatrice's words, especially the request. He had never thought about killing much when on active duty. It was the job, and it was a necessity if other people were intent on killing you. Could he kill a noncombatant? He sincerely hoped it didn't come down to that decision. Beatrice wasn't completely honest with them. Jackson's person in Honolulu had informed Steve that Beatrice was a victim of rape when only a teenager. This was the source of her anger and her life's mission.

Steve nudged Matt and pointed. Diamond Head was in view. Just before boarding, Steve received a text from Jackson. He was on his way to Hawaii. Once the three of them were together, maybe a plan would form. Going to Thailand and spreading money around wasn't much of a plan. Jackson was a pro, and as a former FBI special agent, much better at understanding criminal organizations and criminal behavior.

Matt wasn't a cop. All he needed was a target set and resources; the rest was execution and focus. He wondered as he heard the sound of the plane's wheels squeaking, would he be an asset or a liability going forward? He glanced at Steve. Did Steve see him as value added or as a has-been, a clump of lead to be dragged around out of a sense of obligation?

Matt knew in his heart he was vulnerable to a relapse, but he also knew he had made a promise to Tom and to Steve to see this thing through to the end. And he was a man of his word, or at least he once was such a man.

Matt was happy for the opportunity to get some much-needed sleep after their return from Kauai. The long nap that afternoon had been refreshing, even if his muscles were unusually sore when he woke up. The morning workout hadn't been that aggressive, and Matt couldn't believe such a meager effort had generated what he was feeling all over his body.

Drinking every evening interfered with the concept of dinner, so he'd been living off of breakfast and lunch for two years. He wasn't overweight; he only needed to tone up and gain some operational strength back. As they walked across the street and headed to Benihana's, he decided he would work out every day of this mission. He wanted to feel normal again.

Steve met Matt at the appointed time in front of the hotel. Jackson wasn't due in until eleven, so the two had agreed a good dinner would help the time go faster. It was just after dark, and the city of Honolulu was lit up like it was Christmas, an entire island operating as if it were a Vegas casino. Always open, always ready to show the tourists a good time.

The restaurant was only a few blocks away, but Steve suggested they sightsee a bit before their 8:30 dinner reservation. Matt shrugged and went along with the flow, even though he could feel his stomach rumbling with hunger.

The two men wandered toward the International Shopping Center, but decided not to go inside its make-believe environment. The open air mall was a sprawling mix of medium-sized trees, Christmas lights, eateries, and lots of kiosks of all sizes selling Hawaiian trinkets. The place was packed with families, and the decision to pass it by was a good one.

They walked about a mile toward Diamond Head before deciding to cut up a few blocks to see if there was anything interesting off the main beach strip. Steve followed Matt down a side street that was partially blocked by several dumpsters. Matt heard the whack of wood on bone and then the grunt.

He casually turned to see Steve crumpled on the ground with three men standing over him. The one who hit him had a baseball bat cut down and reshaped so it was big enough to do damage but small enough to conceal. He and one other were local boys, big Hawaiians in their late twenties maybe early thirties. The third man was different. He was well-dressed and looked

Asian. The delicate features reminded Matt of a Filipino. The small man addressed Matt and Steve.

"You two assholes have been sticking your noses in where they don't belong. It stops here and it stops now!"

Matt heard the words, but his mind was racing, assessing the situation and his options. He wasn't small, at just over six foot; but as recent experience confirmed, he was no high-speed operator anymore either. He was unarmed and didn't see a weapon other than the bat held by the man who struck Steve.

Steve hadn't so much as wiggled since he was knocked down, and that concerned Matt more than his own survival. He needed to get that bat and then he'd have a fighting chance. He did the only thing he could think of: he attacked.

The three men were not expecting Matt to come at them, so there were a few seconds of surprise and a failure to react. That was all Matt needed. He reached the man holding the bat in three quick steps and slammed his palm into the lower part of his nose, feeling cartilage crack and then collapse. The nasal bone was thrust up and into the frontal lobe of the man's brain, and he collapsed without a sound. Before he hit the pavement, Matt had the bat in his hand.

The second Hawaiian yelled an alarm and then sputtered in anger at what Matt had done to his buddy. Matt swung around to his right, which placed the big man in between the Asian and himself. He didn't have long to wait for the attack, an emotional war cry, and lunged, closing the distance. Matt stood motionless, waiting for the opening he needed. As the Hawaiian came into range, Matt feinted with a left jab. The man predictably raised his fists to protect his face, and that's when Matt dropped low and swung the bat.

The howl filled the small alley and echoed beyond into the street. The bat took out the big man's left kneecap, and he was combat ineffective, rolling around the pavement holding his now useless leg joint. Matt was sure he'd broken something with the blow; but to be certain, he stepped forward and whacked the man across the back of the head. The howling stopped. There was only one man left.

Matt squared off on the Asian and noted that the man's hand was tucked behind his back. He was wearing a standard short-sleeved flower-print shirt, so there was plenty of room to carry a concealed handgun. The gesture was subtle and the short Asian wasn't flustered a bit, not even after watching Matt dispatch his muscle without breaking a sweat.

"My message to you has not changed. There are a hundred more like these two who will do what I say, even kill whomever I tell them to kill. Your heroics are interesting, but inconsequential. You are both in way over your head, and you should go home. Back to Miami." The little man looked down at Steve's still form. "Or Key West, in your case."

Matt could hear people out on the street talking excitedly. The scream and howls were too loud not to be noticed. He really didn't want the police to find him here holding a bat over three unconscious bodies, and he had to get Steve to a hospital.

"I've heard your message, twice now. What we do or don't do is our business. Now, unless you have a gun and plan to shoot me, I suggest you stop scratching your ass and get the fuck out of here before I try this bat out on you!"

The Asian man slowly pulled his hand forward; it was empty. That didn't mean there wasn't a gun; it just meant he wasn't stupid. He could hear people searching for the source of the commotion, and pretty soon they'd find them standing there.

“I can’t help what happens next. You have been warned.”

The small man backed away, and then turned to disappear down the small side street in the direction of the beach. Matt waited a few seconds then dropped down to check Steve’s pulse. It was strong. *Thank God he was alive!*

Matt tried to revive his friend, but it wasn’t working. He tucked the bat down the back of his shorts and reached down. Steve wasn’t a heavy guy, but tonight he was all dead weight. *Fuck me! I need to up my workout intensity if I’m going to be doing this crazy shit!*

Steve slid over Matt’s left shoulder, and Matt stood up, staggering but not falling down. “Okay, swim buddy, I need to get you someplace where we can sort this all out.” Matt walked to the end of the street and stayed in the shadows. Steve had insisted he download the Uber application, so he had an idea. Five minutes later an SUV pulled up.

“You Matt?”

“Yeah, you Joey?”

“That’s me! Hey, what’s wrong with your friend?”

Matt laughed. “Too much Hawaiian punch!”

He maneuvered Steve into the vehicle and slid in next to him. The last shove elicited a moan. “You know the park near the base of Diamond Head? I don’t know the name, but I saw it when we flew in, lots of palm trees.”

Joey frowned. “Your request said you were going to the Royal Hawaiian hotel.”

"Yeah, but I changed my mind. His wife is there and she'll hit the roof if he shows up like this. I need a little time to get him more presentable, if you know what I mean."

Joey nodded. "Got it! The park it is."

Matt looked outside the SUV and scanned the mass of humanity flowing up and down the main drag. He didn't see the Asian guy anywhere. If they'd been under surveillance, there may be more of the assholes nearby, watching. He needed a safe place, a place with 360-degree views. The park would have to do.

As they rolled down the street, Matt thought about the man with the bat. Fighting on instinct, Matt's training from years ago kicked in, and he'd delivered a strike designed to kill a man without thinking. If that guy was dead, things were going to get messy. Time to grab Jackson and get the fuck off the island of Oahu.

Chapter Eight

Jackson flashed the headlights of his rental car and waited. The park was dimly lit, mostly around the perimeter. The place was filled with Honolulu's homeless population, bodies lay sprawled here and there, on the ground and on benches. He had the driver's seat back as far as it would go to accommodate his six-foot-four frame. He flashed the lights again.

The loud rap on the rear of the vehicle startled him. One glance at the right-side mirror confirmed it was Steve; he assumed the other man was Matt. He hit the electronic door lock and waited for the two men to enter the car.

Jackson ran his hand across his military style hair cut that hid the grey invading his naturally black hair and sighed. "What's his status?"

As the car pulled away from the curb, Matt checked Steve's pulse for the tenth time since the attack. "He's groggy, spoke a few times in the park. No lacerations, only a wicked lump on the side of his head. I wouldn't be surprised if he had a concussion though. I saw the guy swing that bat pretty damn hard."

Steve decided on a plan as he drove the car to the end of the strip and then turned back near the base of Diamond Head to return to the hotel. He hadn't had time to stop and check in, but that was okay. They all needed to get the hell out of Honolulu and fast.

Matt saw Steve's eyes open, close, and then open again. For the first time he seemed to focus on Matt's face. "Where the fuck am I?"

Jackson laughed. “You’re in the backseat of my rental car giving Matt a blow job. It’s my turn next.”

Steve tensed up and his eyes grew wide. “Fuck you, Jax! What the hell happened back there, Matt? Are you okay?”

Matt gave his two companions a blow-by-blow narrative, starting with Steve going down after being hit on the head. When he was finished, there was silence.

“You didn’t check the one guy’s pulse, did you?” Jackson asked quietly.

Matt shook his head. “I didn’t have time. I needed to get Steve out of that alley and to somewhere safe. I don’t know for a fact that I killed the guy; it just felt like I did.”

Jackson looked at Matt’s face in the rear-view mirror. “Nothing we can do about that now. Unless there were cameras focused on that alley, you are probably free and clear. They wanted to hurt you two really bad; and if you hadn’t acted the way you did, you might both be in the hospital right now, or worse.”

The drive to the hotel was short, but Jackson passed the building and circled the neighborhood for a few minutes to allow Steve to regain full consciousness. When he did finally come around, he was pissed.

“Who the fuck were those guys?”

Matt shrugged. “I don’t know. The little guy, the Asian, he said he was there to warn us, said we were causing problems with our snooping around.”

Steve rubbed his head. “I assume, unless it was a case of mistaken identity--wrong alley, wrong time, that he was referring to our little quest to find Tom’s daughter?”

Steve turned the car into the valet lane in front of their hotel. "Okay, gentlemen, time to disembark."

Matt answered Steve's question as he opened the car door. "This wasn't a mistake. The little guy said we'd been followed for some time. I think he was a messenger, sent by whoever pulls the strings on this island, to tell us that we'd worn out our welcome."

The three men walked through the busy lobby and remained silent until in the elevator. "So, now what?" Matt asked.

"We need to get away from Honolulu. Go someplace close to the game, but not in the middle of the game," Steve suggested.

Jackson agreed. "I have a friend in Coogee Beach, in Sydney, Australia. Thomas would put us up in his place, no questions asked. He's a retired federal agent, their version of the FBI. He might even be a valuable source of information about trafficking in the Pacific Rim."

The elevator door slid open with a loud ping. "Beggars can't be choosers. Right, sir?" Steve slapped Matt on the back.

Matt nodded. Moving closer to the nexus of evil in Thailand made sense. Someone must have an idea who runs the pipeline out of the Hawaiian Islands and where those girls end up. Their only hope was that Vicky was still in that pipeline and hadn't been sold and transported to a buyer in another part of the world.

Jackson stopped them in the hallway. "You two should pack up. Let's leave now, tonight. I'll set up a flight to Sydney. We're safer sitting in the airport for as long as it takes, rather than giving those goons another shot at us here in the city."

The flight to Sydney left at six in the morning, so the three men spent the night in the airport. Matt and Jackson took turns watching over Steve. If he did have a concussion, a sign of that condition was sleeping. The fact that it was natural to sleep in the middle of the night didn't deter them from waking Steve every thirty minutes or so. By the time the sun came up, Steve was pissed, completely lucid, and clearly okay.

Matt sat on the large Qantas aircraft and thought about the last week. For two years he was a world unto himself. Now, after saying yes to a friend, he was heading to a place as far from Key West as he could go. He'd been thrust into the murky world of human slavery and possibly killed a man in self-defense. As the wheels left the tarmac, he decided he'd give Tom a call once they arrived in Australia. He deserved to know if they'd made progress or not.

Matt slept the entire flight. When he woke up, they were circling Sydney's airport, waiting for clearance to land. As he studied the city below, he realized that his nightmares had stopped. A curious thing that made Matt wonder if they were gone forever or would return if he started drinking again.

He'd come to the conclusion a year or so earlier that the dreams were punishment, nightly reminders of his failures, and in the end, his breaking faith with himself and the brotherhood. In 2014, he participated in an operation in Somalia. A classified incursion into that country to rescue three American aid workers. The mission had been fucked up from the beginning. He happened to be near enough to the problem to get selected to lead the rescue.

There wasn't enough time to wait for a cohesive unit, so an ad hoc team of twelve SEALs and four Marines were cobbled together and inserted thirty miles inland. Matt's hubris made him confident he would be able to lead, think, or fight his way out of any challenge his force might face. He was wrong.

In the end, it was a bloodbath. Friendly fire deaths of one hostage and one SEAL. The remaining two hostages were fine, but four other SEALs and Marines were severely wounded. Matt had stumbled into a patrol on the way to the target site. Once engaged, he decided to fight through the first issue and push on to the target. They were waiting for him and his rescue force, and all hell broke loose.

The press never heard about the mission, and against Matt's personal wishes, he was awarded a Silver Star for his leadership under fire. He'd always felt it was easier for the chain of command to reward the team rather than admit a mistake on their watch. A medal was like rewarding an arsonist for putting out the fire he started.

The wound he received to his ankle seemed slight at the time, but it was the wound that eventually dictated his early retirement. His other wounds collectively added up to a 70 percent disability rating; the ankle made it 75. Matt thought he'd replay that operation over and over again every night for the rest of his life; but since visiting Tom, his nights were calm and quiet.

Thomas Mallory waited in the international baggage claim area holding a sign that said *FBI Puke.* Steve spotted the sign and laughed. "I think I've found your trusted contact in Sydney!"

Jackson gave Thomas the traditional American bro hug and stepped back. "Thanks for doing this, Thomas."

"What are friends you never write or talk to for, unless it's an emergency houseguest request?" Thomas laughed at his own jab.

Matt followed Steve, Jackson, and Thomas at a short distance. Once he was seated in Thomas's rented SUV, he decided it was time to reach out to Tom. The phone rang three times before Tom picked up.

"About time, sir. I've been pacing the garage for days now."

Matt smiled at the self-deprecating joke. He could imagine Tom doing laps around the perimeter of his driveway. "Sorry, Tom. We've been busy, but we think we're on a trail, sort of. Not sure if it will end up where Vicky is, though."

Matt relayed the events of the past few days, and Tom asked questions from time to time. He was alarmed at the attack in Honolulu. Matt didn't mention his theory about the man with the bat.

"As you know, I reached out to every team guy I knew when Vicky was kidnapped. Yesterday a guy named Gary Conroy called me. Every hear of him?"

Matt was surprised. Gary Conroy had been in his BUD/S training class nearly 15 years ago. "Yeah, I know him. He was in my class. Didn't work with him after we all graduated and split up to our different team assignments. He didn't tell you this already?"

"No, I didn't tell him much. Figured a random team guy I've never met might be solid or he might be a poser. He was referred to me by a guy I served with in team seven. I kept the names and details out of our conversation, but he still seemed willing to help. Only one problem though."

Matt took it all in. "What's the problem?"

"This guy was banged up pretty good. He confessed he can't join the team to help physically, but he mentioned he had access to resources if we were interested in letting him in on the search. He's not far from you right now. Lives in Auckland, New Zealand."

Matt collected Gary's contact information and thanked Tom before promising to stay in touch. He hung up and told his partners what he'd learned.

"I can have him checked out. I have a few friends here that would know a lot about a character like this guy if he lives in New Zealand," Thomas tossed over his shoulder. "Only take a few hours, just let me know."

Matt thanked Thomas for the offer and happily accepted. The four men arrived at Thomas's seaside home in Coogee Beach and unpacked the SUV. Steve was okay now, but twice had complained of dizziness. Jackson told him it was normal for head trauma, and it should recede in frequency in a day or two.

"How do you know so much about this shit?" Matt asked as they entered Thomas's living room.

"I played football at Clemson, then semi-pro ball in Canada for a season before applying to the FBI. The head injuries drove me out of the game. The trainers weren't as informed about the issue as they are today. I spent a lot of time researching the topic on my own."

“That explains why you have a hard time keeping your head in the game.” Nobody laughed at Steve’s attempt at humor, and that was funny all by itself.

Thomas oriented them to the house and then left to take care of a few personal errands. About an hour later, Jackson received a call from Thomas. He took notes and then hung up.

“Did he find out anything?” Matt asked. He knew Gary was a legit SEAL, but why drag him into this if he wasn’t an asset?

Jackson nodded and began to read from his notes. “Gary Conroy, former US Special Operations, lives in Auckland, New Zealand. Left the SEAL teams after losing his lower left arm to a roadside bomb in Kandahar Province, Afghanistan, in 2008.”

“Shit,” Matt muttered under his breath.

Jackson looked up but then continued. “He turned his disability pension into gold after a GI Bill-funded education in programming and network systems at Stanford led to his creation of several patents, something about neural pathways and AI. Extremely wealthy, single, never married. Lives like a king from the sale of his inventions, but Thomas does say this guy has a lucrative side business as an expert hacker.”

Matt wasn’t computer savvy, and nothing interested him less than technology. He used it when he had to and that was it. Apparently, Gary was a geek. Good for him, Matt was proud one of his classmates had succeeded in something other than killing bad guys. But could he help them in their cause?

“Multimillionaire, you went through SEAL training with him, and he’s a hacker. Not to mention he’s conveniently located a skip and a jump from here,” Steve said, observing the obvious rationale for enlisting Gary. "Why not have him join the merry band?"

After a short discussion, the three men agreed to have Matt contact Gary and see what, if any, help he could provide. Jackson's phone vibrated and he glanced at the screen. "My friend in Honolulu just scored. I asked him to get me any information regarding Roger Maddox's activities and operations in the Hawaiian Islands. I specifically asked him to find out who was running enforcement for Maddox. He just sent this to me."

Jackson extended his arm so Steve and Matt could study the image on the small screen. Matt recognized the snide little man instantly. "Son of a bitch, it's that little Asian fucker from the alley! Who is he?"

Jackson pulled his phone back and began reading the short description. "His name is A-wut Onruang. He's a Thai national and middle broker for the sex trade flow through California and Hawaii to East Asia. Operates out of Phuket, Thailand, most of the time and is believed to have close business ties with Roger Maddox. He's less a local Hawaiian boss than a regional one. Odd that he would get his hands dirty."

Matt and Steve looked at each other. Whatever happened after they left the alley likely was cleaned up by this A-wut character. He wouldn't want problems with the Honolulu police any more than they did.

"So, this guy might be worth talking to, if we can find him," Jackson noted.

Matt nodded and walked to the window. They were making slow progress toward knowing what happened to victims of the sex trade, but were they any closer to finding Vicky before it was too late? Too late to save her physically and mentally?

They needed help, and Gary seemed to have the resources they could leverage. Time to give his old classmate a call.

Chapter Nine

Gary Conroy waited on the front porch of his sprawling estate, if you could call a fifteen-by-four-yard space a porch. A twenty-five thousand square foot complex that encompassed all the amenities and functions of a hotel, Gary had purchased it a few years earlier so he could be close to the ocean.

Like all frogmen, past and present, he had a love-hate relationship with the sea. Water was the primary instrument of pain and punishment in BUD/S, and an ever-present component of being a SEAL. Always cold, usually murky, SEALs operated in the wet environment until they learned to respect the power of the ocean.

Most SEALs stayed away after leaving the service, but Gary couldn't. His love of the water went back to his father and his love of jet skiing, surfing, and SCUBA diving. All the Conroy kids were addicted to the wet sports, and he was no exception.

That's why losing his arm had been so devastating. He couldn't stay in the unit he loved, and he would never be as competent in the water again. At least being next to it, waking up to the sound of its majesty, was something he could afford to do.

The van rolled up the long driveway and came to a halt in front of Gary. Two of his security men walked out to open the side panel door and to help with the luggage. Gary hadn't seen Matt Barrett in over ten years. A brief brush past at a retirement ceremony in Coronado was all he remembered.

Matt hadn't been a very good BUD/S officer: too indecisive, always trying too hard, and screwing it up anyway. The enlisted men in the class liked the awkward leader, but they didn't respect him. The mission in Egypt has surprised all of them. Matt had been a brand-new officer in SEAL Delivery Vehicle Team Two when the uprising in Egypt occurred.

When it was all over, Matt was a legend, a winner of the Navy Cross for gallantry under fire; and from everything Gary knew of the operation, his former class leader deserved the honor and then some.

Matt stepped out of the van and stood still while the bags were passed by Steve to Jackson and then to him. A tall blond man, athletic in appearance but not bulky, grabbed the bags and went into the house. He spotted Gary and waved. Even though his smile was the same, Gary was much older than the teenager Matt had known in BUD/S. He'd gone bald except for a little hair above each ear, but he still had the same twinkle in his eye that used to make Matt feel like a practical joke was about to be sprung at any moment.

The van pulled away, and their host stepped down off the porch. "Welcome to my home, guys! I only wish we were gathered for something a bit less dramatic." The three men shook Gary's good hand in turn, then followed him into the house.

"What did you do, rob a bank?" Steve joked.

Gary stopped in the expansive living room and turned back to look at Steve. "I made my first thirty million the easy way: I used my brain to solve people's problems. The bank robbing came much later."

Matt noted Gary's serious demeanor. Bank robbery? The background information Jackson had obtained indicated that Gary was now a hacker of some skill, at least good enough for the Australians to be aware of his activities. Gary had changed, but for better or for worse, Matt didn't know yet.

Gary explained the history of the home, once a British trading headquarters, and how he was able to find and acquire the property. He described the renovation work in detail, a two-year labor of love that resulted in a grand palace. He also described the security precautions installed throughout the estate and briefly touched on his praetorian guard of former Australian and New Zealand SAS special operators.

The rest of his staff were native to the island, Kiwis. They'd been vetted by his head of security, another former government man, and had impeccable credentials.

"I need to have confidence in the people around me, you see. It's quiet here, and I like it that way. When I saw Tom's request for help, I was unsure how to help. Once he told me that Matt was leading a rescue team to find his daughter, I was all in. Please get comfortable."

Gary signaled a waiting member of the staff and the man scurried off on a mission. Matt, Steve, and Jackson chose a place to sit down. Matt was surprised Tom assumed he was the leader of the group. He didn't want that responsibility on his shoulders. After letting Steve down in Hawaii, he was pretty sure the other two didn't want it either.

Steve was the first to speak. "So, Gary, as you might expect, we've read up on your background. Impressive. We've also heard you're well-connected in Asia."

"Knowledgeable might be a more accurate term," Gary responded. "I know a great many people and can get to know a great many more if required. I never leave this place and rarely see outsiders anymore. But, yes, I may be able to help you find others that can assist you."

Matt was still in shock from the size and opulence of Gary's place. He wondered if the armed (and he assumed they were armed) protection was paranoia or a prudent measure to deter or defeat a known threat. His right hand started shaking again.

Matt clasped it in his other hand and waited. The shaking occurred occasionally, but he had no way of calming it down. He had to stuff his hand in his pocket or do as he was doing now, hold the offending appendage in his good hand.

He knew the shaking wasn't an old war wound, or too much coffee, or even stress. It was one of several withdrawal symptoms he'd suffered since Michigan. He did research online, and the truth was confirmed.

Drinking for two years, and hard liquor at that, built up a dependency that sheer force of will couldn't defeat alone. Every time he considered sneaking off to have even one drink, Steve's face appeared in his mind. He didn't want to ruin their long friendship or be classified by the growing team as a liability.

Steve, Jackson, and Gary were in a deep conversation, and Matt should've been paying close attention, taking notes even. He was on the razor's edge. He knew it; and if this job accelerated and went tactical, everybody would know it. Gary stopped speaking and looked directly at Matt.

"What do you think? I'm assuming with your record and experience, these folks have deferred to you as the leader. What's your opinion?"

Matt froze. He didn't have a clue what to say, because he'd been so wrapped up in controlling himself. Now Steve and

Jackson were looking at him, all waiting for him to answer. *Leader? I fucking doubt it after this display.* Steve guessed that Matt hadn't been paying attention, so he repeated the point to set up Matt for a second chance.

"So, Jackson thinks we need to go to Thailand now, without delay. He feels the more time that passes, the colder Vicky's trail becomes. I tend to agree with him. We've seen these abduction cases in the past, and time is everything. However, Gary has pointed out that we only have three guys. He can hook us up in Thailand with a man he knows and trusts; but he feels we need one more operator, you know, like a four-man fire team."

Matt concentrated. On instinct, he liked the idea of one more man. If he couldn't execute, they'd need a fourth man to end up with three. Besides, he also liked the symmetry of a four-man fire team: two-man pairs, one covering the other when necessary, and the ability to put four experienced men on a task together.

"I'm with Gary. Four is better than three. However, you two also have a point. How long will it take to find a guy we trust, who is willing, available, and can drop everything to get his ass here ASAP?"

Gary had been pondering that very point, and he thought he had a candidate. "I know a guy I worked with in the teams who I'd trust with my life. He's miserable right now, working for the frogman who invented that exercise gimmick, you know the electro-abdominal thing. I bet he'd hop on a plane in a minute."

Matt and the others liked the sound of the idea, but Matt knew that getting in touch, flying commercial, all took time. The best he could expect was two days. That was probably too long to wait. He was starting to lean towards the "time is everything" argument.

Steve nodded and wanted to know more. "What were his skills in the teams?"

"His name is Erik, Erik Swanson. He left the teams six months ago to keep his family of six together. This guy was all in; it was the brotherhood all the way. Between ten and fifteen combat tours easy. A guy making that many trips has got to be a little unstable; but he's still shitting Navy chow, so he should be able to switch into operator mode quickly."

Steve glanced at Matt. He probably could guess that Matt was, by Gary's definition, a little unstable. "Is he physically up to speed?" he asked.

"Was wounded early in his career in Afghanistan. Saw action in the Philippines. Got hit last year in Syria fighting those ISIS shitheads. Like I said, he's an operator's operator. Has to still be in great shape. Should be 35, I'd guess."

Jackson was following the rapid back and forth, but he was curious. "So, how do you know so much about this guy? You've been out of the Navy and off the grid for a long time."

"He saved my ass in Afghanistan. Patched me up after I was hit twice, once by an AK round and once by frag from a rocket that just missed four of us. He kept me alive. I've made it a point to stay in touch ever since that day. Besides, who do you think got him that shitty job selling personal shock treatments?" Gary grinned.

Erik was sweating like a pig. He only had three minutes of cardio before his second workout of the day would be over. He pushed his long, reddish-brown hair out of his eyes and focused hard on the digital display as it wound down. Two minutes, one minute, done!

He slowed the pace of the spin bike to a slow and steady rate. He'd cool down for a few minutes and then hit the shower. The only good thing about his lousy job was the freedom to roam without a boss looking over his shoulders. That scrutiny happened on Friday afternoon when he came face-to-face with his dismal sales numbers and had to grit his teeth to avoid clocking the asshole who thought he was a leader. *Leader, my ass!*

Erik toweled off his sweaty face and tossed it into the receptacle provided for such things. That was another perk: free gym memberships all over the place. All the gyms that had bought the company's fitness products allowed its sales guys to join their clubs for free.

Erik stepped on the scale next to the men's dressing room and smiled. One hundred and ninety-five pounds. One pound lighter than the day he stripped off the uniform for good. Working out twice a day was keeping him lean and strong, and of course, preventing him from gaining too much weight. Civilians had it rough, he'd observed.

In the teams, everybody was your fitness coach and critic. There were no boundaries. They all depended on each other to be in warrior shape, and as a result they always were. Civilians didn't have a vicious support group; and even if they did, he doubted anyone would be able to express an opinion without being fired.

He walked into the dressing room and stripped down. Opening the locker door, he decided to check his voicemails and texts for prospects willing to meet with him. There were seven voice messages and four texts. It was the third text that made his jaw drop. *Fuck the shower!* Erik was dressed and out of the building in four minutes flat.

Steve and Jackson were on a run, and Matt had worked out that afternoon, so he had some time to himself. It had been an hour since Gary informed them Erik was a go. Gary had membership in shared usage of various executive jets, and he was in his home office setting one up to bring Erik to them. They'd all decided to stay one night with Gary and leave for Thailand in the morning. Erik would fly direct to meet them all there.

Gary was a godsend. Matt realized that as much as they were driven to succeed, success on an operation like this was expensive. What had the horse lady said? *Take a lot of money and spread it around; you'll get a lead.* Well, so far money had allowed them to pull a great team together and get to where the information was: Thailand.

Gary also had indicated that he owned two Thai banks. He promised to set up a master account with all four of them given access to draw funds. He had a credit card machine on the estate and would produce the cards and activate them in his capacity as administer of the bank.

Finally, he was connecting them with his main point of contact in Thailand. He assured them this man was discreet and highly capable. He suggested they ask him about his capabilities and personal history when they met him.

Steve and Jackson's voices could be heard outside. In a minute they walked into the main living area, sweat pouring down their bodies. "Short run?" Matt poked.

“Hey there, mister BUD/S instructor, I didn’t see your lame ass out there running these fucking hills. Two miles are as good as five miles for a flatlander like me.”

Matt laughed. “You should see me try to do more than ten push-ups. I’m in no way qualified to judge you two. I think Gary is still back in the office area. He’d mentioned dinner at 6:30. That’s only twenty minutes from now, so you might want to wash the road dust off!”

Steve was about to respond to the push-up comment when he was interrupted by the distinct sound of multiple gunshots. Five or six in rapid succession, then four more. All three men looked at each other. There was a gun battle erupting outside the estate.

Chapter Ten

Matt and Steve instinctively started to move to the front entrance. Jackson stood there trying to triangulate the origin of the gunfire. Just as Matt placed his hand on the doorknob, he heard a shout.

"Everyone, get your asses in here now!" Gary's voice was firm and didn't convey panic. Matt froze for a moment then followed Steve and Jackson at a run into the back of the estate, where Gary's business office was located.

As the three men rushed into the 2,000-square-foot area that Gary referred to as the "office," they spotted him standing by an old plantation style rolltop desk made of teak wood. More shots erupted, further from the home, if Matt's ears were hearing correctly.

"What the fuck? We need to find out what's going on out there." Steve stopped in front of the multimillionaire. "Do you have any firearms handy? We need to arm ourselves."

Gary remained calm, serene even. "How long you guys been out of the game, huh? Can you do better than ten former SAS operators in their prime? Because that's what I have out there and in here guarding this place and everything in it."

Matt listened and realized there was wisdom in Gary's words. He hadn't fired a weapon on the range or otherwise in over two years. Steve, like him, was rusty at direct combat, even if he'd kept up his shooting proficiency.

"What if these SAS fail? What if whoever is out there is aware of their capabilities and came here prepared to deal with them?" Jackson's tone was measured but tense.

"I'd feel a whole lot better if the four of us were armed in here, just in case. Alamo and all that shit," Steve added.

Two more shots rang out, this time on the back side of the estate. Gary looked from man to man and then nodded. He went to a section of wall six feet to the left of his rolltop desk and reached into his pocket. He pulled out what looked like a thumb drive and pointed it at the wall.

Matt's jaw dropped when he saw the arsenal arrayed on the walls of the secret room. Everything was in there. Sniper rifles, submachineguns, assault rifles, and every kind of handgun imaginable. Most of the weapons were outfitted with silencers, and all had slings. This wasn't a collection; this was a ready room. Gary was prepared for Armageddon.

"There are mags in the drawers underneath each weapon. They're loaded and ready to go. Stop admiring and pick your poison; the shooting seems to have ended outside."

The three men darted into the small room and went to work. Matt selected a German MP-5 SD 9mm submachinegun. The SD meant a silencer was already an integral part of the weapon. He found a three magazine leg pouch in the drawer and backed out of the room. Steve exited a second later with Jackson close behind. Both men were armed with M4 assault rifles.

Gary went in last. He grabbed a tricked-out Kimber forty-five caliber automatic pistol. It didn't look like a combat weapon, more like a competitive shooting piece. Matt smiled. "Nice forty-five!"

Gary smiled. "I had it made for me personally. It has a hair trigger, two-pound pull, and a compensator. Slightly down loaded match rounds, too. I can squeeze off seven rounds, and the sight doesn't even move. Fuck that double tap shit. One shot, one kill."

Steve was looking at the room to determine where they could go to bunker in until help arrived. Jackson was doing the same. Matt was finishing strapping on the magazine pouch to his leg when he heard a deep voice outside the office.

"November Zulu!"

Gary visibly relaxed. "Fun's over guys. That's the code phrase for all secure." Gary stepped around the other three men and responded, "Uniform Sierra!"

Matt wasn't taking any chances. He raised his weapon and focused on the entrance to the room. Steve noted this and mimicked Matt's readiness, standing with the M4 at a 45-degree angle to the floor, rifle butt secured against his shoulder. A second later a man none of them recognized, walked into the room, his hands empty.

"Keith, report please," Gary said. "Gentlemen, please lower your weapons. Keith is my chief of security."

Keith had scanned the room as he entered and marked everyone's position. He had a bull-pup-style assault rifle slung across his back and appeared calm.

"Sir, the estate team is intact. No injuries."

Gary visibly relaxed. He placed the Kimber forty-five on the rolltop desk and sat down in a brown leather club chair. "I'm very happy to hear that. Please, gentlemen, stand down and relax. My home is secure."

Matt removed the thirty-round magazine from his MP-5SD and pulled back on the small black knob to eject the 9mm round from the chamber. As he removed the leg pouch, Jackson and Steve also down loaded their weapons. A minute later everybody in the room was seated, except for Keith, who was patiently waiting to deliver his status report.

"So, Keith, was it our friends getting a little physical?"

Matt had been wondering since their arrival why Gary felt the need to have a crack SAS squad guarding him. That, plus the gunfire, pointed to trouble. Gary must be into something shaky. Then again, people with money can make powerful enemies.

"Sir, they were not affiliated with …" he hesitated.

"Go on, Keith. I trust these men."

Keith nodded and continued, "They are not affiliated with our, as you put it, 'friends.' There were four men, from what we can determine. The security video might give us more insight as to numbers. Alec surprised one of them, who had started to monkey with the power station on the east side of the estate. The man panicked and shot at Alec. Alec returned fire."

Matt thought it made sense that an estate of this size had its own power station. Jackson was curious about the initial engagement, so he interrupted the tall Australian.

"Keith, my name is Jackson, Jackson Bollinger. This power station, is it a building? A concentration of machinery?"

Keith looked at Gary again before answering. Gary's nod seemed to finally allow the head of security to relax his posture for the first time since entering the room.

"A standalone building, Mr. Bollinger. It is locked and possesses its own security surveillance system. There are other security measures, should anyone gain access; but in this case, they did not."

Steve rubbed his eyes, then asked his question. “Hi, Keith. I’m Steve. You said there were four men. What were the other three doing out there?”

Keith sighed. At this rate, getting his report out would take an hour. “Mr. Auger, gentlemen. There is no need to keep introducing yourselves. My team has been fully briefed by our intelligence officer on each of you--your careers in the American federal government or military and what you’ve been doing since leaving government service.” Keith was looked right at Matt as he finished his sentence.

Matt maintained his poker face, but inside he was surprised for some reason. An intelligence officer? *What the fuck is going on here?* Did Gary know he was a drunk? He couldn’t imagine how anyone could figure that out by looking at the internet or social media. Matt had been off those systems for years. Did Tom say something?

Keith looked at Gary. “Sir, I have some things to attend to, if I may proceed?” The tall man’s irritation with the questions was evident.

“Yes, please continue. Guys, please allow Keith to complete his report.”

Steve shrugged, and the other two guests simply eased back further in their seats. Keith methodically laid out a timeline and a sequence of events that sounded like a military operation. One man was sent to cut power, and three men were staged at the back of the estate, poised to enter once the power was cut.

Keith explained there were two security team members on the perimeter of the main building 24 hours a day. The second man, a former Kiwi paratrooper, saw and engaged the three-man entry team, who were armed with rifles. A firefight ensued. Keith and five more security officers rushed from the house to assist. The three men, realizing the odds had changed, bolted, firing a few shots as they ran.

"Very exciting, sir. Oh yes, we did capture the first intruder, the one at the power station. Alec is interrogating him right now. He's wounded, but will survive."

Gary stood up and walked over to Keith extending his good hand. "Thank you, Keith. As always, your team and your leadership prevail. Let me know if you get anything out of the prisoner."

Matt waited until Keith left the office to press the question: who was trying to get at Gary and why? His question was preempted by Gary. Their host cleared his throat to gain attention and then sat down.

"I have enemies."

"No fucking shit!" Matt responded. "Ninjas, no less."

Steve stood up and began pacing the room. "Are you in serious jeopardy?"

Gary laughed, but the sound rang hollow in the large room. "No, I don't think so. As long as I stay here, in my little security bubble, I should be safe."

Jackson had been staring at the hard wood floor for five minutes trying to soak it all in. His mind was geared toward analyzing crimes, not special operations. His first instinct was to collect data, analyze, and profile. "Who is pissed off enough and crazy enough to send a team into New Zealand after a US citizen?"

Matt recognized immediately why Jackson was a valuable part of their team. SEALs tried to think rationally all the time, but their first inclination was to designate a target and take it out. Emotion and passion came before serious thought. Apparently, Jackson was wired the other way around.

Matt still couldn't help himself. "Yeah, what he said. You don't have a security bubble; you have a fortress with a team of commandos at your beck and call. What gives?"

Gary sighed. "After the sale of my patent portfolio, I was wealthy and bored out of my mind. I began, well, hacking is too simple a term to describe what I decided to do with my time. I was good at it though, really good. At first, I had fun, you know, pranks, just messing with things. Then I became enthralled with the idea of breaking into the tough things, banks mostly."

"You pissed off a bank? Banks don't send hit teams." Jackson's tone betrayed his irritation. The answer wasn't coming fast enough for him.

Gary looked around at the men in the room, then locked eyes with Jackson. "Chinese banks do."

Matt leaned back in his chair. "Holy shit, brother. You stole money from the fucking Chinese?"

"Well, actually worse than just a bank. You see, eighty percent of the banks in China are owned by the government. The Peoples Republic."

"The Communist People's Republic." Steve added.

"Explains the ninjas, or whatever the Chinese call their version of ninjas. How many times have they tried to get at you?" Jackson asked.

Gary raised his hand. "Wait, there's more."

"How could there be more? You started a personal war with China! Ballsy, but stupid." Matt had to make the point on everyone's mind. Gary's genius had strayed into dark places, and his life was at risk because of his desire to beat the system--in this case, China's system.

"The agency became aware of what I was doing. They monitor all electronic activity in China, and they became interested in my success."

"So, they recruited you to do more, right?" Steve had a long history working with the agency. Early in his Navy career, he'd worked in a special task force guided by the guys in khaki and dark sunglasses. He didn't enjoy it, and he never learned to trust them.

Gary nodded. "They agreed to give me immunity for any cybercrimes I committed or may have committed in the past in exchange for my assistance. It was a bullshit deal; I'd never been caught, and in my opinion I wouldn't be. That is until I started doing favors for them."

"Let me guess. They had you penetrate something other than a bank." Jackson thought he knew where the story was heading.

Gary nodded. "Hypersonic missile testing facility. Cutting edge technology and lethal. The Chinese steal from the States all the time, been doing it for years. Most of the technological advances in their military since 2000 have been hacked secrets, information pulled from our commercial contractors' servers. Lockheed, Raytheon, the regular list of strategic technology innovators. It didn't seem like a bad idea at the time."

“So, if you’re so good and all, how did the Chinese figure out it was you hacking shit from them?” Matt didn’t expect the answer to be so stunning.

“The Chinese have over 10,000 of what we call hackers. Brilliant men and women who spend their lives searching for data to steal. But a select few have a different purpose. They search for anyone stealing data from China. These were the ones who found me.”

Steve, Matt, and Jackson remained silent for a good minute, absorbing all they’d heard. Matt’s first concern was for Gary’s safety. His second was mission-related. *Could Gary still help them find Vicky?*

Gary felt compelled to finish the story. “They figured out they were penetrated and started a trace. They let me continue doing what I was doing, but watching and tracking me through the multiple cutout servers I used to blur my trail. As good as they were, they couldn’t get close enough to stop me.”

Steve was confused. “Wait a minute. You just said these guys were the reason the ninjas were sent.”

Gary shook his head. “They didn’t find me directly, they found me indirectly. A mole in the agency found my file, and it didn’t take much to put two and two together. That’s how they found out who I was and where I was.”

“Shit,” Steve mumbled.

Jackson stood up and stretched before speaking. “How many times. How many attempts?”

Gary put up two fingers. “They’ve tried to hack into the security remotely a dozen times, same with my secure server. I stopped everything related to the Chinese when my handler at the agency told me they had been made aware by their sources in China that an American hacker living in New Zealand was the person using their top-secret program as a cyber playground. The attacks started a few months after that."

The sound of footsteps cut off conversation, and all eyes turned toward the entrance to the room. Matt instinctively looked for his MP-5SD. As he did so, he realized his mind was beginning to shift more and more into an operator mind-set. The shakes were still there, but he felt better, normal.

Keith entered the room and stopped a few feet from Gary. "Sir, Alec was able to get a word from the man, only one word. He injected him with a little dose of what the SAS used to call 'happy juice.' He was willing to talk about anything after the injection; but when pressed about who he was working for, he kept saying the same word over and over again."

"What was the word?" Steve asked.

"'Awhat.' The word was 'awhat.' Didn't make any sense. Gibberish if you ask me, sir."

Gary waved his head of security out of the room. "Well, that was a dead end."

Matt sat forward. "It wasn't the Chinese."

Jackson turned. "Nobody else would send a hit team in here; it has to be the Chinese."

Steve chimed in, "I have to agree with Jackson. Occam's razor. When faced with multiple possibilities, the simplest one is usually the correct one."

Matt stood up. "It wasn't the Chinese, and the prisoner wasn't speaking gibberish. He was saying a name. A-wut. A-wut

Onruang. The men sent here tonight weren't after Gary; they were after us. Roger Maddox wants us dead."

Chapter Eleven

The sharp mountain ridges held back the rain, causing it to sit over the estate for hours. Once the clouds expended their moisture, they floated high enough to pop over the elevations inland, allowing the sun to bathe the coastal area in welcoming light.

Matt slept fitfully and woke before dawn. The strange events of the prior day rushed to the front of his conscious mind, and he lay in bed trying to sort it all out. Gary wasn't a criminal, or was he? He'd admitted to stealing money, using his hacking skill to enrich himself. Yes, he was a criminal. But was he a hero too?

The Chinese were on the move across the globe. They'd entered the Sudan a few years back with the goal of becoming a driving influence in the region. They poured money and expertise of all flavors into the poor country; and as planned, soon became a player in a place once reserved for European colonial powers.

Keith never told them the fate of the one attacker who was captured and interrogated. Did Gary's squad of Hollywood killers bury him on the property? Dump his body in the ocean, weighted down to prevent discovery? How does one make a body disappear in New Zealand?

Just before going to bed, Jackson asked if the local authorities would respond to the reports of gun play on Gary's estate. Gary smiled and told them all he'd provided certain services to the national government, and in exchange they looked the other way, that is unless a Kiwi was hurt or killed. They drew the line there.

Matt yawned. As exciting as the evening was, he needed to get back on mission focus. The time since leaving Key West felt like it had zipped by, but only four days had passed. Today was day five. For Vicky, somewhere out there in a cell or locked room, time was different. She had to be terrified. Had she been abused already?

Matt's rough beer math calculated she'd been kidnapped two weeks and one day ago. Fifteen days is a long time. SERE school simulated a prison camp, and by doing so taught young pilots and SEALs how to survive the experience. Even that limited one-week prison phase was enough to drive some people to the emotional edge. Vicky was only a kid.

Matt heard soft footsteps in the hallway outside his door, followed by a clicking sound as someone closed the bathroom door. He wasn't the only one up early. He felt himself dozing off again, but a tapping at the door brought him back.

"Come in."

Steve opened the door and walked to the chair near the window. He sat down and looked around the room before speaking.

"Gary's really an interesting guy, right?"

Matt nodded. The sunlight was struggling to push through the gaps in the curtain covering his large bedroom window, but it was still dark enough that he couldn't see the expression on his teammate's face.

"We need to leave today. We're wasting too much time with all the bullshit. It's been fifteen days by my count."

Steve stretched his arms up and over his head. "Yeah, I woke up thinking the same thing. Jackson spoke to Gary for a while after you and I hit the sack. He was going to lock down the plan for today, the flight out of here, contact information in

Thailand, all that stuff. If Gary is going to help, this would be the time to execute."

Matt sat up and rubbed his eyes. "We won't have the SAS softball team with us in Phuket. That's this A-wut shithead's home turf. We'll have a bullseye on our backs the second we step off the plane."

Steve nodded and leaned back. "We need to get weapons; pistols would be sufficient. Just for self-defense. Maybe Gary's guy can get them for us."

Matt pivoted and swung his legs over the side of the bed. "Just like the old days, right? Once more into the breech and all that shit."

Steve smiled. "I worked with a lot of officers in my day. Academy guys, ROTC, and guys right out of OCS. Never saw a distinction based on where they were commissioned. My only way of judging was to score the quality of their decision making. You were the best I ever worked with; the best I ever experienced actually. I don't know why you lost your way after getting out, but you're back as far as I'm concerned. With you leading us, I know we'll find Vicky; I would bet everything I have on that expectation."

Matt sat there and listened. He might have been all that once upon a time, but now? Shit, he could hardly do more than twenty push-ups. His time in purgatory wasn't over; he felt it on the edge of his mind. Waiting for him to come back to the dark. He didn't see a future where that wasn't the case.

"Nice speech. Jackson should lead this project. It's what he's an expert in--finding kidnapped people. I'm along for the ride, do what I can, whatever that is, to help. Making me lead is a mistake."

Steve Auger stared at his former teammate and commander without answering. Something deep inside told him that if Matt didn't become the leader of this effort, he was a lost soul. He'd fade back into the Key West scenery and eventually, on some lonely night, end his journey. Too many frogmen had taken that path after leaving the service. He'd never felt that level of despair and dislocation. Technically, he'd joined the Bollinger Group before his last day in uniform.

The problem with special operators deciding to check out was that they were so strong-willed, so disciplined. As odd as it was, once a SEAL decided to do something, it was damn near impossible to talk him out of it. Steve had lost two close friends in less than a year. It cut across all eras of SEALs, all demographics.

"Well that's just too fucking bad, sir. You are the chosen one. We didn't bring you this far because of your shooting skills."

Steve got up and checked his watch. "I'm going to see what Gary's got set up for us today. Get your ass dressed and grab your shit. We may be leaving right away. Oh, and wipe the mopey look off your face. Leaders need to convey strength and confidence."

Matt didn't respond as Steve closed the door and left him alone. He wasn't sure if Steve's old school Non-Commissioned Offer bullshit was real or just a weak attempt to shame Matt into action. In any case he needed to take a piss, and that meant movement, however slight.

Jackson, Steve, and Gary waited by the shuttle van for Matt. He saw their looks and realized he'd been fiddle fucking around too long. He tossed his personal bag in the back of the vehicle and walked up to Gary.

"Thanks for everything. You sure these pinup boys you have hanging around here are enough to keep you safe?"

Gary laughed. "They are a bit too handsome now that you mention it. I'll be sure to rotate some ugly thugs into the group to make you feel happy. It was good seeing you again, sir. These guys feel confident you'll lead them to Vicky. I have a feeling you will, too."

Gary shook Matt's hand with his good hand and waved at the others who were already inside the shuttle. Matt jumped in and slammed the van door shut. "Steve, what's the logistics plan for this goat rope?"

Steve smiled and pulled out a notebook. The van left the porch and headed down the long driveway. In the distance, Matt spotted an SAS man near the rear of the estate. Whatever the Chinese had in store for Gary, he was pretty sure Gary would end up on top.

"We're flying out on Gary's plane, a Gulfstream Five. We land in Malaysia to refuel and then on to Thailand. The trip will take about ten hours, depending on the fuel stop. Add two more hours for issues in Malaysia, and we land in Thailand twelve hours after wheels up here."

Matt nodded and absorbed the information. "If A-wut knew we were at Gary's …"

"He'll be watching all Gary's transportation assets," Jackson finished. "That's two fishing boats, a 250-foot yacht, two intermediate range aircraft, and the Gulfstream. He'll be watching, and he'll know we left New Zealand."

"Well, fuck him and his gang of shitheads," Steve spit out. We know they are looking for us and we know they are hostiles. Rules of engagement, commander?" Steve looked at Matt.

Matt snorted. "ROE? We don't have weapons, so I guess the ROE is run away."

Jackson cleared his throat. "Gary gave us the name and bio of his guy in Phuket. His name is Seamus Flanagan, Naval Academy grad, former F-14 pilot."

Matt raised his eyebrows. "A Tomcat jock?"

Jackson nodded and continued, "His career went sideways when he refused to drop dumb bombs on a suspected Taliban position. The target located also had a large number of women and children. Ground forces were supposed to call the target clear of non-combatants; when they didn't, he aborted the bombing mission."

Matt and Steve looked at each other. They'd both experienced their share of ethical dilemmas. It was a part of war. The bad guys in the war had a habit of hiding behind their families, expecting the Americans to hesitate. Somalia, Philippines, Syria, Iraq, Afghanistan, the location didn't matter. Their adversary was fanatical. They planned for that hesitation; it gave them an edge on the battlefield.

Jackson noted the change in his two partners' demeanor, but decided to leave them alone. The details about this contact was affecting them in a way he couldn't fathom. "Flanagan left the Navy in 2007. He held multiple jobs, contracting mostly, before taking a gig in Thailand as an executive pilot for a small South Korean company. He eventually started his own air services company. Goat Air."

"Those ring knockers can never let it go. It's like they can't keep from singing the fight song of that boy's school until the day they die." Steve shook his head.

Matt nodded. "They can't buy clothes to wear unless it's a shade of blue or gold. Sad. But most of the ones I've met had integrity. You could count on them to come through for you. Fucking Goat Air!"

"Gary says he named it after the Naval Academy's mascot. After ten years in Asia, he's deeply tied into the legal and the illegal logistics trade, able to find anything for a client and move it anywhere. Gary says he can get us weapons and give us a place to stay until we sort things out," Jackson added.

The Gulfstream Five sat on the tarmac, glimmering in the bright sunlight. The airfield was near the coast and away from the nearly permanently overcast skies aligned with the mountain ridges. Matt and the others walked up to the pilot and introduced themselves. He proceeded to deliver the obligatory safety brief and then opened the cargo door set into the fuselage.

Steve tossed his bags into the hole and then took a step back to survey his surroundings. He didn't see anyone set up and watching them. He looked toward the apartments off in the distance. It was within reason to expect spotters there on the high ground.

Matt strolled over and joined Steve. "Nothing?"

"No, lots of places to observe us from. Those apartments for one." Steve gestured with his head in the direction of the building in the distance.

Matt looked back over his shoulder at the control tower then at the tail numbers on the aircraft. "I wouldn't worry too much about an observation team."

Steve looked perturbed. "Oh really? Because this A-wut turd is too stupid or you're just hoping for the best?"

Matt winced at the biting sarcasm. "A-wut is Roger Maddox's boy, correct?"

Steve nodded. "So?"

"Maddox is a multimillionaire. He's been operating in Asia for a decade. He's not going to rely on thugs to track our movements this time. He's going to just put this tail number on a flight tracker app and watch us leave, refuel, and land in Thailand."

"As easy as that," Steve said.

"As easy as what?" Jackson joined the two ex-SEALs.

Matt answered, "That's right, as easy as that. A-wut does the grunt work, so I guess he's not the tech guy in Maddox's organization."

"Matt here says the plane will be tracked," Steve brought Jackson up to speed.

"That means they likely will have a welcoming committee at the other end of this flight. We need a plan for getting to this Flanagan guy before A-wut makes his move. I'd feel a whole lot better if I was armed."

Matt and Steve both agreed. Matt thought ahead a few steps further. "We could contact Gary, have him reach out to Flanagan, and have him waiting at the airport for us."

Jackson was in agreement. "Now that's good thinking! We can grab weapons and be ready as we leave the confines of the Phuket airport for any crazy A-wut has in store for us. Sound like a plan?"

Steve nodded. The Gulfstream came with an attractive flight attendant, and she now stood just inside the door at the top of the stairs. She waved frantically letting them all know they were messing up the pilot's scheduled takeoff. The three men climbed up and entered the sleek plane. The interior was all light leather. Each set of seats, more like club chairs, was clustered around a table. The attendant guided them until each was strapped in and ready to go.

Matt's cell phone was out of power, so Steve called Gary on his personal line. After a minute or two, he put his phone down and looked up. "We are good to go! He said to get burner phones in Phuket; Flanagan can help us with that. He's assuming all our phones are compromised, as well as our contact lists. That means Tom, too."

The jet began to taxi to the runway. After pausing a few times for other inbound and outbound traffic, it was lined up on the main runway, ready to depart. Matt went over the plan as far as it went and was satisfied. They'd thought of everything. His one burning need was information. Specific information.

Roger Maddox was the general, but someone in his organization knew the full details of the human trafficking operation. The who, what, when, and where that would lead them to Vicky.

If they didn't get that information--and soon--it would be too late to save Tom's daughter, and Matt could add another failure to his long list of fuckups. He leaned back and closed his eyes. They were going to find her; and if they didn't, Roger Maddox was going to get to meet a couple of Navy frogmen.

Chapter Twelve

Seamus turned sharply, taking the bongo truck around the tight corner, nearly hitting an old man on a bike. *There's fucking people everywhere!* He honked the crappy horn and made two kids look, point, and laugh. *This truck's a fucking joke!*

It was a twenty-minute drive from his place near the western beaches of Phuket, but it was only a distance of five miles. Five miles of tiny roads and a mass of humanity. Everybody was selling stuff, buying stuff, standing around staring at stuff, just fucking off in general. He'd thought getting attuned to the Asian way of life would be easy, but it was getting worse the longer he stayed here.

Seamus often found himself surfing the Internet looking at remote places, out of the way locations like Patagonia and Norway. He was pretty sure it didn't take twenty minutes to travel five miles in Norway. He'd bet on it. His next move would be something as different from Thailand as he could find.

Gary's message had been both clear and cryptic at the same time. His friends needed help finding a kidnapped girl, the daughter of a Navy frogman. That part was clear enough. The rest was about some asshole named A-wut, who was trying to stop them or kill them or stop them by killing them. Seamus didn't ask Gary any questions. He'd pick these guys up and get the scoop from them personally.

The bongo truck tilted as he made another sharp turn, this time to the right, and accelerated the rest of the way. Here the road widened out to accommodate the traffic near the airport. He paused at the service gate to wave at the man who was somebody's idea of a security guard and drove through to the commercial side of the complex. Gary's jet was hard to miss. So much for operating under the RADAR. Everybody within six miles would've noticed that plane flying in.

The Gulfstream Five taxied over to the commercial hangars, following the instructions of the ground crew. It finally stopped in front of a newer structure that was both hangar and business office. Matt released his seat belt and stood up. Steve and Jackson did the same. Matt let them lead the way out and off the jet when the attendant slipped the door out of the way.

The attractive woman stood clear for them to pass; and as she did, Steve stopped for a moment to say something to her. Then he slipped her something and exited the plane. Matt followed Jackson out and was immediately hit with a wave of wet heat.

"Welcome to Thailand," he muttered.

"What's that?" Jackson asked over his shoulder as his feet found firm ground.

"Nothing, just pissing and moaning about the fucking heat," Matt responded. If he was going to be their leader, he should probably start acting like one. Complaining didn't raise morale or do anyone any good, especially him.

Steve turned around and looked at his companions. "What are you two yakking about back there?"

Matt preempted Jackson from repeating his observation about the heat. "Hey, what did you give the young lady in the jet?"

Steve smiled. "My business card. I told her I traveled all over the world; and maybe when our paths crossed again, we could have dinner or something like that. She was very accommodating."

Jackson shook his head. "I don't know if he was like this in the teams, but he's a chick maggot …"

"Magnet, chick magnet," Steve corrected.

"Sure, whatever you say, I was right the first time." Jackson led the way to their baggage, now piled unceremoniously next to the jet.

"Now all we need to do is find this lost soul who used to be a naval officer, used to be a pilot, and used to be an American. Any idea what this fucker looks like?" Steve asked, scanning the hangar area.

Matt looked around, too. Off to the left he saw a stocky man with a grey beard. He was dark, but Matt could tell he was of European descent and not Asian. The stocky man crossed his arms and continued to stare at the three of them.

"I have a funny feeling Captain Ron over there with the long grey hair is our man in Phuket!" Matt said.

"He looks smug enough to be an ex-fighter pilot. Let's drag this shit over there and meet this Seamus Flanagan." Steve took off at a brisk pace, heading straight for the man with the beard. Matt and Jackson grabbed their bags and followed suit.

Matt took a second to surveil his immediate surroundings. If this A-wut guy did track the jet's flight, he'd know exactly when they landed. That meant his goons were either here already or on their way. The airport suddenly had the feel of a kill zone to Matt; he'd feel better once they were off the X.

Seamus sized up the three men approaching him. He'd been around snake eaters a few times in his career. There were

SEALs riding two of his four carrier deployments. In his opinion, the only person in the Navy with a larger ego than a pilot was a Navy SEAL.

With a sigh, he uncrossed his arms and stuck out his hand. “How the fuck are you folks? I’m Seamus Flanagan.”

Jackson gripped the man’s meaty little paw and pumped twice. “Jackson Bollinger. This is Matthew Barrett and Steve Auger.”

Matt and Steve took turns shaking Seamus’s hand. Matt looked over their contact’s shoulder at the parking lot beyond. He couldn’t shake the feeling he’d had since leaving the plane.

“Nice to meet you and all, but we have a bit of a tactical problem. You see, we’re pretty sure our aircraft was tracked; and there are assholes here in Thailand who’d love to see us out of the way, if you catch my drift.”

Seamus jerked his head back toward the parking lot. “What a news flash! Assholes in Thailand!” He chuckled and jerked his thumb over his shoulder. “My bongo truck is right over there. What was it … Matthew?”

Matt nodded. “Just call me Matt. I figured Gary read you in on our situation, but he may not have told you the guys we’re worried about have tried to stop us twice. Once in Honolulu and a day ago in New Zealand. The second time they sent a team of armed men to attack Gary’s place. They are deadly serious, and we’ve been standing around here in the open too fucking long.”

Seamus’s eyes narrowed. “This ain’t my first rodeo, *Matthew*. We’ll head to the truck as soon as I see your lips stop flappin’.” He turned and walked casually toward the parking lot.

"Interesting character," Steve said, pointing out the obvious. "Did I detect a Texas twang? I kind of like the way he says your name, *Matthew.*"

"Fuck you, sport. He's a smartass. Reminds me of you, in fact. He's the furthest thing from a Naval Academy officer I've ever seen."

Steve snorted. "Maybe he was a rodeo clown before he went to Annapolis?"

The three men laughed and hurried to catch up to their guide. Matt and Steve kept their heads on a swivel, marking all the threat points in the open area behind the hangar and across the street twenty yards away. Seamus pointed to the back of the covered bongo truck, and they crawled inside, dragging their gear along with them. Jackson secured the back and banged on the side of the truck to signal to Seamus they were good to go.

"Hey, what about this Erik guy?" Steve brought up their last teammate, and Matt shrugged his shoulders.

"I'm sure Gary gave him the straight scoop on our situation and coordinated with Yosemite Sam up in the cab to have him picked up. Did Gary say when Erik was supposed to arrive in Phuket?"

Jackson shook his head. "Nope. Just said the man would meet us here."

The men stopped talking and focused on holding on. The bongo truck had shit for suspension, and every hole and bump was amplified. After twenty minutes, Matt's ass was numb; but mercifully the truck slowed down, took a turn off the street, and settled into a dark place to stop.

“Everybody out!” Seamus’s muffled shout was all the prompting required to cause them to scramble out of the vehicle.

Matt stepped away from the truck and took a look around. They were in a large warehouse. The floor was old cracked concrete covered in pallets of material. Most were covered in plastic, but several holding stacks of new tires were exposed. Jackson and Steve also soaked up their surroundings.

“This is one of my warehouses. I have six scattered here and there. We’re just outside the western edge of Phuket near the beach. Handy for shipping and receiving shit, if you know what I mean.”

Matt didn’t know what he meant, but that was okay. At least for now, they were safe. “Seamus, did Gary tell you anything about another arrival?”

Seamus slammed the cab door and walked over to Matt. “You mean Erik? He’s at the Katahani. It’s a beach resort about three miles from here. Arrived early this morning, and I didn’t have a place for him yet. Besides, I wanted to hear your plans before dropping all three of you off at a hotel. You might want to stay away from the touristy places.”

Jackson nodded in agreement. “Too easy for us to stick out and for them to blend in at a hotel. Can we get Erik and bring him back here?”

“Sure, I can have him here in a couple of hours. I have a few things to attend to right now, but I can be around to chat when you’re ready to tell me what you need from me. Gary didn’t pass along a checklist or anything. Sound like a plan?”

Steve flashed a thumbs-up, and Gary took that as a yes. He walked away mumbling and soon disappeared into a makeshift office at the far end of the warehouse.

"What do you think of our … asset?" Jackson's tone revealed his opinion.

Matt shrugged. "He's a blank slate as far as I'm concerned. My assessment will be based on performance."

"Got us from the airport to here without getting us shot, so far so good!" Steve tossed out.

"If you guys say so," Jackson responded. "I only thought a naval aviator, and an academy man at that, would be a little more professional."

Matt considered his words carefully. "Some of the best combat fighters I ever worked with in the teams were not, well by the FBI's standards of grooming and dress code, professional. Let's give Gary some credit; he wouldn't saddle us with a loser. My bet is Seamus Flanagan will surprise all of us before this gig is over."

Seamus finished his business, hung up the phone, then called over one of his men. "Blue, I want you to show the new arrivals the bunkroom so they can get situated. Then I want you and Gold to take the sedan, the one with the taxi markings, to the Katahani and pick up a passenger. Here's his cell phone number. Come straight back and note if anyone tails you. Got it?"

Blue nodded. He held up his hand, fingers configured to represent a pistol. Seamus nodded. Blue left the office and headed straight toward the three Americans, now sitting next to the bongo truck. As he walked, he placed his fingers in his mouth and let out a shrill whistle.

Matt saw the short Thai approach and kicked Steve. “Maybe this guy knows where we can take a shit,” Steve said hopefully.

Blue stopped in front of Jackson and gave a short bow. “Suh, my name is Blue. Mr. S has directed me to show you to your living quarters. If you would please follow me. Oh and yes, there is a place you can shit.” Blue said the last line with a mischievous smile of his face. He turned and the three men scrambled to get up, grab their bags, and follow.

Blue wore a yellow tank top, worn out cargo shorts, and flip flops. Matt noted the man was sinewy, lots of muscle, and near zero body fat. He moved like an athlete, so that was a likely reason for the muscularity. Like many Asians, he looked young at first glance, but was probably in his mid-thirties.

A second Thai appeared off to their right. He vectored across the hanger to intercept Blue. When he was twenty feet away, Blue spoke rapidly followed by a hand signal that, to Matt, looked like the American way to depict a handgun. The second man bowed his head smartly and turned to go back the way he’d come.

Blue led Matt and the others through a side door in the main warehouse wall. It turned out there was another building attached to the warehouse. This one was also configured like a warehouse on the inside with one exception. At one end Matt could make out a line of bunk beds and what looked like hope chests made of a light-colored wood.

“Our accommodations, gentlemen!” Steve swept his hand across his body.

Jackson led the way behind Blue, who stopped when he reached the line of beds. “Beds here, clothes there.” He pointed at the little chests, which Matt now realized were military-style foot lockers.

"You take dump there." Blue pointed down the wall to a constructed enclosure. Four walls and no ceiling.

Blue took a minute to look each of them in the eye. "You no hurt Mr. S. We have problem if you do."

Before any of them could respond, Blue had spun around and moved out smartly. Steve chuckled and Jackson closed his mouth, which had dropped open. "What the fuck?"

Matt appreciated Blue's candor. "He's not here to wipe our ass and run down hookers for us. This guy is a hired gun, I'd stake my life on it. The second guy back there fit the same mold."

Steve nodded. "I agree. They look and move like Muay Thai boxers."

Matt saw the connection. "Every kid in Thailand is a boxer, but these guys aren't kids. They're warriors. Street warriors, maybe, but warriors just the same."

Jackson started putting his gear away. "Did you guys pick up on the pistol thing?" Matt and Steve both nodded. "Anybody concerned that might have been an order to take us out?"

"Pretty bold to flash the 'kill the gringos' hand signal in front of the gringos," Steve said jokingly.

Matt listened to the chatter, but his mind had already shifted into planning mode. Time was slipping away, and nobody helping them seemed to care about that fact. He needed to lay out all their requirements to Seamus so they could put together a timeline and create a set of action steps.

He was already forming an opinion, one he wasn't ready to share, that all of this would probably end up with the three, now four of them sticking a gun barrel in Roger Maddox's mouth. It always worked.

Chapter Thirteen

Roger Maddox hung up and slipped the smart phone into his right cargo pocket. He was in Hong Kong on business primarily; but now that his business was concluded, he'd decided to take a break from his hectic schedule and stay for a few more days.

He leaned back in the plush leather chair and clasped his hands behind his back. The Chinese were putting pressure on him. Anyone who did business in the western Pacific in the last ten years had to cope with the Chinese. They acted more like a mafia family than a sovereign nation.

He owed money to several Chinese banks, banks that were beyond the reach of international law enforcement. His businesses' cash flows and asset purchases were cycled through them without risk of discovery and tracking, except by the Chinese themselves, of course. That was the rub. On the one hand he had security; but on the other hand, the Chinese government, which owned eighty percent of the banks in China, could extort favors in return for discretion.

He'd grown up in a simpler era, a South Africa before the fall of apartheid, before technology connected everyone with the rest of the world. Now he spent every day thinking about that same technology. It facilitated his transactions, allowed him to operate under a cloak of secrecy, and gave him the opportunity to do it all from a remote location in Cambodia. Safely under the watchful eye and protection of the Cambodian government. A government well paid to provide this sanctuary.

The call was mildly disturbing. He had over two hundred people working for him around the world. Advisors on every subject under the sun. Logistics experts that knew how to move anything anywhere. And a small cadre of helpful thugs that ensured his enemies didn't interfere with his widespread operations. A-wut was just such a character. A former member of the Thai Army's special forces, he specialized in interrogation and surveillance. He was clever, trustworthy, and good enough at his job to be irritating at times. Times like right now.

A-wut didn't have evidence to support his theory, just a story. He believed a team of low-visibility operators, an American special operations team, was working their way to Maddox himself. A-wut detailed an attempt to scare away two men in Hawaii that went sideways when the victims became the victors. A-wut told him nobody could dispatch the men he had working for him in Hawaii the way these two men did. One of his team was in a coma, probably for life.

Leaping to the conclusion that US Special Forces were involved didn't make a lot of sense, but A-wut's instincts were usually spot on. He took in the information and thanked the man before ending the call. It was the last part of the story that nagged at him. A-wut tracked the men to New Zealand and made a second attempt to engage the strangers. His team went to the private residence where the two men were staying, but were chased away by a very capable private security team.

Whoever had a high-end private protection team was either in the government or very powerful. In either case, if these so-called special operators were staying in a place like that, it indicated they had considerable resources at their disposal. He'd have to do some digging. He had to know if it was the American government or a rival guiding the actions of the men.

He rubbed his jaw, always conscious of his pockmarked skin, a consequence of severe acne as a teenager. It was one reason why he stayed away from social engagement. He was never comfortable dating or even speaking to girls. Instead, he focused on learning. In time, he earned a national scholarship to attend the London School of Economics.

His life in London was simple. After graduation he'd selected the equity markets as the best place to start his professional life. It proved too boring, so in a few years he shifted to the currency markets. Hedging dollars against the yen and learning the way money moved around the world led him eventually to the import-export world. He'd finally found a home.

At age 46, he was now a global broker in anything valuable. Currency, drugs, rare artwork, and at times, people. The people trade was the most dangerous. The world had woken up in the last few years to the exploitation of children in a rampant global sex market.

He'd started small. A favor here and there to grease the skids and succeed in other, unrelated business objectives. It only represented eleven percent of his revenue stream, but it was the part of his financial portfolio that worried him the most.

He'd contemplated severing ties to that whole sordid enterprise many times. The sex trade was human slavery, nothing more. Yes, slavery was a natural part of the history of humanity, but in this day and age it carried a stigma. The western nations vowed to stamp it out, even as their leaders made men like him rich ordering their own guilty pleasures.

His human trafficking operation was a business. He provided his rich clients with their specific and sometimes exotic requirements, and they paid him. It was only a business. But from time to time, he set aside carefully chosen girls to satisfy his own pleasure. Girls that reminded him of the ones he never dated. The girls who laughed at his ugliness as a teenager. So, he relived his past in a very different way.

He was aware there was product in the pipeline heading his way from Hawaii. A girl chosen to his specifications. He would spend a few days in Hong Kong, then go home to Cambodia where she would be waiting. He'd derive pleasure from her for a few days; and when he became bored, she would be taken care of discreetly. He didn't leave loose ends. He was too successful and smart to be that stupid.

A-wut sat in his plush Bangkok penthouse apartment and mulled over the situation. His boss, while curious, wasn't concerned about his theory. He'd been around enough commandos to know an operator when he saw one, and that American in the alley was either a SEAL or a Green Beret. He'd bet on it.

So, he was sitting on the additional information flowing in to him from his resources in New Zealand and Thailand. Best to take care of the problem himself, nip it in the bud so to speak, than piss off his boss with more calls about his fears. The Americans were a team of three now.

Their benefactor in New Zealand had provided them with a way to fly to Thailand, which made it easy for his people to keep track of their progress. He realized with a sigh that these men were not going away. They were, instead, going right to the heart of one of Mr. Maddox's key operations: the slave trade hub he'd helped his boss build in Thailand.

His men on the ground in Phuket had been too late to see the Americans deplane and leave the airport after their arrival. Now he had spread the word throughout the resort city that he would pay handsomely for any information that led his men to the American Special Operations team.

He'd ruled out the CIA when the men left New Zealand in a privately-owned jet. The agency would never move in such a clumsy manner. They had aircraft, boats and other means of clandestine transportation to rely upon. No, these men were soldiers on a mission. Soldiers followed orders, and these particular orders were placing his operations in Phuket in potential jeopardy.

His cell phone rang. A-wut listened intently for a few minutes, then hung up and placed the phone back on the table. He'd used his influence to pull a few strings in Auckland to find out what he could about the owner of the large estate where the Americans stayed while in New Zealand. His request was fulfilled.

The owner was a man who went under several aliases. That meant intelligence agent or criminal. If A-wut's theory held true, then this man was an agent of the United States, providing a safe house for the team to plan and prepare for their trip to Thailand.

It didn't matter what his real name was; the second piece of information confirmed his insights. The team that thwarted his attempt to take out the Americans was made up of Australian and Kiwi SAS special operators. This mission was planned by Americans, led by Americans, and supported by America's allies.

A-wut stood up and walked to the window. The city of Bangkok sprawled beneath him. He was a wealthy man and could quit the business if he chose to. He had money stashed in banks in three countries; the amount in any one of them would allow him to live like a king for the rest of his life. Why give a shit anymore? *Was it time to walk away from the game?*

Maddox would probably let him go unmolested. He might have to promise to do a favor here and there once in a while, but he wouldn't stop him from leaving. He crossed his arms and looked up into the sky. He was ready.

At age 42, he'd given all of his life to his country and then to Maddox. He only had to clean up this last little mess. Maddox wouldn't even know how much danger he was in. A-wut would deal with it quietly, effectively. The cell phone rang again.

Erik reacted to the phone call by jamming his toilet kit and clothes into his backpack, then heading to the hotel lobby. He'd been told to wait near the gift shop entry, and he'd be met by a man he should call Blue. He wasn't sure if the name was a code name or not, but it sounded ridiculous. He pondered all the better choices for a code name as he rode the elevator down.

The double doors opened, and he stepped into the chaos. People were everywhere. In this hotel, a majority were Europeans, Americans, and wealthy travelers from the Middle East. He ran his hand through his long, thick, reddish brown hair and suddenly wished he taken a shower rather than crashed as soon as he'd arrived.

Dodging an old couple bent on entering the elevator, he stepped nimbly to the side and scanned the huge, open expanse of the lobby. He maneuvered toward the street entrance, trying to see where the gift shop was situated. After a minute or two, he spotted the store.

He moved back against the window and spent a few minutes surveilling the store and the areas to the left and right of the entrance. Having spotted no irregularities, Erik sauntered across the lobby and positioned himself a few feet to the left of the open doorway.

"Mr. Swanson."

Erik looked down at the short, yet sturdy Thai standing next to him. Erik was only five-foot-nine, but at 190 pounds of mostly muscle, he was comfortable in most physical situations. However, this guy made him uncomfortable. He gave off an aura, a scent or something. Erik was sure the man was a professional fighter or killer. His eyes conveyed his total neutrality. The eyes of a hit man.

"Maybe. Who are you?" Erik said tactically, gauging the distance between the two men.

"My name is Blue."

"Okay, Mr. Blue. I guess you're who I'm supposed to meet. What's next?"

"Blue."

"What?" Nick responded, puzzled.

"Not Mr. Blue, only Blue. Follow me, Mr. Swanson." With that, the little man turned and went toward the elevators.

Erik wasn't sure if the guy was fucking with him or trying to be funny, but he followed as directed. Blue led them to a small hallway to the right of the elevators and that led to another hallway. He then opened a door and went through, not checking to see if Erik was still in tow. Erik recognized the area as a maintenance accessway that wasn't meant for guests. After moving for two more minutes, Blue stopped at another larger door.

"You stay here."

Erik nodded and waited for what felt like ten minutes, but was probably only half that, until finally the large door opened and Blue waved him out. The sunlight was brilliant, and Erik was blinded for a moment. He squinted his eyes and made out a rusty sedan parked at the curb. They were on the backside of the hotel complex near the loading bays used to move the thousands of pounds of food and drink consumed every day by the guests.

Erik bent low and sat in the back, watching Blue take a moment to scan his surroundings. This simple act confirmed his first thought; whatever the guys were up to, somebody out there didn't like it. Blue completed his counter-surveillance drill and jumped in the driver's seat. A second man sat in the front; he could have been the driver's twin brother.

"Hold on to something, Mr. Swanson. I need to make sure no one follows us."

"Hey, call me Erik, and who the fuck are you worried about?"

Blue laughed. The first indication he was a human and not a robot posing as one. "Everybody, Mr. … I mean Erik. Now hold on, please."

Erik felt the car accelerate and then did as he'd been told, clutching the arm rest and jamming his left foot under the seat in front of him to prevent him from sliding all over the back of the car. Blue weaved in and out through vehicle traffic and pedestrians. He didn't appear to care if he hit anything or anybody; but miraculously, he didn't. The drive seemed to last forever, but eventually the sedan pulled down a narrow side street and stopped next to a huge warehouse.

"Home?" Erik asked.

"My home," Blue responded. The other Thai in the car glanced over his shoulder at Matt with a stern look on his face, as if to say, *shut the fuck up, dumbass*.

They exited the sedan and walked to a roll-up door. Blue raised the lid covering a panel and punched in a series of numbers. The second man jumped into the driver's seat and backed the sedan out of the way.

The roll-up began to move. As soon as it was five feet off the ground, Blue ducked into the warehouse. Erik followed suit, and once inside took a second to get his bearings. As his eyes became accustomed to the dark interior, he heard a friendly voice shout out to him.

"Hey, butt munch! It's about time you made it to the fucking party!"

Erik looked to the source of the taunt and spotted three men standing one hundred feet away, near a makeshift camp of sorts. Beds, tables, and bags instantly made him feel at home. In his professional life, he'd spent many a day in hangars and buildings like this waiting for the green light to whack some asshole. He smiled.

"Fuck you, whoever you are. I took my time because I knew you lame turds couldn't start without me."

Matt laughed. Having another team guy around was just what he needed. Such familiar irreverence was a tonic for his soul. Now that they had the entire team assembled, it was time to act. He walked over to join Jackson and Steve in shaking Erik's hand. Time was running out on them all.

Chapter Fourteen

Seamus pondered Gold's message. His warehouses were safe as far as basic fire and security went, but they weren't fortresses. He always expected that someone would try to break in to steal something; but most of his stock was bulky and heavy, not the sort of pick up and run items a thief might want to take. So, it was concerning that his neighbors saw surveillance being set up outside his main warehouse in Phuket.

Logic dictated that he toss out a criminal motive and select the obvious reason: the new arrivals. He was fifty miles away at his private residence, a twenty-thousand-square-foot, two-story building that sat on a peaceful bluff overlooking the ocean. It was originally a country home for the British ambassador to Siam, Thailand's former name. It was designed and constructed in a classic English style. It was the only thing in Thailand that reminded him of home.

He went out on the broad wraparound front porch and sat down in a wicker glider big enough for two people. Seamus swirled his bourbon gently as he stared out into the beautiful blue water. He did his best thinking out here, and he needed to think now.

Blue disappeared somewhere, leaving the four Americans to themselves. "Here we go again," Steve muttered. "Hurry up and wait, hurry up and wait."

Jackson was getting more concerned by the minute. "I thought we were going to get weapons from this guy. So far, I've seen one skinny kid with a pistol. If the A-wad guy tries something here, we're not in a good position to do anything about it, gentlemen."

Matt had been thinking the very same thing. Besides wasting time and accomplishing nothing toward their goal, they were sitting ducks. He assumed Seamus was trustworthy, but that was based solely on Gary's endorsement. What if this guy was playing all sides here in Thailand? Maddox was a powerful man. It wouldn't be a stretch to allow an accident to happen for the right price.

"Steve, take Erik here and see if you can't find one of those skinny kids, and ask them for weapons. If they refuse, we may need to unass this place and find our own safe house."

Steve stood up, then froze. "That sounded like a take-charge-get-some-shit-done speech, sir. Welcome back to the game!"

Matt ignored the barb. He watched the two former SEALs leave the berthing area and head back into the main warehouse. He hadn't unpacked, but Jackson had. He promptly began to repack his gear without asking questions. Apparently, Matt was now in charge for real. It felt good and scary at the same time, but Matt pushed the negative thoughts aside. He needed a plan B if Steve and Erik came back empty-handed.

Ten minutes later, they both heard the sounds of someone approaching. The door to the main warehouse opened, revealing Steve and Erik, each lugging along a large sports bag. Matt swung his legs over the edge of the bunk bed and stood up.

"I hope those bags aren't filled with soccer balls or some other playground shit."

Jackson snorted. "Might be the next best thing if they didn't bring back weapons. I'm bored out of my mind."

Steve closed the last few feet and unceremoniously dropped the bag on the cement floor with a clunk. Erik placed his bag next to Steve's with a bit more care.

"Miss us?" Steve grinned.

"That depends. Were you successful?" Matt answered.

Steve bent down and unzipped each bag in turn. Reaching into the first he drew out a small automatic pistol and placed it on the table. He continued to pull out pistols and then suppressors for the pistols. The movies called these devices "silencers," but there was no such thing as a completely quiet firearm.

A suppressor was just that, a piece of gear that dampened the noise created by a bullet exiting the barrel down to a sound too subdued to be associated with a weapon being fired. Professionals referred to all suppressors as "cans." There was one for each of the four handguns on the table.

"What do we have here? It doesn't look familiar." Jackson reached down and picked up one of the automatics. It looked tiny in his oversized hand. "Nice balance though."

Steve picked up a gun, dropped the magazine into his other hand, jacked the slide to the rear, and locked it back. A quick check to ensure the chamber was empty finished the safe handling drill. He looked around the group to make sure each man was paying attention.

"This is the model 3830 9mm Security-9 pistol. It's made by Ruger. It's their most popular concealed carry sidearm. Reliable and sturdy, while being one of the lightest nine mils in the world. I was surprised to find one, let alone four, in this crazy place. Our newfound friend, Seamus, has quite an arsenal hidden here."

Matt stepped over and picked up one of the cans. The cool, finely-milled steel alloy felt oddly calming. “Barrel length?”

Steve picked up a can and began screwing it onto the threaded end of the barrel. “The barrel is three-and-a-half inches long. Not a long-range weapon, but for around here, where everyone wears shorts and T-shirts, a practical solution for self-defense. The can adds another five inches.”

“We have ammo, additional mags, and concealed carry holsters in this bag here.” He tapped the bag in front of him with his foot.

“Any sign of our benefactor?” Matt asked. It was nice to finally get the weapons, but they needed to get moving.

“Mutt and Jeff wouldn’t answer our questions. I’m pretty sure they understand English, but they weren’t giving up any information regarding their boss. They did give us the name of the second skinny guy; his name is Gold.”

Jackson didn’t react, but Matt shook his head. “You’re shitting me, right? Seamus named his tow pets Blue and Gold?”

Erik smiled. “Yeah, but not like a team guy would. It’s not about the old reversable blue and gold dive shirts the frogs used to wear. I guarantee you it’s academy bullshit.”

Matt nodded. Goat Air, now this. Why the hell leave the US if you’re so damned lonely for Annapolis? He checked his watch. “Guys, let’s get the mags loaded and spread the gear out. We’ll put any additional shit we don’t carry on our bodies in one of the sport bags. If we don’t hear from Seamus in the next hour, we’re going it alone. We’ve wasted too much time here as it is.”

The other men nodded in agreement and began checking the equipment. No one spoke, and after twenty minutes, they were ready. The small concealed-carry holsters were made by Ruger for this specific gun. They had a tube made of elastic on the outside of the nylon pocket where the gun rested. It accommodated the five-inch-long suppressor, holding it snugly in place.

A door closing caught their attention. Blue entered the large room and walked up to the four Americans. “I hope you are satisfied with the tools we have provided. Long guns are difficult to move in the city. You are much better off with these.” Blue pointed to the table where the pistols lay.

“Yes, these are sufficient. Thank you. Where’s your boss?”

Blue looked at Matt and narrowed his eyes. “He doesn’t ask me permission to come and go, and I don’t ask him questions. It’s better that way.”

“I think what he means, sport, is why haven’t we received the information we were promised?” Steve’s tone was combative, but it accurately reflected their emotional state.

“I have been told to say this to you: Go to the Chinese district. Find a woman there. Her name is Greta Schumacher. She has the information you are searching for.”

Jackson took a step forward, and Blue’s head swiveled to stare at the tall former FBI agent. The look was cold, hard. Blue wasn’t as simple as they’d all assumed. Matt wondered if he was he more than an errand boy in Flanagan’s organization.

“We’re running out of time, and it’s already dark outside. Where do we find her and how do we get to this Chinese district?" Jackson used a more soothing voice, the same voice he was trained to use when negotiating with hostage takers.

Blue smiled a thin eerie smile before answering. "You will find her at The Gate. It is a restaurant and a hotel. I cannot help you with transportation. Our two vehicles have been compromised. I will call you a taxi; it's better that way."

Matt looked down and realized they weren't ready. After all the wasted time, they still required a few minutes to get their shit together. "Blue, we need five minutes to prepare. Can you have a taxi here in five minutes?"

Blue nodded. "My cousin owns a taxi and is standing by, waiting for my call. So, yes, in five minutes then." Blue turned and left through the door that led into the big warehouse.

"Okay." Matt's voice shattered the silence and alerted the rest of the men that he was about to give them directions. "In five minutes, I want us standing tall, ready to walk out of here. Do a buddy check once you're comfortable with your holster placement. We don't want folks to freak out because they can see we're packing. Make sure you have your personal documents and money. Leave the backpacks here. We might not be back for a long time. Questions?"

There were no questions, and the sounds of rapid preparation filled the room with clicks and slaps. The team cross-checked each other when ready, a few making adjustments until the weapons were positioned correctly. On cue, the far door opened and Gold stepped forward, waving to them. It was time to go.

The taxi ride was uneventful. It turned out that the Chinese district wasn't much to look at. Unlike Chinatowns in the US, the district only covered three city blocks. The driver remained silent throughout the trip; and when he finally stopped in front of a dark building, he simply pointed. It was time to get out of the car.

As the taxi drove away, Matt looked around to get his bearings. The dark building wasn't The Gate. The hotel restaurant was across the street and half a block further down. The streetlight above them was broken, and Matt saw the wisdom of leaving them here. They were in a position to watch the street for a moment or two, undetected, and work out their plan of action.

"Let's split into pairs, frogman style. Steve and Jackson, you two go in first and get a table. Erik and I will wait five minutes and then come in and do the same. I'll wait another ten minutes before asking about our contact. Everyone good?"

The men all nodded; there was no need to speak. They had all been government professionals, and they knew how to take direction and how to execute. Matt appreciated the depth of experience represented in the team. Nothing would shake up these guys.

Matt pointed across to the restaurant and nodded. Steve and Jackson sauntered to the other side, casually scanning the rooftops, alleys, and the street in both directions. Matt saw them pause to look at the menu posted next to the door, then watched them disappear inside. He checked his watch; it was 8:55.

Matt and Erik waited ten minutes, then mimicked the first pair's counter-surveillance technique as they approached the entrance to The Gate. As they entered, Matt immediately realized there was a problem. There was only one other table occupied in the moderately-sized dining area. A man and a woman, Middle Eastern by Matt's guess, sat near the bar. According to plan, Matt selected a table as far from his teammates as possible and next to the restaurant's entrance.

After a few moments, the waiter came over and filled their water glasses. Matt could see that Steve and Jackson were just beginning their meal. So he held the waiter's attention and ordered something simple, emphasizing mild. The waiter smiled a knowing smile. Americans couldn't stand Asian-spiced food. In the United States, Chinese restaurants served bland versions of their much hotter mainland China recipes. Here in Thailand, there was no reason to do so. Erik gave the man his order and the waiter left.

Matt discreetly checked his watch. He would wait until after his food was served before inquiring after Greta. If this was a dead end, the team would have to abandon Seamus Flanagan and try another route. Maybe Gary had someone else in Thailand who could really help them find Vicky.

When the food did come out, it wasn't carried by their waiter. Instead, their plates were delivered by a thirty-something brunette with a killer body. The woman wasn't dressed like a restaurant staff member, and she flashed a smile at Matt that nearly stopped his heart. Definitely movie star material. What the hell was she doing in a place like this?

"Good evening, gentlemen." Her subtle German accent alerted them both to the possibility the server was in fact, Greta Schumacher. For some reason, Matt had expected a much older woman, like the old witch out of "Hansel and Gretel."

Matt nodded, speechless, as the woman placed their orders in front of them. "Would the two of you like to stay here, or perhaps you would prefer to sit with your friends?" She gave the smallest movement with her head, as if to indicate where Steve and Jackson were sitting across the room.

Matt shook his head. They were made, but he was sticking to the plan. "I assume you are Greta?"

The leggy brunette nodded, then sat down next to Matt. Her scent was subtle, but still potent enough to make Matt's nostrils flare ever so slightly. He realized he needed to get out more. He took a look around the room.

"You are safe here, at least for the next few minutes. Maddox has friends in high and low places. You four are known to his people, and they are searching for you. It is very dangerous."

"If it's so dangerous, why meet with us out in the open like this?"

Steve's question went right to the point. Did Greta have information for them, or was she at their table simply to warn them of the obvious?

"Our mutual friend told us you might be able to steer us toward our objective …"

"The girl you seek. Yes, I know your mission," she interrupted. "There are many girls in Thailand, girls from all over the world. The ones taken against their will and brought here are associated with three organizations. I understand you believe it's Maddox's people that took this girl. Correct?"

Matt nodded. "We've been fucked with for the last few days by a man named A-wut. We know he works for Maddox."

Greta leaned back. "Yes, he does; but he is also an independent player. Does business on the side for his own profit and amusement. Maddox apparently doesn't mind. So, it's Maddox then." She sighed.

Matt reached out and touched her hand. "Her name is Vicky, and she's fourteen years old. She was snatched off the street in Honolulu two weeks ago. We've followed her trail to you. Can you help us?" Matt gave Greta's hand a gentle squeeze.

Greta looked first at Erik and then back at Matt. "I can help you."

Chapter Fifteen

Matt asked Greta to call them a cab, then leaned back in his seat to ponder the information she'd provided to the team. It was no surprise that Maddox was using commercial ships to store his human product. They'd been told that ships were the preferred method of transport in the human trafficking business.

They were independent of territorial law once beyond the recognized line of maritime sovereignty. They were self-contained villages, with food, water, kitchens, and storage hidden from aerial view. Why expose an illegal operation by moving the kidnapped girls around on dry land?

Greta named two of the four commercial maritime ships known to be owned and operated by the Maddox Corporation in the Pacific. These two, she said, were known to frequent the harbor in Bangkok, Thailand, specifically. The large commercial harbor facility was home to hundreds of ships of all sizes and shapes. Maddox's vessels were midsized, 200-foot, general cargo vessels. Not too big and not too small.

As he thought it through, he came to the conclusion that those smaller ships were not the entire transport system. They were sturdy, but best used for short distances. That meant they probably linked up with much larger ships offshore before coming into Bangkok. Ships capable of crisscrossing the Pacific effortlessly.

He gave the guys at the other table a thumbs-up, indicating he had the information they'd been searching for. Erik downed his beer in one dynamic move and slammed it on the table. Just then a waiter stepped through the door to the kitchen and whistled. Their ride had arrived.

The team exited in reverse order, with Matt and Erik leaving the restaurant first, pausing to check out the street. They waited a moment then waved the second pair forward. Steve and Jackson came out and followed Matt and Erik into the waiting vehicle. Matt sat in the front passenger seat to guide the taxi driver once they got close to the warehouse. He wanted to stop a few blocks away and walk to their safe house, in case they could get lucky and spot any surveillance on the location.

Greta, or one of Greta's people, had given the cab company their destination address already, avoiding a clumsy communication exercise between the Thai driver and the Americans. The ride back was quiet. Matt didn't want to fill in the other two in the car. For all he knew, A-wut owned the taxi company. He would wait until they were all safely back at Flanagan's warehouse retreat.

When the taxi was a few blocks from the warehouse, Matt placed his hand on the driver's arm and pointed to the curb with his other hand. The driver nodded and slowed to a stop. As he opened the passenger side door, he was hit with an intense smell. The acrid scent of something burning, and it wasn't barbecue.

The other three men poured out onto the street. As the taxi sped away, they all stood and stared at the red glow pulsing in the distance. The safe house was a blazing inferno. Steve moved first. "Keep your heads on a swivel. If this is intentional, then the assholes who did it might still be around!"

Profound wisdom coming from the Senior Chief, Matt noted. He and the other three moved out smartly, scanning threat points, such as roofs and spaces between buildings. They spread out a little and all of them checked their pistols, a soft touch to verify its position, in case they needed to defend themselves. In less than two minutes, they arrived at the warehouse.

“Shit! Our stuff!” Erik said what was on all of their minds. The part of the building engulfed in flames was the area of their makeshift headquarters. It was useless to try putting it out; the fire was well on its way to destroying the entire warehouse. All their gear and what little personal clothing and effects they’d brought to Thailand were now toast. They were down to the clothes on their backs and their pistols.

A sudden rapid popping sound caused the four men to duck and move to cover. Matt saw Erik smoothly draw his pistol, and then remembered the man had been an operator only a few short months ago. It showed. His instincts and training were clearly not dulled by years as a civilian. Matt drew his gun a bit more stiffly and pondered his next move. The sound of sirens wailing in the distance interrupted his thoughts.

“Put the guns away.” Jackson’s firm tone had the effect he intended. As the two fire trucks and one ambulance pulled up in front of the warehouse, the four Americans holstered their firearms and slid over to the opposite side of the street, facing the building. There was a tiny eatery on the corner that offered a commanding view of the scene unfolding in front of them.

“In here!” Steve called out.

The proprietor saw them coming toward the building front and, sensing their intent, hurried to close the door. “Closed!” he said even as Steve jammed his shoe into position, blocking the door from moving.

“We need an hour. We’ll pay,” Steve growled, his face only a foot from the old man’s. He was intimidating, and the message was clear; they weren’t taking no for an answer.

The owner looked at Matt and the others as if calculating a per head rate. “One hundred dollars.”

Steve smiled and shook his head. "I'll give you fifty and that includes a beer for each of us."

The old man started to say something, then thought better of it. He opened the door and stepped out of the way as Steve led the team inside. Matt trailed in last. He closed the door and stood there watching the firefighters get to work. The others had grabbed a round table near the window, but not too close. Matt shut off the lights and locked the front door. No one could see them observing the chaos.

The beers arrived in short order, and they sat in silence. After twenty minutes, Erik pointed out that the paramedics had a victim in tow heading for the ambulance. Jackson volunteered to go out and get some intel on the status of the fire, the cause, and the condition of the man they brought out. He unlocked the front door and walked across the street. A few minutes later he returned, his head lowered.

"The guy we just saw was Gold. He's suffering from smoke inhalation and two gunshot wounds; both are superficial, and they said he'll recover fast. The other person they found was dead. The description sounds like Blue."

Matt didn't react to the news. He sat there and soaked it all in. His instincts were screaming the obvious: the attack wasn't by one of Seamus Flanagan's competitors, it was conducted by men looking for his team. Seamus's two men just got in the way. The fire was probably a way to cover up the evidence, start a diversion, or both. Could he have saved them if his team hadn't gone to Greta's?

"I know what you're thinking, boss," Steve growled. "This isn't on you, or us for that matter. This is squarely on Roger Maddox and his gang of shit birds."

"Steve's right, Matt. It sucks, but the only way we could have prevented this was to be here instead of searching for Vicky." Jackson put his hand on Matt's shoulder.

Erik nodded. "We can't get sidetracked, and we can't fight everybody. This guy Maddox is getting desperate to stop us for some reason. Sounds crazy since we have no fucking clue where Tom's daughter is. These assholes are acting like we are a major threat, instead of a bunch of frogs looking for information."

Matt thought it through. "We need to get a hold of Seamus. What's the best way to do that?"

"Call or text Gary. That's my guess," Jackson offered.

"Okay. Steve, contact Gary. Tell him … tell him we need to contact Seamus immediately. Tell him we'll be staying in the hotel he put Erik in when he arrived. Let me know what he says. In the meantime, let's split up into pairs. Get away from all the commotion and rendezvous at Erik's old hotel. Get one room per pair. We need to stay together until this all gets sorted out."

There were nods and murmurs in agreement all around the table. Matt grabbed Erik, and they left the small eatery first. Matt led the way without speaking, his eyes darting everywhere. They were marked men, and he had no idea what the enemy looked like. No uniforms, no unique weapons, no way to identify them in a crowd. It was an odd feeling.

Fifteen minutes and ten blocks later, Matt signaled a passing cab. The trip was short, and the hotel thankfully had accommodations despite the short notice. Matt and Erik went up to their room and waited for Gary's response. Almost an hour after Erik's outreach, Gary sent back a text. Seamus was aware of the incident and was glad to hear they were okay. He promised to connect with them soon at the hotel.

The next morning, Matt woke up to the sound of the phone ringing. Erik rolled over and reached for the offensive device, but Matt was closer.

"Hello?"

"It's Steve. I'm in the lobby restaurant. Seamus is here."

Matt looked at the desk clock; it was six o'clock. "We'll be right down."

Steve was sitting with Jackson and Seamus near the back corner of the large hotel restaurant. Matt and Erik joined them. "This place doesn't look open," Erik observed.

The owner is a friend of mine; you might say a partner in this establishment," Seamus answered. "Steve just filled me in on your escapades since we last saw each other."

Matt noted the look of sadness in Seamus's eyes as he spoke. Gone was the cocky assuredness and bravado of the retired fighter pilot. He was hurting inside. Was Blue that close a friend?

"The cook comes in at 6:30, so we can order food in a few minutes. Steve said you already know about Gold's injuries. Thank God he's going to be alright. He was Blue's younger cousin, you know. Probably the smarter of the two, and in many ways the more mature one."

Matt leaned forward. "We made the assumption last night that Blue was the fatality." Seamus only nodded, acknowledging the truth of that theory.

Jackson was aching for a cup of coffee, so he kept looking up every time he heard a noise that might indicate someone had arrived to work. He settled down and cleared his throat. "We're very sorry for all of this. It wasn't our intent to bring this to your doorstep."

Seamus turned his head slightly and looked at Jackson. "You being here isn't justification for what happened last night. What happened last night was an attack on me, on my people. Whatever the reason, the end result is a war with me; and if there's one thing I do well, it's war."

Matt was surprised. Seamus was serious. The man was half movie character and half crime lord. What could he possibly do against a man as powerful as Maddox? The best option would be to continue to assist the team in their search for Vicky. Matt knew in his heart that both roads led to the same villain.

The information Greta gave them about the two slave ships in the Bangkok harbor had to be acted on and quickly. However, in his gut Matt had a feeling there was a need to tear the weed out of the ground at its source, and that was Roger Maddox.

"Seamus has offered to get us a private plane so we can fly to Bangkok," Steve informed Matt.

"That would be very helpful. We're doing a piss poor job of managing the timeline as it is. It feels like taking three weeks to respond to a car accident. Way too much time has passed since Vicky's abduction."

The patter of footsteps was clearly heard by everybody at the table. A face popped out from behind the kitchen door. "Ah, Mr. Flanagan! Welcome!"

Seamus waved his finger in a circle and held up five fingers. In minutes, there were hot cups of American style coffee on the table. They ordered breakfast; and when they were finished eating, Matt got back to the business at hand.

"Okay, it's 7:20. All our stuff was lost in the fire, so we're ready to leave whenever you give us the word, Seamus."

Flanagan nodded. "I have a maintenance van parked in valet parking." He reached into his pocket and pulled out a ticket. I want you to take the coast road south out of the resort area. When you get ten miles out, you'll see signs with an airplane on them. The commuter airport is small; but it's next to the coastal road, so it's impossible to miss."

"I assume you have a plane there we can use to get up north?" Erik asked.

"I do. By my rough calculations, you can be in Bangkok ninety minutes after we take off."

Matt raised his eyebrows. "We? Are you coming with us?"

Seamus nodded. "Who the fuck do you think is flying the plane?"

Jackson weighed in. "That's a thoughtful gesture; but considering how things are unfolding, it might be dangerous to even be seen with us again. Maybe you should stay here and let someone else pilot the plane."

Seamus wiped his mouth with the napkin, placed it neatly on the table, and stood up. He looked down at Jackson and then scanned their faces. He paused, as if considering his words carefully. When he did speak, he revealed something none of them had guessed.

"I'm not afraid of Maddox or his lackeys. Blue was my adopted son. I took him in off the streets a year after I arrived here. He died defending me, my property, his home. He will be avenged, and I will be there to deliver that revenge or to watch one of you do it for me. No, I'm flying that fucking plane and I'm joining the four of you until I, we, see this through to the end."

A-wut listened to the full report, then dismissed the man by waving his hand toward the door. One dead and one wounded, both Thais. The Americans were there, his sources were sure of it. How could he have missed such a perfect opportunity?

He would hear about the fire. Many politicians drew their support from the lower classes in Phuket, people who performed a myriad of tasks for the local tourist industry. The fire had been clumsy and unnecessary. It had posed a threat to the families living all around the warehouse complex. He would have to spread money around to get this behind him.

At this point, he was sure the Americans were keenly aware they'd been the targets. They wouldn't be sloppy in their habits from this point forward. He needed to reacquire their whereabouts. Right now, the trail was cold; but he was confident his network would flush them out.

The Americans had a couple of choices now. Go to ground and hide until enough time passed to move safely about the city again or leave Phuket. The warehouse complex belonged to a Thai corporation, but his sources believed an American was the true owner. If that was true, he must be helping the others.

Maybe Maddox was right. Maybe the CIA or some other American law enforcement agency was behind all of this, starting back in Honolulu. It didn't matter to him who was behind the team of Americans; they were snooping around Mr. Maddox's operations and that had to be stopped.

He'd make a few calls. If the Americans were being assisted by the owner of the warehouse, then the man might have other resources the Americans were using as a safe place to hide. The sooner he tracked down this information, the sooner he could end this once and for all. Maddox would be pleased, and he could take a few weeks off. He needed a little A-wut time.

Chapter Sixteen

The team arrived at the small rural airport and was informed by the driver that they should enter a light blue, corrugated tin hangar, located twenty or so yards away and wait. When they reached the building, Matt was impressed. The hangar was nice. An access door to the left of the main doors allowed them entrance, and they stopped just inside to survey their new surroundings.

"No fucking plane," Steve mumbled, looking at the empty structure.

A snort from behind Steve caught Matt's attention. "I'm afraid it is my destiny to spend a good part of my life waiting in hangars." Erik's comment earned laughter from his fellow SEALs and even brought a smile to Steve's sour-looking face. Special operations units routinely used hangars as staging and mission planning centers. The hurry-up-and-wait game drove operators crazy, while a constant stream of changing intelligence meant plan A became plan B, then plan C. Hangars sucked.

It made sense, even for blue water commandoes. An airfield had power, water, communications, and it provided a wide range of mobility options. Helicopters could load rubber boats or sling load larger maritime craft underneath the airframe and take the SEALs to their mission insertion points. Matt laughed with the others. Yeah, hangars sucked sometimes; but in a way, he felt like he was coming home.

"Well, the man said to wait, so I suggest we all get comfortable. No telling how long before Seamus shows up." Matt's suggestion was greeted with grunts and nods. Erik, the youngest on the team, went over to a water pipe attached about six feet off the ground along the far wall of the hangar and began to do pull-ups.

"Youth," Jackson mumbled as he followed Erik and waited his turn. Within minutes the two men were working out together, all body weight exercises; but as Matt knew, or used to understand, working out was always a great way to burn off frustration. He felt a twinge. He should get over there and join the workout; he needed it more than any of the others. His flash of motivation quickly died, and he let the impulse pass.

They were all tired of the delays and the inability to make headway against Maddox's efforts to stop their progress. Matt was thankful that so far, none of the team had been injured or worse, but it was only a matter of time. In Thailand they were targets, big American targets, surrounded by the unknown.

Trying to read the Asian body language was a waste of time. None of them had ever been immersed in the culture sufficiently to pick up the sixth sense they had acquired in the Middle East. He knew in his gut they needed to seize the initiative. Bring the fight to the bad guys going forward, but how? *And where the fuck was Seamus?*

Vicky sat in the corner of the huge room, hugging her knees and rocking back and forth, back and forth. She'd been doing this for hours now. She thought anything would be better than the cargo hold of the ship that brought her from Hawaii. That monster vessel was dark and dirty, with a disgusting crew that eyed her up every day of the journey. She wasn't naïve; she knew what boys wanted, and men were probably worse.

By now she was under no illusions. She'd expected to be raped right after her abduction, then when she was bundled onto the large ship and placed in the hold. But it didn't happen. All she'd suffered was the indignity of being stripped bare to pose for a few photographs. Nobody touched her, and she couldn't figure out why. What was preventing them? After they left, she'd put her clothes back on and waited alone in the dark, rocking.

When it came time for her to be switched to the second, smaller ship, things improved. It was not so smelly, and they were kept in a storage room instead of the cargo bay. It was much nicer. It was there she met the other girls being held onboard with her. The guards didn't seem to care about them chatting all day long. They were allowed out on deck each night where the stars shown with incredible brilliance in the dark Pacific night.

They were never allowed topside during the day, only at night. The guards would bring them up and tether each of them to a piece of the ship so they wouldn't attempt to jump off the vessel and attempt to swim away or worse, commit suicide. Most of the girls were American, but a few were Canadian.

Those short visits on deck sustained her morale. After that came the much darker storage room and nearly twenty-four hours before the next topside visit. The crew were all Asian; but as much as she tried, she couldn't determine their specific country of origin. She only spoke a little Spanish, so there was no way to eavesdrop on their conversations. She realized she could be anywhere by now.

Vicky tried to stay positive, to think about happy things. Her dad must be going crazy; she knew he would be furious. Furious that she was in harm's way and furious he was physically unable to save her. In her heart, she knew he was doing something. He wasn't the kind of man who hoped for outcomes; he made them happen.

Her mother, on the other hand, was useless. Beautiful and well aware of that fact, she specialized in playing the helpless victim. Batting her eyes and flashing her cleavage to attract attention and sometimes more. She appreciated the genetic inheritance and was aware she was attractive, but she was happy her dad's personality ruled her mind and spirit. She was a fighter like him; and if she was going to survive this, then she would have to fight.

She knew her mother loved her, but she couldn't see her trying to find her. She was most likely sitting in a bar with an off-duty Five-0 cop telling him her sad tale. Vicky adjusted her hips a bit to allow the blood to flow. There was a perfectly good bed, but she felt more secure in the corner with her back against the wall.

Her dad used to demand a seat in every restaurant that backed up to a wall and looked at the door. "No surprises," he used to tell her, running his hand across her hair. Two days earlier, the guards brought an old Caucasian man to her room. She was terrified that this was it, that her time had come to suffer the pain and humiliation she'd dreaded since her capture. Instead, it was a medical check.

The physician was calm and gentle, and she didn't struggle. The two guards watched from a few feet away, and she was sure they would have held her down if she'd resisted. The touching and the probing went on for twenty minutes, and then, just like that, he was gone and she was alone again.

She'd remembered old war movies, the ones her dad loved. There were a few that were about prisoners of war, and she recalled they tracked the days with marks on their walls. She started that on the first ship and continued the ritual when transferred to her current prison. Another thing she remembered was exercise.

Every day Vicky walked through all the kick, knee strikes, elbow strikes, and punches her dad had taught her. The practice made her focus on survival. She might have only one opportunity to escape, and these guards would not anticipate that their female prisoner could hurt them. After twenty minutes of shadow boxing, she exercised: push-ups, sit-ups, body-weight squats and lunges, jumping jacks, whatever she could remember.

At first, she did these things once a day. Lately it was three times a day, and she was starting to do boy push-ups instead of the girly ones. But there was always more time to sit and think. At some point, something was going to happen to her. It waited for her just beyond the door. She began to cry.

"Fellow fuck sticks!" Seamus's voice boomed across the empty hangar. Behind him trailed Gold, a bit pale, but mobile and smiling.

"Holy shit, look what the fuck just washed in, an old sailor and his trusty Asian sidekick. You two look like the Green Hornet and Kato." Steve laughed at his own joke as Matt walked over and shook first Seamus's and then Gold's hands.

"Good to see you up and operational!" Matt smiled at the young Thai. "How're you feeling?"

Seamus waved and answered for his ward. "He's hard as ironwood, this boy! He'll be an asset when we are in Bangkok. He blends in, not like all you professional athletes."

Matt immediately saw the wisdom in Seamus's statement. They did stick out, and they would need to deal with the two ships in a very discreet manner. He saw that Seamus's arrival pulled the others from their workouts, and now the entire team was standing in a semicircle.

"Next steps?" Matt asked the old tomcat jock.

Seamus checked his watch, a fancy upscale timepiece made by Brietling. "We are wheels up in thirty minutes, lads. I need to do flight checks and file a flight plan. When I'm ready, I'll send Gold over to get you guys. Be ready to leave."

"Don't worry about that, old man. We'll be ready." Erik smiled and turned to walk back to the wall. "That means we have time to do a few more sets, Jackson!"

Jackson groaned and followed the younger man. "That's a nice-looking watch you got there," Steve observed, pointing to the Breitling.

Seamus looked at his wrist. "Yeah, it's a Brietling emergency. Linked to satellites, so if you need to be rescued, you just twist this oversized stem and pull. The whole world will know where you are and that you're in trouble."

Steve took a better look. "What's that mark on the watch dial?"

Seamus smiled. "This was a gift from a former employer. It's their corporate logo. Only a hundred or so in existence. Now if you don't mind."

Steve swept his hand across his body and toward the door. "Sorry to detain you, captain."

"Commander, I was a commander. I didn't make captain," Seamus muttered as he left the hangar.

"Touchy subject," Steve noted.

Matt heard the exchange, but he was already thinking about Bangkok. The ships were in the harbor as of yesterday, according to Greta's information. He had the names written down; but no matter how hard he tried, he couldn't pronounce either one. One was a Malaysian flagged vessel and the other was from India.

The plan was basic and in need of target intelligence. Which pier or piers? Lighting? Guards on the pier? Regular security? Guards on the ships? And could they access the ships by boat or would they have to swim? Gold's involvement was a godsend.

He would load the man up with EEIs--essential elements of intelligence--bullet points to collect on. They would need to see the targets at night; so depending on their arrival time, it would have to be done at the same time Gold was collecting up close and personal.

He heard a loud coughing sound, then another. Seamus was firing up a pair of engines, and they were nearby. He walked to the hangar door and stepped out. The hangar doors one building down were open, and the sound was emanating from there. He walked closer, and once at the opening he peered inside.

The Beechcraft King Air was like a piece of handcrafted jewelry. Mat was awestruck by the lines of the fuselage and the dramatic blue on white paint scheme. The sound he'd heard were coming from a pair of Pratt and Whitney engines. *Class act!*

The twin-engine commuter aircraft was probably capable of speeds over two hundred knots. Matt had a clue as to the cost of such an aircraft, but it was only a guess. This was a multimillion-dollar plane, and Seamus owned it in addition to the hotel and his other buildings and business interests. Someday he'd have to find out just what the hell the old bird was doing to make his money.

Gold came around the wing; and upon seeing Matt, he waved. Matt nodded and jogged back to get the others. The team exited their hangar in time to watch Seamus taxi out of the second hangar and swing around toward them. Matt waited until Seamus stopped and waved them forward from the cockpit.

Gold pulled the stairs out of the side compartment and stood by until all four of the Americans were onboard. He then climbed up and pulled the stairs up behind him. He secured the door and found a seat.

The plane had the capacity to seat twelve people, so there was plenty of room. When the door signaled shut, Seamus radioed the tower and began to taxi to the runway. Once there, he ran up the big engines for a minute and then rolled onto the main runway. After a few seconds pause, he punched the plane forward with a jolt. Within twenty seconds, the nose was up and they were in the air.

"Fucker still thinks he's flying Tomcats!" Erik shouted out.

Matt turned his attention outside the Beechcraft. He focused again on the plan to board and search the ships. Even as he mulled over the details, his subconscious was forming a plan B. Maddox would be the primary target if Vicky wasn't on the ships. He'd decided first things first: act on Greta's tip. But if she wasn't there …

A-wut's cell phone rang, and he scrambled to find the damn thing. He tossed two couch pillows and snatched it from behind the lovely thigh of a girl he was just about to enjoy. She lay there silent and obedient as he answered.

"Yes, what do you have?" A-wut listened intently for a moment. He thanked the voice on the phone and hung up. This person of interest, Flanagan, owned a plane and had filed a flight plan for Bangkok. His aircraft was more than capable of carrying the four Americans, and his gut told him they were onboard. This was good news.

He'd reacquired the targets and had a specific location and probable time of arrival in Bangkok. The young beauty rubbed his leg and slid her hand under his robe, reaching for his cock. The slap surprised and startled her, and she began to cry while rubbing her red cheek.

"Not now, bitch!" A-wut walked over to his computer and sat down. He accessed the encrypted email system used by all Maddox's businesses to send orders to his men in Bangkok. The Americans had picked the worst possible place to go. A-wut had over fifty operatives in the city. He'd make the order clear: no survivors.

In five minutes, it was done. He pushed himself away and it was then he heard the quiet whimpering. He felt bad for hitting the girl. She was innocent and stupid but likable. She didn't have a life or know the world outside of the one created for her by A-wut. Maddox liked to refer to them as the children. Girls taken when they were only toddlers and raised for one purpose and one purpose only: pleasure.

He needed to calm her down. It wouldn't do to have her fearful. He trusted these girls, but rarely did business in their presence. They knew they were expendable and that just one indiscretion would result in a sudden and painful exit from this world. Once they were older and used up, they would be sold on the secondary market, likely to Arabs who didn't mind used goods.

He would have his way with the girl and then send her away. He started thinking about packing. He needed to go to Bangkok tonight. He needed to be there when it was over. A-wut walked over and cooed gently. He held her hand for a tender moment and then ever so slowly raised her up off the couch. Holding her hand, he led her step by step toward the bedroom. Her hands began to shake.

The sounds of violent slaps and fists hitting flesh were muted by the soundproof walls in A-wut's apartment. The girl knew better than to scream. Her groans and grunts were not the sounds of pleasure. She knew she might not make it through this night alive. It was her fate, what she was bred to do, and it was likely the way she would die.

Chapter Seventeen

Seamus eased the nose down and settled onto the still hot concreate at Don Mueang International Airport. Matt had never visited Thailand, but here he was in Bangkok, the city made famous in song and film.

Jackson had mentioned that there were two city airports now. The new one took in most of the modern commercial and international traffic. Don Mueang was an aging facility, catering to smaller commuter aircraft and regional commercial flights.

Seamus had remained silent throughout the trip, focusing on flying. He was a strange old bird, Matt mused. A man of mystery, yet apparently known by everybody in this country. The former naval officer didn't look or act like the result of the prestigious academy.

Was it all a show? Did the obviously wealthy and prosperous man go home every night to a spacious mansion, drop the pirate character and the ratty clothes, and wear a silk robe while sipping on fine wine? Matt smiled at the image he'd conjured up. He doubted it. Seamus seemed genuine in a disingenuous sort of way. He liked him, and now he had to trust him.

The Beechcraft came to a halt, and Seamus cycled down the two big engines. "Final stop, lads! Bangkok, the city of dreams awaits you."

For a brief second Matt thought of gear offload, and an image of Steve directing the event flashed through his head. Then he realized they didn't have any gear, no equipment, no extra clothes for that matter. Flashing back to the good old days in SDV Team Two, when things were confusing for the young Matthew Barrett, and Chief Petty Officer Steve Auger had an answer for everything. He sighed and got in the short line exiting the aircraft.

Gold had flown in the co-pilot seat, so he and Seamus were the last to deplane. Seamus gave instructions to the ground crew to refuel, then sent Gold off at a jog toward the space between a large commercial storage building and the tower facility.

"I hope you sent him for pizza," Erik grumbled. It had been a long time since their last meal.

Seamus shook his head. "Just a precaution. I'm assuming we are going to be tracked from Phuket to here. Gold can mingle into the crowd outside the airport and then double back to watch over us and whoever might be conducting surveillance."

Matt watched the young Thai until he was out of sight. They needed a place to plan and prepare. "I don't suppose you own a convenient warehouse here in Bangkok? One we can use to set up and get our shit together?"

Jackson, Steve, and Erik all looked at Seamus. They were curious, too. "I can do one better than that. I have a boat, well almost a yacht, over there in the marina. It's 75-feet long and sleeps six. Once Gold checks the outer perimeter of the airport, we'll drive over in an airport maintenance van. It's a short drive from here to the harbor. The boat's just big enough to justify a crew of sorts. But my guess is we won't be traveling far tonight, correct?"

Matt nodded. "We should get off the tarmac and into a building. No reason to make it easier for them to spot us here."

Steve chuckled. "That's hilarious! They tracked Gary's plan from New Zealand to Thailand and likely tracked the

Beechcraft to here. You don't have to be very sharp to follow this gang of misfits."

Seamus nodded in agreement. "The plane is mine; and if they are on to my connection with your team, they no doubt put eyes on all my known mobility platforms. That's planes and shit for you slow FBI fuckers."

Jackson's eyebrows shot up. "Okay then, smart ass. What's preventing them from knowing that you have a boat in the harbor?"

"Two reasons," Seamus explained. "First, Gold will scrub the area close to the plane to identify anyone who looks too interested in us. That's a good reason to stay right here on the taxiway until we hear from him. Second, my boat is owned by a friend. The friend is me under an assumed name, not any of my companies, mind you. It's my personal get out of Dodge plan, in case this country ever goes to shit on me."

Matt was vaguely aware that Thailand was far from a stable political entity. He'd lost touch with such things since leaving the Navy, but he was schooled enough on the subject to know the power here didn't reside in a stable democracy.

The players in Thailand were a mix of traditional ethnic clans and powerful families who controlled a vast amount of the businesses in the country. A fragile balancing act was all that stood between calm and chaos.

Gold sat in the café chair and waved off the waiter for the third time. The shop's proprietor was getting angry, and he knew he'd have to move or order something soon. Seamus had picked the observation point in the cockpit, pointing out that there was only one narrow gap where somebody outside the airport could place the arriving Beechcraft under surveillance.

Gold could see the plane and the five men standing near its nose clearly from his vantage point, but his attention was on the two men seated a couple of tables away. Both wore short jackets, strange in the heat of the day. They were probably armed, hence the need for the jackets. They were not trying to hide the small pair of binoculars, and their façade would be humorous if the situation wasn't so serious.

Each man took turns looking all around, up and down the street before settling on the gap between the airport structures. After a minute or so, the binoculars were placed on the table before the routine was repeated. Gold had watched the men get out of a small sedan in the alley next to the café. He had a good description of their car and the two men. Time to check in with his boss.

Seamus answered the cell phone and waited until Gold's report was finished. He told his ward to wait and placed his hand over the phone. "Two men, armed. They have us under direct surveillance from a café right behind the hangar. Gold says they arrived in a forest green Subaru sedan, parked in the adjacent alley. There are obstacles in the alley blocking the car from view, but it's there. What do you want to do?"

A few minutes later the men walked to the hangar, and Seamus summoned the airport van. He watched his watch carefully. Four minutes later the van pulled up; and as instructed, it stopped short of the hangar, right in the gap between the two buildings. Once the passengers were loaded inside, the van made a tight turn and headed back the way it came.

Gold stood up and walked across the street without looking at the two men. It didn't matter. As soon as the van stopped in plain view the two men wearing jackets jumped up, slapped a few bills on the table, and hurried toward the alley. When Gold subtly glanced to his left, they were gone.

A minute later, the airport van rolled up and stopped. Matt slid the door open long enough for Gold to jump in. The van accelerated and went down three blocks before turning left and traveling two more blocks. The stoplight held them there for a count of ten; when green, the van turned left again.

A-wut's surveillance team covered the two hundred feet down the alley to their car. The taller of the two men reached in his jacket pocket for the key. He opened the passenger side door and slid across the front seat. The second man waited impatiently until the way was clear for him to get into the car.

He sat down and pulled on the car door, but it wasn't budging. Just as he tried to pull even harder, he heard a mechanical clinking sound and a clacking near his right ear. The first man into the car slumped over the steering wheel, two small holes in his temple oozing blood. The second man quickly looked to his right. Clack, clack.

Erik unscrewed the silencer from the Ruger and placed both in the concealed holster under his shirt. Steve walked in front of him as they exited the alley on the backside. He spotted the van coming down the street and led the way across the traffic to the other side. The van paused curbside and then roared to life.

Matt gave a thumbs-up, and Steve and Erik nodded. Now they had a fighting chance to get to Seamus's boat without being followed. Maddox's men in Bangkok would have something else to think about now. The team was armed, and they were through playing nice.

Matt's plan had been bold and readily accepted by everyone. Each man knew they'd stepped over a line. Men were dead on both sides now. Matt hoped it was a sufficient deterrent, but doubted it was. Now it was time to plan for the marina takedowns.

Seamus's boat was more of a ship. At 75 feet in length, the power yacht was more than impressive. Matt decided Seamus was a drug lord or something close to it. How the hell could he have amassed such a fortune? The team moved onto the yacht one at a time in five-minute intervals to lower their signature. Anybody seeing a group of men boarding together might become suspicious and get the word out. Matt wasn't taking any chances.

Seamus directed them to the largest cabin, one that could serve as a planning area. Once inside, Matt gained their attention. "We have two vessels to search tonight. *Search* is the operative word here, gents. This might feel like a good old-fashioned takedown, but we only fight if forced to protect ourselves. Understood?"

Everybody nodded; Erik, however, was smiling while he did so. Matt didn't personally know Erik. He'd have to pair up with the younger man to help curb his enthusiasm a bit. Seamus came into the space, carrying a large harbor chart.

"Right on cue!" Matt noted, spreading the chart out on the bed. "Seamus, can you orient us a bit? Where's your ship berthed?"

Seamus stepped closer and pointed. "My ship has a name: Gladiator." The men shared winks and grins.

“What happened to using female names?” Steve asked, tongue in cheek.

Seamus shrugged. “Too long a story to retell here. Another time perhaps.” Seamus pointed to the chart again. “This is where we are: pier twelve. The Gladiator doesn’t get out much; and when she does, she stays out for several days. I suggest we stick to that profile. Do your searches. If you find Vicky, bring her to the ship and we’ll figure out the next move at that time. I don’t have enough fuel to get very far, but far enough, I should think.”

“Where are the two vessels we’re looking for? Greta said near pier alpha nine.” Jackson asked the question on everyone’s minds. Should they access the target vessels by land or by water? Could they use the Gladiator as a mother ship and speed up the process, or would her presence in the area of the commercial piers raise scrutiny?

“Right here. This is alpha nine.” Seamus pointed to a spot across the harbor from the Gladiator.

Matt nodded. “So, we need to come up with a plan. It’s 4:20 in the afternoon. It gets dark around 9:30. I want to hit the two vessels at the same time, so that means splitting up. Erik and I will take the Indian ship, and Steve and Jackson the Malaysian ship. Seamus will command the Gladiator, and Gold will drive a van. Seamus, we need a van.”

Seamus nodded. “I think I can work that out for you. Do you need me here for this, or can I go begin to make arrangements? I assume you turds are hungry, too?”

Steve’s face perked up at the mention of food. “I knew I liked you, Seamus. Always looking out for the men.”

Seamus grumbled, "Fuck that noise. I'm starving. May as well feed you at the same time." The stocky ex-fighter pilot left the berthing space and headed toward the ship's galley.

"Charming asshole, isn't he?" No one answered Erik.

Matt cleared his throat. "Okay, let's get serious here. My initial thought is we approach the ships the only way we know will be effective and give us the highest probability of surprise."

"Fuck. We're swimming, right?" Steve was a true frogman. Team guys worked in the water, but hated being cold and wet. Of course, it went with the mission and the whole Navy thing, but Matt felt the same way Steve did. How long had it been since he even took a casual swim?

Matt nodded, confirming Steve's guess. "That's right, tadpole, we're all getting wet. The only question to be resolved is where do we insert? Do we use the quay wall or come in from the open end of the harbor?"

There was silence as each man pondered the options and studied the chart. Matt's preference was to find a dark section of the commercial piers and enter the water there. Keep low visibility in and out. His biggest concern was getting Vicky off the vessel safely. Could she even swim?

"You think Tom taught his baby girl how to swim, boss?" Erik was reading Matt's mind.

"I don't know. I was just thinking the same thing."

"Maybe we could come in from the shore side, but use the Gladiator's RHIB boat to take us and her off the ship on the harbor side," Jackson offered.

"Now that's a great idea!" Steve responded. The RHIB's long enough to carry us all and Vicky in one trip. It's a stable platform, too. The rigid hull below the water line and the inflated main tubes on top make it fast and sturdy. That's my vote. Use the RHIB as the extraction vehicle."

"That means Gold's van is the insert platform on the land side and the secondary extraction vehicle if we run into any problems using the RHIB," Erik finished.

Jackson was rubbing his chin and staring at the chart. "I'm not a rootin' tootin' Navy SEAL, but I can swim. How do we actually get onboard once we are in the water next to the hull of the cargo ship?"

In unison the three SEALs said the same thing, "Hawsepipe!"

Matt smiled. They'd insert on land using the van and enter the water wherever they could find an area bathed in shadow. Two teams of two men each would swim to the vessels, find the anchor chain, and use the links as a climbing ladder until they were onboard.

Once on deck, the search teams would move throughout their assigned cargo vessel looking for Tom's daughter. Once they were finished, they'd quietly climb back down the anchor chain and reenter the water, with or without Vicky. He needed to tighten up the role of the Gladiator in the final phase, but the plan looked solid as a fully fleshed out set of mission phases.

"Hit the pause button, guys. I smell food!" Erik exclaimed.

"Now you're talking!" Steve was gone in a flash. Matt sighed and nodded to Jackson. "Not smart to think on an empty stomach. We can come back to this later. After you." Matt waved his hand toward the door, then followed Jackson to the galley. The old feelings of paranoia mixed with excitement surged through his brain. They could fuck this whole thing up, and he was painfully aware of that possibility. But the feeling of working with committed professionals again served as a counterweight to his fear of failure. In the case of Vicky, the poster said it best: fear was not an option!

Chapter Eighteen

The harbor waters were calm. The cloudy sky helped by blocking what was to be a full moon, and Matt could see several places along the commercial quay wall that were not illuminated by overhead lighting.

The two ships were relatively close to each other. The Malaysian vessel was the farthest out, hugging the very end of the broad commercial pier, and on the opposite side of the Indian ship, which was tucked in very close to Matt and the van.

Gold had scored a food truck for their insertion vehicle. It wasn't conspicuous among the hundreds of trucks coming in and out of the pier area, and that was a plus because Matt felt like they were being watched every minute. He knew in his gut that was paranoia and not grounded in fact, but he couldn't shake his apprehension.

Would A-wut connect their arrival and the deaths of his surveillance team to their mission? If so, he could have a nasty surprise waiting for them on the two ships. Matt and the others had considered this possibility during their final briefing, but decided it was a fifty-fifty shot A-wut didn't know who they were searching for or why they were in Thailand in the first place. So, it was time to execute, execute, execute.

After a short debate, Matt directed Gold to maneuver the food truck to the first dark area on the pier complex. The location was close, but not too close to the first ship. Matt waited until the vehicle came to a complete stop, then cracked open the back door.

"Good luck, guys. See you on the yacht!" Matt slapped Steve and Jackson on the back as the two men exited the truck. They slipped into a space between two stacks of containers as

Matt shut the truck door and directed Gold to pull out for the far end of the pier.

Matt had selected the Malaysian ship for himself and Erik because it was the most difficult challenge. They would have to drive near the vessel in order to see a suitable place to enter the water, and that meant exposure to the crew and any security that might be in place.

As Gold maneuvered the truck around a large crane, Matt sat in the space next to him so he could survey the possibilities through the front windshield. "To the left. Do you see that dark spot near the orange canvas?"

Gold didn't answer the question, but turned in response to Matt's instructions. The dark spot was isolated over the area of a large collection of industrial materials. The orange tarp covered what appeared to be a huge electric generator. Was the cargo deposited for onloading? Or a shipment heading inland? Matt didn't have a clue, but it offered what he was looking for.

"Stop here!"

Gold complied and remained silent as Matt and Erik left the food truck. The entire event took seconds; and to anyone watching, the food truck appeared only to pause rather than stop. Gold drove away and turned toward the city.

He'd stage the vehicle as instructed, near the commercial piers, but not too close. If the two swim pairs needed him for an emergency extraction, he would be in position. He glanced down at the blanket beside him. The Belgian belt-fed machine gun was ready for use if needed.

Matt and Erik moved to the far side of the stack of metal tubes and stopped short of the open area beyond. To their right was a small tug, small relative to the much larger Malaysian flagged cargo ship on the other side.

The area was dimly lit. Not as dark as Matt would like, but dark enough for their purposes. He nodded at Erik, and the former SEAL casually walked across the open space to the edge of the pier. He sat down on the edge for a moment, then slid over the side. Matt looked around waiting for an alert call that never came. He waited two minutes, and then mimicked his partner's routine.

The water was warm, and to a frogman that was welcome news. Matt glided over to where Erik clung to a piling. They had two choices. Go out and around the tug or try to navigate the complex array of pilings under the pier. Erik held up a fist to tell Matt to wait and he pulled himself inside the pilings to check things out. A minute later he came back shaking his head.

"There's crap blocking the way through. Even if we could get through it all, we'd lose too much time. We'll have to swim around."

Matt winced. More exposure and more chances to be spotted. It didn't even matter if it was A-wut's men who saw them. Anyone swimming around here at night was up to no good. They'd be reported, and the harbor police would be on them in minutes. Matt began to ease away from the pier, with Erik following a few body lengths back. He suddenly had an idea and angled in toward the tug, instead of away to open water.

A few powerful strokes put him next to the working boat and under the curve of the broad hull. They were invisible to anyone on deck, and even better, invisible to anyone looking out into the harbor. Basic combat swimmer shit. Erik nudged him and whispered.

"Smart move, boss!"

Matt didn't answer. He edged himself along the hull until it ended. The Malaysian cargo ship was twenty feet away, across an open patch of water. The ship cast a dark shadow, giving Matt an idea. He took a deep breath and submerged, angling left until he bumped into a piling. He turned to follow the pier and when everything went black, he slowly surfaced under the bow of the cargo ship.

A few seconds later, Erik popped up next to him giving Matt a thumbs-up. The anchor chain was aft near the stern. In many harbors, large ships dropped their anchors as they came in, allowing the chain to play out onto the seabed. In shallow ports, they used the anchor to winch them back and away from the piers until they were in deeper water, instead of powering back and risking sucking in silt and muck into their power plants. Now all they had to do was climb.

A-wut got dressed in a hurry. Maddox was in Bangkok and he wanted answers. It was late, but he knew his boss kept odd hours. He debated telling him about the dead surveillance team. The hit was professional, up close and quiet. He'd been able to cover it up with a few well-placed phone calls and a bribe, but the act did smell of American CIA. Maybe Maddox was right.

He'd picked up on these guys in Hawaii after a tip from a contact in Kauai. Why did they go to Kauai? He needed to follow that lead and see what turned up. Maybe he could figure out why this team was in Thailand and why they seemed interested in Roger Maddox.

The limousine pulled up in front of the luxury hotel where A-wut was staying, and he jumped inside. He dialed a number and waited for someone to pick up.

"Hello?" The female voice on the other end was calm, mature.

"I need a favor. That contact in Kauai. I need you to find out why the Americans were on the island. I need details. Use whatever means necessary to get the truth. Mr. Maddox is interested."

The voice on the other end had a tinge of irritation. "If you say so. It might take a few days."

A-wut let his emotions take over. "You don't have a few days. Make it happen now! I want fucking results!" A-wut snapped the cell phone shut, ending the call. He decided he wouldn't tell Maddox about the hit. He needed more time to turn all of this shit around. Time to come out as the hero and not the fuckup who let Maddox down.

Steve Auger was a good swimmer, and he'd kept himself in excellent shape after leaving the service. Jackson Bollinger, on the other hand, was not having a good time. The swim was a mere thirty meters, but the choppy water was giving the FBI man a hard time. The sputtering was pissing Steve off.

"You need to shut the fuck up, man. The whole harbor thinks there's a whale surfacing."

“Sorry!” Jackson said, taking in a mouthful of oily water. He fought the gag reflex and waited a five count before regaining control of his stomach. “I’m good, I’m all right!”

Steve wasn’t so sure, but what choice did he have? He maneuvered to the bow and began to follow the edge of the hull toward the stern. The Indian vessel was a bit shorter than the one Matt and Erik were boarding. In no time at all, he was gripping the anchor chain and pointing up.

Jackson was right behind him and nodding. He waited until his swim buddy was six or seven feet up the chain before following him. The climb took less than five minutes. At the top, Steve eased through the large hawsepipe and slithered onto the deck, making room for Jackson. Jackson was better off on the climb. He was in great shape; and in few seconds, he popped through the hawsepipe and joined Steve.

Both men reached under their shorts and pulled out Ziploc bags containing their pistols. The silencers were in place. After making eye contact and receiving a nod, Steve came up into a low crouch and began moving across the deck.

The way was clear into the superstructure, and Steve followed at the same steady pace. They’d discussed the likely places to find the girls and hopefully Vicky among them, so Steve avoided the upper decks and went down the first ladder he found, his pistol extended and at the ready. The ship was quiet, and at this time of night, sitting pier side, there was no reason to expect a watch or a guard. If there was security, then it would be collocated with the girls.

Jackson followed the SEAL further and further into the ship, checking rooms until they reached the main cargo bay. Steve didn’t think the girls would be kept there, but he needed to be sure. He waved Jackson up close.

"The cargo bay might be full and difficult to move through. I'll watch everything on the horizontal, but I need you to look up. Most of these types of ships have overwalks and mezzanines around the perimeter of the cargo bay. Ready?"

Jackson patted Steve on the shoulder and nodded. Steve didn't hesitate, but opened the hatch and stepped into the large cargo storage area. He saw immediately that it was empty, but in the pitch black he couldn't tell where the exit hatches were located. He felt Jackson's hand grip his shoulder. Smart, they could lose each other in here. He wasn't sure of the time, but it felt like it had been hours since getting out of the van. He began to move down the wall.

Erik nudged Matt and began to pull his pistol out of the Ziploc bag. They both stank. The mixture of dirty oil and trash in the harbor coated them both in a slimy wetness that made their shirts stick to their bodies uncomfortably. Matt already had his weapon out and up, scanning the upper decks for signs of life.

The ship was large and impressive. He wasn't sure where to go from here. In the teams they'd had access to ship layouts, professional schematics of target vessels. That way they could choreograph the takedowns and minimize wasted time. This ship was a maze of rooms on multiple levels. *Well, it is what it is.* Matt stood up and moved over to the nearest bulkhead.

Erik tapped Matt's shoulder and pointed to a hatch that was barely visible on the level right above them. They crouched low and made their way to the external ladder and began to climb. Somewhere deep within the vessel a hatch slammed shut. They were not alone.

Roger Maddox hated Bangkok. The city had a smell that stayed with you days after leaving. It was in the air and all around him. He had to placate the powerful from time to time to keep his business in good standing, so here he was. The meetings were scheduled for the morning and required no preparation on his part.

The other reason he was in Thailand was to speak with A-wut in person. The nagging premonition he'd been having about the Americans wouldn't go away. A-wut said he was handling the issue, but the silence these last few days indicated something was amiss. He needed to look in the man's eyes to see the truth of the matter.

The doorbell tone was muted, but it echoed throughout the penthouse suite. Maddox waved his hand at the bodyguard; and the former boxer took a few steps to the door and opened it, revealing A-wut, right on time.

"Come in, my friend. Take a seat, get comfortable. Would you like something to drink?"

A-wut shook his head and looked around. There was only one bodyguard visible, but he knew Maddox traveled with two. He tried to suppress his nervousness as he sat down on the sofa across from Maddox.

"So, how are things going with the American situation?" Maddox sipped his glass of red wine and smiled.

A-wut tried to smile back, but he didn't think it was coming across quite right. He needed to give the man something, anything. He had a thought.

"We lost track of them in Phuket. I had a team hit their safehouse, killed one for sure. My guys torched the place and left.

I'm pretty sure the survivors went to ground, at least for now. I have eyes everywhere, ready for when they pop up again."

As A-wut spoke, his confidence rose. It was all true, well mostly true. It showed he'd taken the initiative and struck a blow. Surely Maddox would appreciate this news. He watched the South African swirl his wine around and around, pondering the report and thinking through all the possible ramifications.

"I'm pleased, A-wut. Very pleased. The Americans hate disruption, and they hate being exposed. You're probably right about them going underground, but my guess is they won't pop up again. At least not these same men. Are you sure you won't have a drink before you leave?"

The question was both an invitation and a polite dismissal. A-wut was happy to leave. If Maddox was happy with the information, then he was off the hook, at least until the Americans showed themselves again. He declined the drink and stood up. As he rode the elevator down, he smiled. He was getting pretty good at handling Maddox.

The limousine ride was short. As the car pulled into the valet parking lane in front of his hotel, his phone rang. "Yes, what is it? It's late!"

"I have the answers you seek, unless you want me to call you in the morning." The soothing voice on the other end was almost taunting.

"Go ahead," he responded.

"The Americans are searching for a girl."

A-wut wasn't sure he'd heard correctly. "A girl? What fucking girl?"

"An American teenager kidnapped four weeks ago in Honolulu. I don't have a name, but I'm certain it was four weeks ago. Does that mean anything to you?"

A-wut struggled to make a connection. A teenager, four weeks ago in Honolulu. Suddenly his face registered full understanding. They were not CIA or any other organization. They were a rescue team, probably privately hired and paid by the family of this girl. But why were they in Thailand and why did they come to Bangkok?

The voice asked the question again, but A-wut simply hung up. Why Bangkok? He searched his memory and then it hit him. The ships! They were after the fucking ships in the harbor looking for this girl!

Chapter Nineteen

Jackson grabbed Steve's shoulder and held him back. Both men stopped and listened intently. They were halfway down the last section of compartments near the bow, and there was no sign of life, crew or otherwise. Jackson whispered into Steve's ear, and Steve checked his watch. Steve nodded. He needed to pick up the pace. Twenty minutes of searching the ship's interior had flown by, but they spent much more time onboard.

Five minutes later, Steve stopped. They'd reached the bow and completed their inspection of the vessel's spaces. No Vicky. It was time to get back to the to the stern and off the vessel before a crew member showed up and spoiled their night. Steve climbed a set of stairs and exited the superstructure on the darker, harbor side of the vessel. He waited until Jackson joined him topside. Together they moved to the back of the ship, careful, but not wasting any time. It took three minutes to move down the steel deck to their original entry point.

Before descending the anchor chain, Jackson turned and crouched down, covering their rear security while Steve pulled out a waterproof flashlight and went down on one knee. The lens was taped up, leaving a small area of lens uncovered. This allowed a limited amount of light to shine through, just enough to do the job.

Steve pressed the power switch on and then off, on and then off again. He repeated this until he'd flashed the signal five times leaving a three second pause between each signal. The message to Seamus on the yacht was clear: no joy. No recovery of Vicky, or anyone else for that matter. They were ready for pickup.

On the yacht, Seamus watched, using a pair of ordinary binoculars. They worked for this task well enough. Night vison goggles would only enhance all the backlit features of the harbor and wash out the tiny signal he was anticipating. As he scanned from the back of one target vessel and across to the other one, Seamus thought he saw something. A tiny flash of light? A second later he spotted it again and knew it was the signal. No luck for Steve and Jackson. Now it was up to the second team.

Steve went down the chain first, followed closely by Jackson. The rough metal tore at their wet hands as they descended and finally bobbed side-by-side on the surface of the harbor. The water was colder this time. It wasn't rational, but sometimes being wet in the open air sapped the body's warmth. Confirming this observation, Steve felt a chill run down the length of his body.

Jackson was tough, but he wasn't a frogman. Hypothermia was a torture device used in SEAL training to weed out the unworthy and harden those who decided to stick it out. Once students became SEALs, they slowly appreciated the use of cold water to select the men who would wear the fabled gold SEAL trident. SEALs were destined to be cold until the day they retired or left the service.

According to the prearranged plan, once Seamus received signals from both teams, he would send in the RHIB for their pickup. Waiting was going to suck; waiting for a water extraction always sucked. Jackson checked the time. Thirty-two minutes had elapsed since they'd exited the van.

Matt and Erik had a longer swim to accomplish and a larger ship to explore. Given that, Steve estimated they'd require at least another twenty minutes before they were ready for pickup, even longer if they ran into difficulties. All he and Steve could do now was hang onto the slippery chain and play mental games to ignore what exposure to the water was doing to their core temperature.

Matt moved slowly toward the light. The low power lights in the passageway were dimmer than the light escaping the compartment on the right. It was occupied. The voices were muffled, but proof someone was on the ship and awake at this late hour. He turned to Erik, but Erik simply nodded. He'd taken in all the visual and audio information and came to the same conclusion. Matt eased up to the hatch and peaked inside.

Three men sat around a table and played cards. Matt spotted rifles in the far corner, stacked too far away to reach, but he noted each had a magazine in place. They were ready for use. Why? Who needed firepower like that on a cargo vessel? He spotted the grip of an automatic pistol sticking out of the waistband of the nearest crew member. These guys were on guard duty, but what or who were they guarding?

Matt backed up several steps and looked back at Erik. He first took his left hand and tapped his Ruger pistol. Then he held up three fingers. Erik understood the old Vietnam hand signals immediately. Three guys with weapons were in the compartment. Matt thought through the next steps carefully. He remembered the old saying that when one considered everything, the simplest answer was usually the correct one.

He concluded that wherever you found guards, you'd find something worth guarding. Instead of skirting the compartment to continue their search, Matt decided on a bold plan. They would enter the room and ask. If they resisted, Matt and Erik would deal with that quickly and quietly.

He made a talking gesture with his hand and Erik nodded. The two former SEALs were calm. Matt felt like he was doing what he'd been born to do. He felt alive and locked into a zone that he'd missed for several years. He started to move. Erik placed his free hand on Matt's shoulder, and they entered the compartment together, separating left and right as they went in.

A-wut knew there was inventory on one of the ships, so it was easy to choose which one to warn. Ironically, Maddox was in town for a second purpose, which involved the inventory on that same ship. A-wut sighed with relief that his boss had received his shipment earlier in the day and was unlikely to care much about the ones left behind on the ship. He grabbed his cell phone and began dialing.

The phone rang and rang; after a minute he hung up and made a second call. This time the person on the other end answered immediately. "We have unwanted visitors on the Berharap. No one is answering the phone onboard, so assume the visitors have interfered with our operation. Get a team there as fast as you can!"

A-wut hung up. Maybe he should go, too. Show a little bravado. It might come in handy when he explained to Maddox why one of his precious ships was boarded. He suddenly had a thought. The Berharap had taken on a shipment of inventory recently that included two girls his people in Hawaii had grabbed about four weeks earlier. He knew one of them was a thirteen-year-old Japanese tourist. The second one, however, was an American.

Matt looked down the barrel of his Ruger and smiled. He took the palm of his left hand and extended it outward, gesturing in a way that conveyed they should all place their hands on the table. The two closest to him complied, but the third man furthest away was hesitant. He'd had a hand under the table when Matt entered the room, and it was still there. He waited a short count and made the gesture one more time.

The hand moved rapidly; before Matt could react, he heard the classic sound of two suppressed rounds being fired to his right. The man's face opened up as the 9mm bullets entered near his left eye. He jerked back and groaned before sliding to the deck.

Matt couldn't argue with his partner's decision. In that small space, any asshole with a gun could get lucky and hit one of them. He moved close to the man on the right and crouched to pat him down, placing the Ruger's silencer firmly against the man's temple. Not finding a weapon, he backed off and waited as Erik disarmed the second man, tossing the pistol out into the passageway.

"Now what?" Erik was calm, almost serene. There was another door to his right; but before opening it, he needed to know what Matt's plan was.

By way of an answer, Matt stepped forward and struck the guard closest to him across the head. The man slumped over unconscious. Erik took the cue and struck the second man. They both stepped back for a second to survey the compartment. It was time to check out the other room.

Erik moved to the door and listened for a moment before nodding. Matt moved up to the opposite side and waited for a three count before checking to see if it was locked. The door swung open to reveal a dark room filled with cushions. Matt's eyes didn't adjust at first so he waited a moment before entering.

Erik followed him in and they stepped left and right. A muffled scream alerted them to a body lying in the fetal position to their right. Matt looked around for a light switch and flipped it on, illuminating the room. There were three girls blinking back at them. One in each back corner and the one in the fetal position in front of them.

"Vicky?" Matt spoke in a comforted tone.

The three girls looked at each other and then back at Matt. One of them spoke up. "She's gone. They came for her this morning."

Matt felt a wave of despair. So fucking close! Erik checked his watch. "We need to get the hell out of here, boss. Vicky or no Vicky. We've been on target for over thirty minutes."

Matt shook off the bad feeling and nodded. "Okay, ladies, we are here to escort you to safety. I need you to follow my instructions exactly."

"She doesn't understand English that well." A short brunette pointed to a dark-haired girl in the corner. "She's from Japan; we've been calling her Sam."

Matt nodded. "Okay, you, what's your name?"

The brunette spoke up. "I'm Christy and that's Anne over there. She's really freaked out."

Matt smiled at Anne, but the girl just stared at the gun in Erik's hand. "We are friends. Former American military. We were sent to rescue Vicky; but now that we've found the three of you, we need to get you out of here and fast."

Matt spent the next five minutes briefing the girls on the method of movement and the climb down the anchor chain. The two Americans said they could swim, but the Japanese girl refused to indicate her ability either way. Matt decided to take charge of her and directed Erik to lead them out.

The trip to the stern took forever as the conga line of connected bodies negotiated every ladder, turn, and hatch. Erik stepped out onto the deck, and after a second waved the others outside. Matt took the lead. When he arrived at the hawsepipe, he pulled out his flashlight and signaled Seamus. A series of three quick flashes of light followed by a ten-second pause, then repeated. Satisfied Seamus would get the message they had found someone on the ship and were ready for extract, he waved at Christy, indicating he wanted her closer to him.

A shout in Thai surprised all five of them. Matt looked back toward the bow and spotted three armed men running toward them on the weather deck. Erik jabbed his finger at the hawsepipe and growled. "Move!"

Matt took aim at the closest man and dropped him with a shot to the chest. He heard Erik open fire as he turned and ushered Anne through the hawsepipe to follow Christy down to the water. The Japanese girl dropped into a ball and began crying, making it impossible to move her to the chain. Matt looked back over his shoulder and saw Erik drop the second man with a shot to the head. The third man ducked behind a section of firehose and opened fire in their general direction.

"Get the fuck out of here, sir," Erik yelled as he moved forward to get a better angle on the third man. Another set of voices rang out higher up on the ship. The sound of the Thai's weapon was guiding more men to the stern. They couldn't fight all of them, so he made a decision.

The Japanese girl was light and easy to toss over the side. Matt tried to swing her body out far enough to avoid landing on the anchor chain but he didn't have time to look. More shots zipped past his head and rounds ricocheted off the metal all around him. Erik finished off the third man, but was nearly killed when a new face popped over the railing above and opened fire.

Matt fired three times before hitting the newcomer, allowing Erik to move away from the railing to rejoin Matt at the far back of the ship. Matt heard the sound of a speedboat roaring closer. "Let's hope that's Seamus and not reinforcements."

Erik nodded. "You go first, Matt. We need to get off this fucking boat."

Matt had an idea. "You know the fastest way down, right?" He smiled and turned. Placing his foot on the four-foot-high gunnel, he gripped his pistol tight and launched himself into the air. On the way down he heard a rapid series of shots above him and feared the worst. Then Erik hit the water three feet from landing on him.

"That was crazy!" Erik sputtered.

Matt swam over to the three girls who were hugging the chain links as briefed. The Japanese girl was right there with them. Either she was capable of swimming or the other two teens had helped her get to the chain.

The RHIB screamed across the water and sprayed the group with a wake as Seamus brought the boat to a stop. "Let's go! There's assholes up there shooting at me!"

Matt and Erik pushed and shoved the girls up and into the boat. Then they grabbed the safety line that ran around the perimeter of the boat. "Gun it, Seamus!"

The RHIB spun around in its own length and jumped as Seamus pushed the throttle forward. He kept the speed up until he was two hundred yards away from the cargo ship. Matt's hand raised up and Seamus grabbed the pistol. Setting it down, he helped Matt into the boat. They both helped Erik, and then Seamus returned to the console and powered forward at a more sedate pace.

The ex-fighter pilot looked back. "Vicky?"

Matt shook his head. "They took her off this morning. These girls are what's left of ten that were originally moved to the Malaysian ship from other vessels. That means we were too late to save Vicky and six others."

Seamus turned his attention forward again. "At least we saved these three. I'll get my friends here in Bangkok to put out feelers. They're bound to come up with something. Half a day behind isn't a bad thing. Have the girls been … ?"

Matt wasn't sure how to answer the question, so he turned to Christy. "Are you three okay? Did they hurt you?"

Christy shook her head. "No. They pushed us around a little, but I think they were afraid to touch us. I kept waiting, but …"

Matt nodded, his face set in anger. It was likely Vicky also was unhurt, for now. The goons guarding these girls were afraid to spoil the cargo. That meant someone with power and money was willing to go to extreme lengths to get girls who were untouched, unspoiled. The method pointed directly to Roger Maddox. That was where they'd find Vicky. He was sure of it!

Seamus completed the trip to the yacht sitting just outside the harbor at anchor all alone and unmanned. While Matt and Steve assisted the girls, he went aboard and pulled out his cell phone. Gold's voice answered immediately. He listened while Gold confirmed that Jackson and Steve had arrived at the secondary extraction point and were now shivering in the back of the food truck. Seamus hung up. Tomorrow he'd have answers.

Chapter Twenty

It made sense for everybody to stay onboard the yacht for the night. It was safer here at anchor. There was sufficient room for the three girls in one stateroom, and the five men found places to lay down or sit. They were all tired, and sleep came quickly.

Matt woke with a start. The sudden bump of the yacht against the pier signaled that they were back. Seamus must have risen early with a plan. Matt stood up and stretched his back. Frogmen can sleep anywhere at any time, he remembered. Apparently, the rule wasn't true for old frogmen.

A quick survey of the rest of the team revealed all were awake, with Jackson topside having coffee with Seamus. The three girls were still asleep, huddled together in a ball. They must be exhausted, Matt thought. Much like a SEAL unit coming out of the field after a long multi-day mission. The stress management brain function gave way all at once. The body shut down and deep sleep followed. He closed the door to their stateroom and headed up the ladder.

Steve and Erik had beat him to the coffeemaker, so he decided to skip making a new pot. Instead, he looked at the harbor and realized that with the residential and commercial high rises surrounding their current position, A-wut and his band of merry assholes could watch their every move. He hoped Seamus's expectation of privacy was well-founded. He had his doubts. A-wut didn't need technology to find them; he could just put the word out on the street.

Seamus was on his cell phone speaking to someone in Thai. When he hung up, he smiled. "I think we have a solid lead on where Vicky was taken."

Matt and the others gave Seamus their full attention. "Where?" Steve asked.

"My resources say that the select few, who are destined for the high-end market, are taken to a hunting camp in the interior. A place I've only heard about. There was a shipment yesterday presumably destined for that camp."

"That's it, then! We need to get there before she's moved again!" Erik tossed out. "Do you have assets out that way, Seamus?"

Seamus thought for a moment. "No, but it isn't impossible to get there. The camp itself will likely have a helicopter pad and a rough airstrip to accommodate wealthy customers going there to hunt. I need to see a land map to find another way to get a plane in there. A straight road could work, as long as the overhead jungle canopy allows for a landing."

Jackson and Erik asked more questions, with Steve adding his own observations as to the difficulty associated with operations in the jungle. As the four men discussed preliminary planning, Matt pondered the intelligence they'd received. Seamus's people were no doubt reliable and loyal. But the profile didn't make sense.

Maybe his personal pet theory was wrong. Maddox didn't have to be the end customer. It just felt right for some reason. Yet, here was evidence he was wrong. One thing was for sure: they couldn't ignore the tip from Seamus's informant. It looked like he was headed to the jungle.

"Hey, boss! Why so glum? This is good news!" Steve poked.

Matt sighed. Steve was right. He didn't have an alternative set of facts to act upon. "I'm just mulling over the difficulty of getting there, undetected, then dealing with the potential security force that's bound to be in place, protecting the inventory. The time factor is a problem, too. We are a full day behind the transfer event. They took Vicky yesterday morning. Even if they used ground transportation, she'd be there already and presumably under lock and key."

Erik grunted. "Sounds like a typical day at the office to me, Matt. Let's take each piece one at a time. Assuming Seamus can find a place big enough for that Beechcraft, we need to write up a gear list. A full set of requirements for four, from head to toe. Then we try to assemble as much of the list as we can until Seamus solves the insertion challenge."

Matt listened intently. There was once a time when he would have said the same words, with confidence and surety. Just like Erik. He was thankful for the new blood on the team. He felt better with each passing day, but he still wasn't the old Matt Barrett, Mr. Navy Cross. He was a recovering alcoholic with brain trauma issues and a severe lack of self-esteem.

Seamus asked them to stay onboard while he went into the city to find a good topographic map of the interior. He directed them to email him the inventory of essential equipment when they were finished compiling the list. He'd discreetly procure a few things, like tactical radios and maybe camouflage uniforms in Bangkok, but the weapons were back in Phuket.

Matt and the others knew time was critical; so after Seamus departed, they devoted the next hour to mission planning and creating the list of support items on a per-phase basis. SEAL missions were generally based on a five-step process.

First came the insertion: the manner or method of getting the mission team to the general area of the target. They decided to defer to Seamus and his access to a plane for this phase. Since he would be landing the aircraft, there was no need for special gear such as fast ropes or parachutes.

The second classic phase was called infiltration. This took the mission team from the insertion point to the target. In this case, the method was jungle patrol. Presumably they would execute the fourth mission phase, exfiltration, in the same way. They spent most of their hour on these two phases, leaving the third phase, action at the objective, for last.

Matt knew the three SEALs in attendance had similar skills and tactical backgrounds, but he was unsure of what Jackson brought to the table on this mission. He knew if they attempted to choreograph the target takedown, Murphy's Law would probably intervene to derail their plan. So, he focused on the basics.

Jackson would be able to hang if the team flowed from one structure clearance to the next, taking them in a linear fashion. This would be more time-consuming, but it couldn't be helped. They really didn't have enough operators to do it any other way; and it allowed for new information to be processed by the team in real time, as opposed to tightly planning every step and later finding the stumbling blocks they hadn't anticipated.

Steve read the gear list out loud and waited for objections, comments, or alibis. Hearing none, he sent the list by email to Seamus and looked around. "Hey, is anyone else fucking starving?"

Gold had rejoined the team on the yacht, and he agreed to go into the city to purchase food. Matt's stomach was grumbling, and it made him think about the girls. *When was the last time they'd had a meal?* Matt asked Gold to hold up while he checked in with their young wards. When he came back, he added a few things to Gold's shopping list and then waved him away to accomplish his mission.

An hour later, Seamus returned, carrying a cardboard tube under his arm. Matt checked his watch. Gold was taking a lot longer than he'd expected. His stomach noises were now part of a chorus of similar protests emanating from the other men on the boat. Seamus came onboard and immediately pulled a topographic map from the unmarked tube.

"Here it is, boys! A good 1:50,000-scale military topographic map. Plenty of detail. And while it doesn't show the buildings at the camp, it does show the roads leading into and out of that place."

Matt and Steve stretched out the curled map as Jackson and Erik grabbed objects around them to weigh down the corners. Once in place, the five men studied the green-colored depiction of the Thai jungle. Swirling lines marked the contours with numbers, indicating the height of ridges and, in a few cases, higher than normal hilltops.

The camp was set back from an old logging road, widened near the camp entrance, but shrinking and becoming narrower north and south of the facility. Seamus looked for a place he could land a plane. His finger traced road after road to determine a straight portion long enough to use as a landing strip.

"Don't see anywhere you can land that big ass plane of yours, Seamus." Jackson stated what they were all thinking. If they couldn't fly in, they'd be left with using trucks. That would take at least a full day of travel. Besides, flying in and out gave them an edge they desperately needed. The roads back to civilization would be peppered with ambushes within hours after their raid on the camp. They needed to fly.

"I have access to more than one aircraft, my friend. I only need to find a place suitable for one of them. A place not too close, but close enough that the four of you don't have to cover too much ground to get to the target." Seamus continued to stare at the map until he suddenly stabbed a spot to the east of the main road. "This is it!"

Matt leaned forward and tried to see what Seamus was indicating. "Where, Seamus?"

"Right here," the former fighter pilot said, grinning. "This east-west road has a straight section where I can land and take off. Might be tricky if the winds are north-south, but I've dealt with that before."

Steve cleared his throat. "What sort of plane could land in there?"

"A CASA 212. It looks like a mini C-130 military cargo plane. Wings on top, tail rail for easy cargo or personnel on-load and off-load. It's a workhorse here in Asia."

"South America, too!" Erik pointed out. "I've worked with them quite a lot, and he's right. That airframe is versatile and rugged. You sure about this, Seamus?"

The old pilot nodded. "As you say, the CASA will do the trick. I have access to one in good condition through a friend. He'll let me fly it, no questions asked, as long as it's available. Let me call him right now. If the CASA is available, I'll figure out the rest of the logistics. We'll need to get the heavier firepower from one of my warehouses in Phuket, so we need to fly back there first."

"Sounds like a quick schedule. Go make your call. Oh, by the way, what about our gear list?" Matt asked.

Just then they all heard Gold's voice letting him know he was back. "Belay that question, Seamus. Food first," Matt said.

Nobody disagreed with Matt's priorities. Seamus went aft to make his call, and the others ambushed Gold, grabbing the bags of food and pouring the contents out on a table. It sure wasn't a gourmet lifestyle, but anything was better than nothing. Matt pulled out some bread, jam, and fruit for the girls and took it down to them.

Matt heard the voices stop as he approached the stateroom door, and he knocked respectfully before opening the door. "May I come in, ladies?"

In an instant, Christy was on her feet and pulling the door open from her side. "I could smell the food before I heard your footsteps. We are famished!"

Matt deposited the food on the bed and took a quick look around. The Japanese girl was more relaxed, but she never took her eyes off of Matt. Anne was warming up to him, even as she helped Christy sort out the food and handed an orange to the Japanese girl.

"We are working on a plan to get you safely out of Thailand and back to your homes," Matt lied. They'd been so focused on Vicky since waking, nobody had given the three teens a second thought. He'd rectify that oversight as soon as he rejoined his team topside. "Enjoy!"

Matt closed the door and as he did so, he noticed the odor. The girls needed to bathe. He walked down the passageway and looked around until he found the bathroom, one equipped with a shower and ample supplies of soap and towels. He walked back to the stateroom and knocked again, entering when Anne gave him the okay to do so.

The girls were happy hearing a warm shower was only a few feet away and that they had freedom to wander about the boat, as long as they stayed inside and didn't go up to the main weather deck. Matt left the room once more and went straight up the ladder and to the control room where Seamus was explaining the results of his call to the others.

"Hey, Matt, I was just telling everybody about the CASA. Good news! It's currently located at an airfield twenty miles west of here. My friend is having it flown to where my Beechcraft is parked so we can fly from here straight to Phuket. I've already forwarded the weapons and ammo list to my people there, and the supplies will be waiting for us on the flight line. A quick refuel and we're gone."

Matt did the math in his head. "I'm not a pilot, and I'm not familiar with the time distance calculations for these aircraft. In layman's terms, when is the earliest we can be on the ground at the insertion point?"

Steve answered for Seamus. "That's what we were figuring out when you showed up. It's ten in the morning. The gear Seamus procured for us here in Bangkok should be at the airport and staged in the hangar near the Beechcraft by noon. The flight in the CASA is ninety minutes max. So, we load, refuel, and leave Phuket no later than three in the afternoon."

"That puts us on the ground at 5:30 tonight," Erik finished. "We change clothes on the flight and move to the target as soon as Seamus opens the tail ramp. He'll fly to another airstrip an hour away and wait for our call for pickup."

Matt smiled. "That all sounds good. But we have another problem." Matt turned to look at Jackson. "We need Jackson to stay with the three girls and use his connections to get them out of Thailand."

Jackson opened his mouth to protest, then slowly closed it. Like Matt, he'd completely forgotten about the girls. As much as he wanted to see Vicky's rescue through to the end, he knew what Matt said made sense. "Are you sure the three of you can do this by yourself?"

Erik snickered. "Your primary role was to yell, 'FBI, everybody put your hands up!'" The others, including Seamus, laughed at the image of Jackson ordering A-wut's camp guards to honor the badge and give up.

"That's right," Steve added. "I will keep practicing the line until we get into the camp. It won't be authentic FBI shit; but those little fuckers won't know the difference, I promise!"

Again, the space was filled with laughter. "All right, you shitheads, I get it. I'm not a badass bone frog." Jackson looked back at Matt. "I'll make sure they stay safe and get home, Matt. You can count on that."

Matt nodded. "Okay. We have a timeline, an insertion platform, and gear to gather up, check, and prepare, all before boots on deck tonight at 5:30. I suggest we finish off the rest of this food. We may not see another meal like this for quite a while."

Chapter Twenty-One

The drive to the auxiliary airfield was short on distance but long on pain. The roads outside of Bangkok deteriorated rapidly into narrow, potholed pathways, filled with vehicles of all types and sizes. A fallen tree could block traffic for an hour or so. Matt settled in and tried to ignore the pain he felt in his back every time the SUV hit something.

An hour and a half after leaving the harbor area, the Chevy Tahoe pulled off the unimproved road and entered the confines of the small airfield. The facility was home to many utility aircraft--planes designed to carry fuel, food, and many other kinds of material into the country's interior.

As Matt looked through the window, the SUV swung in an arch and aimed for a small metal hangar, a shed actually, on the far side of the airstrip. There he spotted a dirty white CASA 212 tethered to the ground with ropes secured to large stones. The SUV came to a stop near the tail of the aircraft. "This is it, gents. Let's find the gear and get to work. Seamus, how much time do we have before we leave for Phuket?"

Seamus had exited the Tahoe, but leaned back into the SUV to answer Matt's question. "It should be fueled up, but I need to check. Then run down the preflight checklist. My guess is fifteen minutes if everything is good to go. That's fifteen minutes to wheels rolling, all gear and personnel onboard and strapped in."

Seamus didn't wait for a follow-up question. He closed the driver side door and walked to the CASA. Matt got out of the vehicle and waited until Steve and Erik joined him near the front grill. "You heard the man. Find the gear, change our clothes, and rig what you can into the vests or harnesses, or whatever they found for us as tactical wear. I'll give everyone ten minutes; then we need to drag the shit onto the CASA, ready or not."

The equipment and materials the team requested were staged inside the small metal shelter, more storage shed than hangar. When Matt separated and opened the box of clothing, what he found inside made him chuckle.

"What's so funny?" Steve asked as he began pulling sets of simple halter-style magazine holders out of another container and handing them to each of the men.

Matt shrugged. "Funny to me, anyway. You remember those old pictures of SEALs in Vietnam? They wore tiger-stripe-style camouflage fatigues."

"Yeah, so?" Steve finished handing out magazine holders and bent to open another box that contained preloaded thirty-round magazines for the classic AK-47 assault rifle.

Matt pulled a set of fatigues from the box. "We are going old school, gentlemen!"

Erik laughed. "Holy shit! Tiger stripes? Really?"

The roar of the CASA coming to life stopped the laughter, reminding them time was running short. The three former SEALs quickly changed into the camouflage. Each man set aside a rifle from the weapons container and then found boots that fit them from a large canvas bag. The last step was to don their magazine carriers.

The carriers were also a throwback to an earlier time. Made of thick cotton dyed a dark green, they went over the head like a bib. Three magazine pouches were arrayed vertically across the front of their body. A waist strap connected the lower end of the harness to the body. A cheesy rig by modern standards, in Matt's opinion, but it would have to do. He checked his watch.

"Grab everything and let's load up!"

The other two men immediately reacted to Matt's command. In a minute, they were walking up the tail ramp of the CASA 212 and getting situated. Once they were strapped in and the excess gear was secured, Matt picked up the crew headset complete with boom microphone. Placing it on his head, he got a comms check.

"Hey, do you have a callsign? All you flyboys have one, right?"

Seamus looked back and smiled. "It's Skid Mark, and don't ask."

Matt smiled back. "Oh, don't worry. I get the picture. I don't have a standing callsign. What should I use?"

Seamus raised the tail ramp and continued his checklist procedures. "Why don't I just call you Tiger?"

Matt rolled his eyes. "Well, I guess that fits now, doesn't it?"

Seamus set aside the checklist. "Tiger, this is Skid Mark. We are ready to depart. You're the mission commander. Am I cleared hot?"

Matt felt a tingle run up his back. Up until this point, the adventure felt like a cheap detective story filled with corny bad guys, a damsel in distress, and a loosely defined group of military has-beens. In that one radio call, Seamus had reignited a spark deep in Matt's soul that he thought had been extinguished forever.

"Skid Mark, this is Tiger. You are cleared hot for phase one insertion."

"Roger that, Tiger. Rolling!"

Vicky sat quietly in the large room and thought about her escape plan again. Since being moved off the ship, she'd been transported in all manner of vehicles. It was scary to be sure, but she found that as time went on, she was less concerned for her life and more concerned about how her dad and mom were doing.

Her mom wasn't all together to begin with, she knew. Alcohol and one-night stands were her prescription for happiness and a semblance of control over her life. Her dad, on the other hand, was the opposite. He would control every aspect of his world if he could. His first, second, and third options, when faced with a challenge, was to attack, take action, and complete the mission.

Her dad had finally turned the corner after dealing with his injuries, and something like this might drive him back into a dark place. It was all her fault. He was the one who taught her that the first rule of self-defense was situational awareness. Knowing your routes, understanding both your larger and your immediate environments. To avoid threats and risks was ninety-five percent of security.

When she was kidnapped, she wasn't following her dad's rules. She'd had a fight with her mom, who wanted her to remain with her, wherever they went in Honolulu. Vicky had rebelled against the idea. She was old enough to go to a store or look at a monument. She didn't need an adult for those things. So, after a protracted argument, she'd worn her mom's resistance down.

The win was moderate, but it was a win. She would be allowed to leave the hotel after they shared breakfast and go to the International Marketplace. She'd read about the expansive Polynesian-themed retail mall under tree canopies and couldn't wait to see and experience the place. The walk from the hotel was short, only ten blocks. Once there, Vicky happily roamed the market, looking at everything and eventually focusing on a delightful puka shell necklace.

The necklace was stunning, and she was sure it was more than she could afford. As she touched it and imagined herself wearing the jewelry, a woman approached her. She was friendly and businesslike. Vicky liked direct and serious people; so she explained her attraction to the necklace, and the woman agreed it might be a bit pricey.

Vicky agreed to follow her new acquaintance to the back of the market, where she had a friend who owned another kiosk, selling many of the same items. She intimated that her connection might result in a healthy discount, a discount that would allow Vicky the opportunity to own the precious necklace.

Vicky followed the woman, oblivious to any risk or potential threat. It was a bright and sunny morning in Hawaii. What could possibly go wrong? Once at the kiosk, everything went sideways. The little shop was tucked away in a side alley in the very back of the huge market. The woman allowed Vicky to enter first. She called out her friend's name and stood behind Vicky.

The last thing she remembered about the abduction was a hand clamping down on her nose and mouth from behind. Her first reaction was surprise. Then she felt the needle. The pain alerted her to danger and she tried to struggle, but the woman was strong, really strong. And the effects of whatever was contained in the shot affected her in seconds. The kiosk faded; she felt herself slumping, her legs going dead.

Situational awareness. In her hurry to act grown up and get away from her mom's wild mood swings, Vicky had acted like a stupid little girl, clueless and drawn into a trap by an impulse to buy a necklace. It was a lesson she would never have to learn again, if she survived her current predicament.

She heard the guards outside talking again. The walls and doors were thick, and there may have been additional sound dampening materials added. Vicky couldn't make out a single intelligible word. She eyed the only weapon in the room and began to fantasize about her escape plan again.

The two small chairs in the room were of basic design and simple construction. Vicky had explored every corner of the room for a way out, and then for a means to defend herself. As she examined each piece of furniture, she discovered the legs of the two chairs were screwed into the seat.

She tested one leg; and as it budged and began to rotate, her heartbeat increased. She was able to unscrew the leg completely and grip it in her hand. The piece of wood was now a club; she held a weapon in her hand.

A sound outside the door had startled her, and she'd quickly replaced the leg, only turning it a half turn. It looked normal sitting there, but she knew the weapon was available if needed. Since that discovery, she'd focused on what to do once she incapacitated the guard with the club and stepped out into the area beyond the door.

She began to doze off as the options swirled around in her head. She'd lost all sense of time. What day of the week was it? What month? Her attempts to keep track by scratching hashmarks on the wall of her compartment in the ship were washed out by her transfer to another vessel. She tried to continue the discipline, but fatigue muddled her mind. Vicky gently fell into a deep sleep.

Ten minutes after takeoff, Matt calling up to Seamus. "Hey, Skid Mark! Can we finish jocking up?"

"We can drop the stupid call signs, Matt. Let's save them for the extraction comms. What the hell is jocking up?"

Matt smiled. Seamus was a former Navy pilot, not a frog. "It's an old Navy diver term that means getting your dive rig on in preparation for a dive. We use it generically to mean getting our shit together."

Seamus flashed a thumbs-up as he replied, "Sure. Do what you have to do."

The space in the CASA was small. Matt didn't have direct comms with the other two using a radio, so he fell back on hand signals. He nudged Steve who sat next to him; and when Steve looked, Matt signaled for him to undo his seatbelt. Matt pointed to Steve and then to the pile of gear and boxes stacked on the centerline of the cargo floor and twirled his finger in the air.

Steve nodded and followed the directions. He stood up, as far as he could stand up, and went to the pile to finish his preparations. Matt watched as Steve slapped three pre-loaded AK magazines into the harness pouches, strapped on a nylon utility belt with a hunting knife hanging off his right hip and a canteen hanging just behind his left hip, and pulled a small radio and earpiece from a smaller bag.

Steve finished by picking up an assault rifle, inserting a fourth AK magazine into the magazine well, and slamming a round into the chamber. He held the rifle with the muzzle pointed down toward the cargo deck and returned to his seat. Once there, he nodded at Erik. Erik got up and repeated the drill, sitting back down when he was done. Matt was last, and once back in his seat, he informed Seamus of their status.

"We are all set back here. We'll get comm checks between us first, then you and I can do a comm check on the extract frequency."

Seamus didn't respond, but instead held up a thumb. Matt pulled the small line-of-sight, VHF radio from his cargo pocket and inserted the earpiece into his ear. The earpiece was both microphone and receiver. A Bluetooth connection made the radio a convenient piece of equipment. Gone were the days of bulky headsets or wires running from the radio to the earpieces.

Matt poked Steve and pointed to the radio. Steve pulled his radio out, inserted the earpiece, and turned it on. They'd agreed to use numbers instead of names, since the radios were not encrypted. Their numbers were assigned based on their position in the patrol. Erik was first at point, then Matt, and finally Steve at rear security.

"Three, this is Two. Over." Matt waited for Steve's response.

It was loud and clear. "One, this is Two. Over."

"I read you five-by-five, boss man," Erik replied. Five-by-five was an old school method used to convey a signal was a level five in volume and a level five in clarity, based on a one-to-five scale.

Matt nodded. He was still wearing the CASA headset over one ear. "Switch to extract freq for comm check."

Seamus leaned forward and twisted a knob a few turns, then flipped a toggle. Aircraft communicated using satellite or UHF frequency radio settings. When he was properly lined up, he responded on the tactical VHF frequency.

"Two, this is Skid Mark. Radio check. Over."

"This is Two. Read you Lima Charlie, loud and clear!"

With the preliminaries over, Matt leaned back and ran through the mission's phases of execution. The insertion would be hairy from Seamus's perspective. Landing on a narrow jungle road was tough enough during the day, but at night?

He knew Seamus had procured a set of decent night-vison goggles for the trip and that would be helpful. Night vison had been on his list for the tactical team, too, but only one set could be found in the limited time they'd had back in Bangkok.

The infiltration was simple but challenging, because patrolling in the jungle at night was a struggle. The distance to the target was reasonable. Matt believed that, even with the patrol through the heavy undergrowth, the team would arrive in time to do a solid recon of the camp before rolling in hot.

Matt checked his watch. The green glow of the watch face was more visible now as Seamus killed the cargo bay lights, allowing him to don the night-vision goggles. If Seamus was on track, they had five minutes left before his descent to five hundred feet.

They all had their seatbelts on tight. Once Seamus began his final landing approach, dropping down from five hundred feet, one of two things would occur. Either the CASA would land and slow down long enough for them to exit or a wing would slam into a tree alongside the road and rip the plane apart. A few minutes passed and Matt felt the nose tip downward.

Chapter Twenty-Two

Seamus took the altitude changes in short deliberate steps, one hundred feet at a time. The saving grace was that there was little to no wind. He was pretty sure as he approached the dirt road that any cross wind would have been a disaster; the road was too damn narrow!

At two hundred feet, Seamus gave Matt the last call. The mission commander Rogered up and took off the headset. He tapped Steve, then put his arms, crisscrossed, against his chest. Steve nodded and passed the signal to Erik: brace for impact.

Seamus throttled back inch-by-inch, slowing the CASA and at the same time lighting the nose slightly to adjust for the reduction in speed. A plane required lift to fly, and the wings could act as a mechanism for that lift or as a brake to slow the aircraft down.

Flying the CASA was nothing like landing a Tomcat on the pitching deck of a Navy carrier out at sea. In a jet, you were trained to drive the plane right to the deck and then power back as the arresting wire snagged the tail hook. The combination stopped the warbird quickly.

The CASA was not a jet. Seamus needed to float and then flare the wings a bit upon contact with the road, to ensure he slowed down sufficiently to allow the team to exit without coming to a complete stop. He glanced at the altimeter: fifty feet. The power reduction made the plane sluggish to control. He was going to pull this off he realized, that is unless a random tree limb laying on the road sent the CASA flipping end-over-end.

He pushed the tail ramp lever and lowered it just before his final flare to land. He'd almost forgotten to toggle over to the VHF mission freq and did so now. The tires hit hard and the plane bounced. Seamus waited until the aircraft stabilized before applying the brakes slowly and carefully. He saw the speedometer slow down to thirty, twenty, ten miles an hour. He would wait until Matt gave him the all clear before throttling forward again to take off.

Matt was the last one off the ramp, and he hit the ground hard. The forward roll was planned; all three men did it upon exiting the CASA. It was a variation of the traditional parachute landing fall or PLF taught in basic jump school. He rolled twice and came to an abrupt stop. The jungle was pitch black. The only reference was the roaring sound of the CASA's engines.

"Skid Mark, this is Tiger. All clear. I say again, all clear."

Seamus heard the transmission and immediately throttled forward. The CASA jumped as he waited for his air speed to build up. He stared ahead and hoped the road stayed straight for a little bit longer. Even as he thought this, the night vision googles spotted a long dark object in the road.

The CASA was almost there. He needed only a few seconds more, just a few, and he'd be airborne before hitting the object in the road. He was a hair under the recommended takeoff speed when he jerked the column back and felt the plane struggle to gain lift. Whatever the object was, he never saw it again as the nose pulled up and the CASA propelled itself into the inky darkness of night. *Good luck, Matt. God be with you!*

The three men sat in a triangle on the edge of the road. Matt waited for the sound of the CASA to fade into the distance and then checked his watch. This patrol would be straightforward. Standard operating procedures or SOPs. Wait ten minutes to look, listen, and learn. Then, if everything was cool, get up and begin navigating toward the hunting camp.

It only took three minutes for the jungle to come alive all around them. Matt nudged Erik and then squeezed his shoulder twice. It was too dark to use hand signals so they'd reverted to close-quarter battle squeeze signals. It was simple and it worked. Erik stood up and held his compass in his left hand. It was dark enough for him to see the illuminated face of the navigation device, and he slowly began to move forward.

Matt squeezed Steve twice and stood up to follow Erik. The three of them kept near constant physical contact as they made their way through the thick jungle underbrush. Seamus did them the favor of being on time with his insertion, so they had plenty of time to do this right. Besides, this wasn't a war zone. The main threat was the camp itself.

The heat was both boon and a curse. Matt felt at home in the jungle. Leading a combat patrol was exhilarating. He felt more alive than he had in several years. He wondered if Steve was having the same emotions. Steve was a warrior of the old school. He was tough as nails; and no matter how any times he'd been injured or wounded, he always bounced back.

Erik was a mystery. The closer they'd come to actual direct action, the calmer and more mature Erik acted. His smart-ass personality was likely a reflection of the true Erik; but when it came down to doing the deed, Erik was all business. Matt liked and trusted him more and more with each passing day. It was too late to have doubts now, anyway. They had to gel as a team and get Vicky out of that camp.

As one hour became two, Matt settled into the rhythm of the jungle around him. The SEALs referred to forest and jungle undergrowth as "wait a minute" bushes. Small knee- to waist-high plants that conspired to tangle, trip, and in some cases, stick a person's legs while they moved forward. The darkness made it infinitely worse. At least during the day, you had an opportunity to weave in and around the undergrowth. Not so at night.

From time to time Erik would stop and pause, listening to the natural sounds and searching for any indication of a threat. After three hours all three men were drenched with sweat; and when Matt saw Erik stumble twice, he called a halt. They each took a knee and drank from their canteens.

Being a point man was intense, especially when you added the requirement to physically break trail using your body like a blade on a bulldozer. Matt checked his watch. They had been on patrol for three hours now. He estimated they were better than halfway to the camp from the insertion point. Time to swap Steve and Erik; he needed a fresh point man.

The swap made; Steve used his compass to get his bearings then squeezed Matt once to indicate he was ready. Matt squeezed Erik twice and then repeated the signal with Steve. They moved out at a steady, ground-eating pace, and Matt began to run through the reconnaissance in his mind.

The hunting camp wasn't well-defined on the map Seamus procured. They had an impression of circumference, but nothing definite. Several scenarios ran through Matt's head. They could get into a dominating position and see the entire camp well enough to identify where Vicky and perhaps other girls were being kept. The map gave Matt hope. It showed a low ridge running north and south just to the east of the camp. That elevation might support the first recon scenario.

The second scenario was more likely. The heavy jungle presumably covered the ridge, too. Line of sight from that vantage point and from everywhere else around the perimeter of the camp would be blocked by the heavy foliage. Matt and his team would have to get right up to the edge of the camp and step out of the jungle to allow them to see anything.

The ridge was the best bet for sure. However, if they couldn't use this terrain feature, they wouldn't have a perspective or a clear view of all the buildings in the camp. To Matt, that outcome meant they would be forced to perform a shorter recon followed by a much longer and more dangerous clearing operation of every building until they found Vicky.

Matt prayed the camp wasn't heavily guarded. The three men were better fighters than most, and he had no doubt they could clear the entire camp tactically; but their small personal supply of ammunition didn't support a protracted gun battle. If they were spotted before they found Vicky, bad things could happen. Bullets flying in every direction would be a direct threat to the safety of his team and her.

At four hours and thirty minutes into the patrol, Steve stopped and froze. Matt didn't need a hand signal or a squeeze to know why; they'd all been listening to the rising sound of running water for that last twenty minutes or so. First it came as a whisper, a mere hint of something different in their environment.

Then it developed its own sound, distinct from the symphony of jungle sounds they'd become accustomed to since exiting the CASA. Steve was standing on the edge of what was a sizable stream or small river, a surprise not indicated on their map. Matt took a knee, and the other two followed his lead. They were only thirty minutes away from the camp and had another ninety minutes of darkness before the sun rose. They didn't have time to waste looking for a dry crossing. It was time to swim.

The camp watch officer listened intently to the person on the other side of the conversation. He acknowledged the other person's directive with a nod and a curt yes in Thai. He was used to being browbeaten by the privileged class. Years of verbal abuse hadn't broken his resolve to save enough money to buy a restaurant.

He hadn't decided where to buy the restaurant just yet, but he was close, very close to his targeted amount of savings. Twelve years of sacrificing, waiting, and enduring. After he hung up the phone, the camp watch officer pondered how much more time was needed. Maybe only six more months of special pay out here in the middle of nowhere would be sufficient to meet his goal. Six more months.

The phone call was about his guests. The new arrivals were quiet and for the most part they kept to themselves, huddled up in two buildings. He'd been told to keep his nose out of their business, and he'd dutifully complied. He warned his security team to stay clear of the strangers.

He was thankful they were only here for one more day. The caller had informed him they would be leaving later in the day after two or three in the afternoon. He checked the clock on the wall of the security shack. It was only an hour or so until sunrise.

The hunting camp didn't store anything of value, unless you counted a small armory of rifles and ammunition for the clients. But it was worth protecting. Marauding bands of thieves, cutthroats, and drifters moved about freely in the interior of the country, where the military and police forces were spread thin. The camp would make a great base of operations for illegal smuggling. Rare flowers, live exotic animals, and pelts for the fur market. Tiger claws were a sought-after item and could fetch quite a sum in Hong Kong or Singapore.

The watch officer decided to make a last sweep before preparing for his turnover. He walked out to the edge of the dimly lit perimeter and passed his flashlight back and forth against the trees. His right hand rested on an automatic pistol. He was more afraid of wild things than he was of criminals in the jungle. He stayed alert and continued his walk.

"We don't have any flotation. No life jackets and nothing that's buoyant." Erik whispered what everyone already knew. Even if the map had showed a river, they wouldn't have had time back in Bangkok to find three inflatable vests.

Matt bit his lip as he tried to think his way through the challenge. The weapons weighed approximately twelve pounds, fourteen with a fully loaded magazine inserted. The other three magazines on their chests represented another six pounds. That was twenty pounds of fighting weight before other equipment, boots, and clothes. All in they came in at thirty pounds of dead weight per man, and no flotation.

Matt checked his watch. They'd been stationary for five minutes on the edge of the waterway. "Steve, how many feet of para chord do you have?"

Steve calculated what he had in both cargo pockets before answering. "If we tied them together, we'd have about fifty feet. Why?"

Matt had an idea, and it should work. “Okay, here’s what we are going to do …”

Erik swam the last few feet to the far bank of the river and grabbed hold of a twisted tree root. The current was worse in the center channel, but here it was manageable. He hoisted himself up the tree root until he sat on the bank. He waited a minute or so, listening for any hint of something out of the ordinary, before untying the para chord attached around his waist and wrapping it around the tree.

He took a hold of the line and pulled hard three times, pausing in between each pull. In a flash, he felt two hard pulls. Matt and Erik were on their way. Steve rolled over on his belly and crawled a few feet into the trees. He lifted his AK and focused on protecting their small beachhead.

Four minutes later, he heard a splash and a grunt as Matt grabbed the tree root. A second later, Erik pulled up alongside. They’d followed the para chord to Steve’s position. Now they began pulling the line toward them hand-over-hand. It took a few more minutes, but the bundle of weapons and tactical vests appeared, tied to the other end of the line.

Matt and Erik pushed and pulled the bundle up onto the river bank and lay back to catch their breath. “Well, that was fun,” Erik whispered sarcastically.

Matt nodded in the dark. “Let’s get this gear sorted out. We need to pick up the pace; the sun will be up in forty minutes.”

The three men took turns getting dressed. Erik finished first and replaced Steve as point security. Steve edged back and donned his vest. Matt was the last finished. The idea had worked, but they’d lost a lot of time. He squeezed Erik’s shoulder twice then squeezed Steve’s. The patrol stood up and moved out, gently pushing aside the stubborn jungle. Despite the delay, Matt was optimistic. This was action, no more asking questions and waiting around in warehouses and hangars. He was ready to finish the job.

Chapter Twenty-Three

It was getting late. Matt became conscious of their tight timeline, as minute-by-minute the dark mass all around them began to take on shape and then definition. The sun was on the horizon and fully up, but the effect on the pitch-black jungle was dramatic.

Matt had stopped looking at his watch. Late was late, and now the issue was being too exposed when they entered the camp. The idea of a thorough recon was long gone. They'd have to learn about the target by walking through it, without the cover of darkness to protect them.

Their wet clothes threw off steam as they dried. The sun wasn't beaming down on them, at least not yet, but the temperature in the jungle was already ten degrees warmer. Steve had rotated to point, pushing Erik to rear security. Matt maintained left and right security, now that he could see enough to distinguish the difference between a tree and a man.

Matt wasn't an old man, but he'd abused his body for two years. The physical exertion was draining him more than he'd realized was possible. In his head he was capable of doing almost anything that required physical stamina. But now … *On the map, the distance to the camp from the insertion point looked so easy.*

Steve froze and raised his left hand in a fist. He slowly sank down to one knee and maintained his rigid posture. To Matt and Erik, the message was clear: Steve saw or perceived a threat. A threat close enough to their patrol to warrant caution. All they could do was trust Steve's judgment and wait for his next move. If they were about to be attacked, the next signal would be the sound of Steve opening up on the adversary.

Matt waited for two minutes, fighting the urge to go up and see what Steve was looking at. Just when he couldn't wait any longer, Steve relaxed his left hand and use it to subtly wave Matt forward. Matt slowly rose until he was standing and then crept softly up to where Steve was kneeling. He saw it before reaching the point man; they'd reaching the north-south road.

Matt waved Erik up, and the three men huddled in the tree line together. "We should be half a mile south of the camp, give or take a few hundred yards," Matt whispered. The navigation plan was designed to angle to the south of the camp, so that when they intersected the prominent north-south road they'd simply turn right and move until they found the camp.

They were forty-five minutes to an hour late. If they tried to smash their way through the half mile of jungle on either side of the road, they would make too much noise, take too long, and stumble right into the camp perimeter with little warning. Matt had always contemplated patrolling up the road to maintain sound discipline and to aid in finding, and then conducting a recon of the hunting camp. Now he had no choice.

He decided they would use the road. They needed to dramatically pick up the pace to reach Vicky before the whole world woke up. He knew it was a big risk. With the sun bathing everything in light, they were exposed on the road. SEALs were successful for two key reasons: stealth and surprise. By taking the road, they were giving up one of those advantages. Surprise was all they had left.

"We're taking the road. I want both of you up forward at point, staggered file formation. I'll lay back a few steps and cover our six o'clock. Sling the rifles and use the 9mm pistols. They're silenced, so we might still get lucky if you have to engage a threat before we get to the camp."

"And when we get there? The recon's out the window. Do we just start clearing each building as we get to it or do you have another idea?" Erik questioned.

"You have a point there. Let's see what we can see once we reach the camp. A quick thirty-second assessment, that's all. Then I can answer you. It all depends on what we find."

"Situation dictates," Steve muttered.

Matt nodded. An old SEAL maxim, but stubbornly true in every war since the SEAL teams were created by President John F. Kennedy in 1962. The situation did dictate tactics. It was why special operators to this day relied on visual reconnaissance for the final look. A satellite or drone might pick up most of the target scenario, but real professionals could see everything they needed to be successful once they were eyes on target.

"Situation dictates," Matt agreed. "Check your shit. We move in sixty seconds!"

The camp was soothing this early in the morning, the way the rising illumination of the dawn created shadows and allowed color to replace the darkness of the night. The camp watch officer had completed his last round and was sitting on the front steps of the administration building.

There were twelve structures of one kind or another, but the administration building was the only one with a communications link to the outside world. Cell phones didn't work this far into the jungle and neither did smart tablets and wireless devices. Truth be told, his primary job, the one he was uniquely suited to perform, was technician.

His resume didn't have a single line related to security, law enforcement, or military experience. He was here to keep the machines running and the communications center operational. The owners of the camp had problems with trespassers in the past, so they came up with the idea of duel tasking the technical position by adding security to the job description.

He wasn't expected to fight or lay down his life to protect the camp; he was only a deterrent. His presence alone was expected to dissuade outsiders from committing random theft and vandalism. He didn't even know how to use the pistol sitting in the leather holster off his right hip. That was a deterrent, too. He yawned.

Down the slope of the camp he spotted a flicker of light from the farthest building, a cabin used for lodging the rich clientele who came to hunt, drink, and get away from their wives. For the last few days, the cabin was occupied by a group of men. The message he'd received before their arrival was cryptic, but clear in one aspect: ignore the new guests.

He watched the light come back on again and thought he'd observed movement in the space between the cabin and the utility storage building to its right. He rubbed his eyes. It was still too dark to see well, and he was tired. With a sigh, he rose and entered the administration building; it was time to update the camp's logbook. Another boring day had come and gone without incident.

Matt was gassed. Up until now, he'd been operating on adrenaline and then pride, but now his poor physical condition was defeating him. In the jungle, the pace was ridiculously slow, a mild but manageable challenge. However, jogging down the road in fifty pounds of wet clothes and gear, he was beginning to realize he was a liability to the team, to the success of the mission.

Several years back, he'd been stationed in Coronado California, at the Basic Underwater Demolition SEAL school known as BUD/S. As a phase officer he was required to attend and act as shift leader for Hell Week, the daunting rite of passage all SEAL candidates must pass before becoming frogmen.

He realized after working his first Hell Week that he'd forgotten most if not all of his own experiences. The memories were fleeting and spotty at best; maybe under such stress the mind suppresses memories or simply focuses on survival and not collecting impressions. Either way, Matt couldn't remember much, but watching the tortuous event in real time was humbling for the young phase officer.

His breathing was now loud enough that the other two had to know he was in trouble, yet they didn't slow down. BUD/S was both an experiment in progress and a foundation based in tradition. Over the years the formula had been tweaked here and there, but only with reverence and only when most agreed a change was needed to keep pace with the world.

One thing hadn't changed: BUD/S sucked. The students spent the entire course dog-tired, beaten down physically, and challenged psychologically. The prolonged physical pain and deterioration in stamina drove the mind to a place where self-preservation was increasingly sufficient justification to quit.

Quitting was the obstacle. Not the distance ran, or the height of the waves during surf passage. Quitting was the real pain. The word *quit* sat there in the student's mind, at first watching and waiting, but then beckoning. It was only a matter of time for about seventy percent of the students.

The course was brutal and it was unforgiving; it had to be. One at a time initially, then in pairs and even entire boat crews, the course took its toll. The majority of the young men crawled into the space in the mind where the bright, warm word waited for them: quit. Matt shook his head. This wasn't as bad as BUD/S. He'd been more tired, felt worse despair in Coronado than here in Thailand. It wasn't about muscle strength and energy; it never had been. It was about force of will, his will to push on. *Fuck it!*

Matt almost ran over Steve. The two men leading the team had slowed to a tactical patrol pace. He backed off a little, embarrassed that his mind had wandered from the task at hand. The road was passing from grey to a dark brown as the sun climbed higher. He checked the time; it was 5:40 in the morning. The world was awakening.

Steve stopped and Erik did, too. The retired senior chief waved at Matt to come forward for a talk. "We're here." He pointed to the left and Matt spotted the low metal fence.

"Let's keep moving. Find a spot on the other side of the fence that's clear enough of jungle vegetation for us to see the camp and conduct a short assessment of the layout."

Steve swept his arm across his body. "Go on, youngster. You take point."

Erik snorted and assumed the lead position in the patrol. The vegetation remained thick for another hundred yards, then suddenly dropped away. Erik paused, trying to determine if it was a small clearing or the camp proper. Matt waited until he saw Erik climb the metal fence and drop down on the other side.

Steve and Matt followed Erik in turn, and they reassembled into a file formation. Matt could see under the trees now that the sun was higher in the sky. He could barely make out the dark spots, likely buildings in the camp, as he followed Erik deeper into the cleared area. A few minutes later, Erik casually held up his left hand in a fist and sank to one knee. The body language didn't seem to indicate an immediate threat, so Matt crouched and moved up next to the point man.

"What's up?"

Erik pointed to a building straight ahead. It appeared to be near the main entrance to the camp and was probably a headquarters or greeting facility. From this vantage point, Matt could now identify seven other structures.

"That's a lot of buildings to clear," Matt mumbled.

"You got that right, boss!" Erik replied.

Steve crawled up to the pair and took a look. "We're burning daylight, sir. Let's make a fucking decision here."

Matt smiled. Some things never changed. As exhausted as he was, he had value to the team; he was the designated leader. It was his job to make the call.

"Okay, smartass. We are able to see seven buildings. The farthest is down there, at the bottom of the slope." Matt pointed to his left. "We ignore the large building by the gate. Unlikely they would house the girls there. That means we have six structures to clear."

Erik nodded. "Roger that."

Steve put his hand on Matt's shoulder. "I definitely think you're right! Let's hit this place!"

Matt nodded. "If we find the girls, we stop. No need to clear the whole camp. We stop when we've located the girls.

Once we have them in tow, we go to the north side of the camp and push until we hit the north-south road. When we get there, I'll make the call to enter the jungle or run the road. Depending on the level of pursuit. We all good?"

Again, both men nodded. Matt nodded in return. "Erik lead us straight to the first building on the left. Quiet entries. I'll be happy if no one ever hears us in the camp. Only shoot if you have to and use the pistols unless we get into a dick dragger of a fight. Then use the AKs."

"You finished talking, sir?" Erik was grinning. "You sound like a talking head on TV. Let's just fucking do this shit!"

Matt stood up and the other two men did also. He pointed forward and that was all Erik needed. The younger man crept toward the first building to the left of the main structure, crouched down low. Even in this awkward position, he quickly covered the intervening distance. Within seconds, the team was entering the first structure.

The building was dark and empty. "Clear!" Erik whispered out to the hallway. "Move!" Steve whispered back, and they moved to the next room. It took all of thirty seconds, and they were back on the ground moving to the second building. This one also proved to be empty. As they assembled outside, Matt scanned down the slope and studied the four remaining structures. He spotted a strange light, just a hint or flash, and then it was gone. His neck tingled. Something didn't feel right.

Erik swapped out with Steve and they entered the next building. Even though it felt empty, they conducted a thorough search. Matt grabbed Steve before he exited the building. "Hold up a second!"

Steve did as he was directed. Erik pulled in tighter and listened, anticipating Matt was going to change up the plan. "I spotted a flash of light down near the last building in camp. I don't know if I was seeing things or it was just a reflection, but I want to take the next building slowly. If the security force knows we're here, they could be setting up on us."

Steve gave a thumbs-up, and Erik patted Matt on the shoulder. Matt took a deep breath and nodded to Steve. The older ex-SEAL nodded back and opened the door to the outside. There were only two buildings left. He was getting concerned that the intel was wrong, stale, or even possibly a misdirection.

As Matt stepped down the short set of stairs, he glanced at the last building one more time. There was movement, a lot of movement. It was near the building and over to their left flank, too. What he saw froze the blood in his veins. "CONTACT LEFT!"

Chapter Twenty-Four

A-wut strolled across the veranda sipping English black tea, a taste he'd acquired as a young man trying to appear more continental, more European. His upbringing was rough, and there were several times when he thought death was a better path than surviving day-to-day on the streets of Bangkok. Then things began to turn around.

He had a skill, a knack for inspiring others. At just the right moment, he collected his first follower. Having a sidekick was alarming and somehow soothing at the same time. He was now responsible for someone else. From that point on in his life, A-wut never felt sorry for himself again.

The dawn was brilliant from the vantage point of his penthouse overlooking the sprawling city of Bangkok. The orange ball of light and heat was now above the horizon. A magical time of day, beautiful yet muted. In an hour the temperature would rachet up and the moisture all around the city would vaporize, creating a stifling humidity. This was a glorious moment.

His rise on the streets of Bangkok was meteoric. After his first disciple, there were more, many more. He learned to plan, to think ahead. This skill and the group dedicated to him allowed for direct actions that enriched his new family. The more successful the plan, the greater his recruiting power became. By the age of seventeen, A-wut led a criminal gang numbering in the hundreds.

Three years later, he met Roger Maddox. Maddox was setting up operations in Southeast Asia. He initially saw A-wut as a threat, a competitor; but his business sense kicked in, and he soon cultivated a relationship with the young Thai. A-wut didn't discriminate regarding crime; anything that made money was fair game. Maddox was more organized, more deliberate, and smart. In time he mentored A-wut, guiding him until, somehow, he found himself working for the South African.

At first, the loss of independence was alarming. A-wut was his own man; he led a criminal organization he'd built from the bottom up. In time he relaxed and saw the long-term benefits of working with and then for the business mogul. His personal wealth skyrocketed under Maddox's tutelage. The results over the years were impressive. This was the first time since the beginning of their relationship that A-wut truly questioned Maddox's competence.

Most criminal activities had passive victims, people who lost an article of material value and either replaced it or mourned its loss temporarily. Kidnapping young boys and girls to be sold into the sex trade was a different thing altogether. It was the kind of crime that felt evil. Stealing money from a rich person didn't feel evil. His distaste for the whole business was at a tipping point. This mess over the American girl was about to push him over the edge.

When you jacked a high-value car or stole a shipment of goods, the victim simply called their insurance company and moved on with their life. Abducting a child, stealing that child away for a terrible purpose, that act created a vengeful and righteous chain of events. A potential risk that wouldn't go away.

The American rescue team was one of those adverse potential outcomes. Over the years, A-wut and Maddox had dealt with the random parent searching Thailand for their lost child. These people were distraught but harmless. In time they left and embraced the reality that their loved one wasn't coming home.

This was the first time, however, that someone had hired a professional team to find their child. A-wut was sympathetic to their cause and would have preferred to lay low until the team failed to find their prize, but Maddox had other ideas. Directing A-wut to close down the search for the American girl, a girl Maddox wanted for himself, had exposed him and his organization. It was stupid, and that's why A-wut had decided to retire from his life of crime. Things were getting too risky.

He was set financially. His assets were scattered across three continents and distributed in as many as nine countries. Maddox had taught him how to hide his money--not only geographically, but also by using different asset classes to launder and hide the wealth. He purchased companies that purchased raw materials, land, and even small banks. He was set for the rest of his life.

A-wut looked at his watch and smiled. It was almost six in the morning. His plan to eliminate the pesky Americans was being executed according to his meticulous schedule. Every detail was critical, right down to the quality of the misinformation spread around the city. The false trail had to be believable, and in the end it worked. The hook was set, and all he needed to do was wait for the call, the call that would set him free to pursue a new life. He sipped the last of his black tea and smiled.

The bullets ripped across the building's thin wood covering. Matt and his team immediately swapped their pistols for the long guns and returned fire. The problem was that fire was coming from at least three directions. *A circular ambush?*

The darkness that had protected them was now gone, and the cheaply constructed structures in camp were worthless as cover from the withering attack. Steve had determined this first; and he ran to their left, where a metal utility shed sat apart from the main buildings. Matt and Erik covered the movement with their AKs and waited until Steve was in position. Steve opened up, covering their sprint to join him.

Matt's mind raced with panic. He'd been under fire before, he reminded himself. He realized the sense of helplessness wasn't based on fear of injury or death; it was fear of failure. Vicky couldn't be rescued against these odds. He calculated that they had less than three minutes at this rate of fire before his team ran out of ammunition. He took a deep breath.

"Move back! Head for the main building by the front gate!"

Erik bolted first, dodging instinctively to make himself harder to hit. He reached the closest building and hit the ground shooting. Matt slapped Steve on the leg and both men jumped up. The adrenaline coursing through Matt's veins had eliminated his fatigue completely. As soon as Matt hit the ground and began firing, Steve and Erik leapfrogged to the next building. Once there, they eased out to the inside corner and opened fire.

The camp watch officer was out cold in his chair when the explosion of gunfire jolted him upright. He'd only heard the sounds of combat on television and in the movies. This sounded similar, yet different at the same time. More like firecrackers.

He moved to the front door cautiously and peeked outside. He saw men running and moving everywhere. Most looked like the guests who'd arrived recently, but there were three men who were dressed differently. They looked like soldiers. This small group was moving backward toward him.

The camp watch officer realized he was in trouble. He didn't understand why these men were fighting each other, but he was certain doing something about it was well beyond his job description. He looked around for the keys to the camp vehicle, an old Volkswagen van lifted six inches and equipped with oversized mud tires. It was parked behind the administration building and gassed up, ready to go. He found the keys and headed for the back door.

Matt leapfrogged back past his teammates toward the main building. That's when he saw a figure dart out and disappear around the backside. As he was about to go to ground, he heard the sound of an engine roaring to life. He got an idea. "ON ME!"

Matt continued forward, increasing speed. As he rounded the backside of the main building, he executed a tactical corner check, rifle up to his shoulder and ready to shoot any threat he found. Instead of a threat he saw an incredible sight.

The camp watch officer grabbed the stick and placed the transmission into first gear. Before he applied pressure to the gas pedal, the passenger side door whipped open revealing a snarling face covered in black. It wasn't the face that froze his movements; it was the dark muzzle of the rifle.

The back door opened violently, and he saw two other men with weapons jump into the back of the van. "Matt! We don't have much time. Those assholes are maneuvering up behind us and three were running to the right side of the gate. We've got to get the fuck out of here!"

Erik's voice registered in Matt's mind; but he had only one thought: mission first. He poked his barrel into the ribs of the driver. "You speak English?"

The watch officer nodded nervously. “Yes, a little English.”

“Where is the girl? The young girl? Which building do you keep her in?” Matt poked him again, this time a bit harder to make his point. Spill the information or get shot.

The watch officer’s eyes grew big. “No, no. No girls, no boys. This is hunting camp. No children here.”

A round hit the back of the van, and Steve slid back out of the vehicle and shot two rounds, both hitting an advancing rifleman in the chest. “Boss, it’s time.”

Steve’s calm voice made sense, but the Thai diving the van might be lying. Could they just run away and leave Vicky here? He tried one more time. “Who are those men, the ones shooting at us?”

Two more rounds struck the building right behind Matt, and he pivoted. Steve was still standing there covering his six, but he’d made his decision. “Steve! In the van, NOW!”

Steve fired three more rounds at a new threat and then jumped into the van. He and Erik crouched in the open door, their rifles at the ready. Matt hoisted himself into the old relic and shouted at the driver. “GO!”

The Thai watch officer was so startled by Matt’s shout that he jammed his foot down hard on the gas. Just then an armed man stepped out in front of the van and leveled his rifle. It was a stupid mistake. Matt felt the van rock as it ran over the shooter and leapt forward toward the front gate. Erik and Steve began picking targets the second the main building was behind them. A team of four shooters were in position near the gate and firing back.

Matt rolled his window down and rotated so he could free his weapon to engage. The attackers were not very accurate, but at this range anyone could get lucky. He heard bullets bouncing off the harder parts of the van and had no doubt most of the rounds were going right through the van. He took a quick look down the slope and saw several bodies lying on the ground. It was hard to underestimate the value of superior marksmanship. SEALs were drilled until every man was an expert in precision shooting. It showed.

The gate was unlocked but closed. As the driver slowed, Matt punched him in the shoulder and pointed to the gate. The Thai knew what Matt meant and braced for the impact. The Volkswagen punched through the gate, causing it to shimmy sideways for a few feet before Matt's hand grabbed and jerked the steering wheel hard to the right.

The van raced south down the very same road the team had used to approach the camp. He poked the driver in the arm. "Who were those men?" he asked.

Steve closed the back door. "Yeah, we're all good back here, boss, just thought you might like to know that." The former senior enlisted man's tone was mocking. An officer was supposed to look after his team. Matt got the message loud and clear.

"Roger that, Steve. Just trying to get some clarity from this guy up here. By the way, thanks for asking. I'm good to go too!"

Steve and Erik both laughed. Matt turned his attention back to the driver. "Who were those men?"

The camp watch officer was aware his life was probably over either way. He knew his job was for sure. He took a breath and began answering the big American's question. Matt listened intently. The Thai driving the van explained that two days ago a group of eight men, carrying long thin plastic cases and wearing black backpacks, had arrived in camp. He told Matt he was only a technical guy, who also watched over the camp when it wasn't in use. He'd received a call from Bangkok telling him to ignore the men and go about his normal business. That's all he knew.

For some reason Matt believed the driver. There wasn't a thing about the man that felt professional. He wasn't a part of the crew that ambushed his team back at the camp. "What about the girl?"

The driver's face told Matt what he feared was the truth. "No girls. Only the men."

Matt leaned back and took stock of what happened. It was a setup, plain and simple. The assholes back there were inserted into the camp to allow them to hit Matt and his team, something they knew was going to happen. They were there before the CASA even took off from Phuket.

The intel Seamus received was bogus. Worse than that, it was calculated to push the rescue team headlong into a prepared ambush. Who generated the misinformation? More importantly, where was Vicky?

Matt pulled out his map and then leaned over to check the gas. The tank was almost full, which meant they had options. The map showed that the north-south road continued for twenty miles through the jungle before hitting a crossroad, running east and west. If they headed east, they might make it to the staging airfield where Seamus waited for their extract call.

Taking the road to the west sent them deeper into the wilderness of Thailand. He made his decision. The twenty miles were covered in no time, as the driver had never slowed down after hitting the gate. The suspension of the van was upgraded to handle what the locals called roads, but the ride was still a jarring and painful experience.

Matt put his hand on the driver's arm and squeezed. "Slow down. We're near the crossroad."

The man complied; and when they could both spot the feature, he looked at Matt expectantly. "Which way?"

"Turn left. We are going here." Matt held up the map and pointed to a small town. "You know this place?"

The Thai nodded. "Yes, it is very small. Only a few people there." He hesitated as he slowed to a stop at the crossroad. "You are going to kill me?"

Matt smiled. "Shit no, my friend. You just saved our lives. Get us to this town, and we'll let you go on your merry way."

The driver smiled a great big toothy smile and turned left. Matt settled back into the seat, fatigue washing over him in a wave. First things first. They need to get to Seamus and then back to civilization. They needed rest, food, and then information.

He was going to hunt down the son of a bitch who set them up. Whoever that person was, they knew the truth. They knew where Vicky was taken when she was pulled off the cargo ship. His eyes closed. He'd only take a short nap.

Chapter Twenty-Five

Seamus dozed in the cockpit of the CASA 212, his headset askew. One ear listened for the team's extract radio call while the other was free to hear anyone approaching the plane. The last time he'd checked the time, he realized there wasn't a fixed pickup window. Matt and his team had left the extract open to allow them flexibility. Their desire for flexibility was causing his stress.

The radio crackled to life in his right ear, and his eyes popped open. He waited … nothing. He was tuned into the VHF line of sight frequency; and he knew that had limitations, especially in the dense jungle terrain between his current location and the target. The radio crackled again. This time he distinctly heard a voice.

"Tiger, this is Skid Mark. Tiger, this is Skid Mark. Over."

Nothing. The VHF tactical radios the team carried were underpowered, but they were all Seamus's contacts in Bangkok could find in the short notice they'd had. The radio made noise again, and again Seamus thought he heard words. Garbled, but words nonetheless.

He thought the problem through. The jungle might be inhibiting Matt's extract call. At least two attempts had been made to contact him, so he had to believe the team was off target and at the extract site. If he got airborne now, he'd be over their position in ten minutes and probably have VHF comms in five. Seamus made the decision.

He tossed the headset and exited the CASA. He was already fueled up, and he didn't need to check out with anyone here at the airstrip. All he needed to do was pull the blocks of wood from under his tires and crank up the bird. The old Tomcat jockey bent over and pulled one chunk of wood away, kicking it clear. As he walked around to the opposite side of the plane his ears picked up the sound of a truck or perhaps an old car. Bad guys?

Seamus had an AK in the cockpit, and he rushed back into the aircraft through the tail ramp. He grabbed the rifle and searched his flight bag until he found two magazines. He slapped one into the weapons and placed the other in the pocket of his cargo pants, then eased his way back to the end of the tail ramp. What he saw caused his jaw to drop.

The Volkswagen van hopped and bumped across the uneven ground that bordered the small airstrip. Matt had directed the camp watch officer to turn off the road and cut straight across the open ground, shortening the trip to the CASA by a few hundred yards.

His attempts to raise Seamus on the radio for the last fifteen minutes had been fruitless. At one point he'd thought Seamus was responding, but the transmission was so distorted and weak that there was no way to confirm this as fact. He was relieved to see the plane was on the runway. He'd half expected to find Seamus had gotten airborne to get closer to the extract point. That would have been a big problem; but he was still here, or at least his plane was still here.

"Hey, is that a guy with a rifle in the cargo bay of the CASA?" Steve shouted out over the noise of the old van.

Matt looked hard and confirmed Steve's observation. There was a man hiding inside the CASA. On a hunch, he grabbed the driver's arm and shouted for him to stop the van. The driver complied immediately, sending the team flying forward.

"What the fuck!" Erik yelled from the back. "Nobody said to slam on the brakes, asshole."

Matt patted the driver on the shoulder and smiled. "Don't worry about him. He's just getting old, bones getting brittle."

The driver didn't smile; he hardly grasped the point of Matt's words. He'd been happy to drive, and the trip had soothed his nerves considerably. He didn't fear these men. They were not going to hurt him. All he needed to do was follow orders, and he'd be okay.

Matt opened the passenger side door and stepped out of the van holding his arms up. He'd left his rifle in the vehicle and wanted to look as peaceful as possible. If his hunch was right, then there was a chance the man in the plane might shoot first and ask questions later.

"Seamus!" Matt yelled and waved his arms. "Seamus!"

Seamus recognized Matt as he stepped out of what looked like a cross between an old hippie van and a modern off-road SUV. He stepped down the ramp and lowered the rifle. A quick wave acknowledged the team as friend and not foe. He saw Matt jump back into the vehicle.

"Go to that plane!" Matt ordered, pointing for additional emphasis. The driver nodded and engaged the clutch. The van stuttered forward and then roared to life. In less than thirty seconds, the team was reunited with their extract platform.

"Where the hell did that come from?" Seamus yelled, as the team exited the Volkswagen.

"Our friend here from the camp was gracious enough to bring us here. I'm never one to turn down a free ride!" Matt said, laughing. Steve followed Matt to the tail ramp, and they both shook Seamus's hand.

"Looks like you were expecting a fight," Steve observed pointing to the AK.

Seamus nodded. "It was boring here until I heard the racket that thing made approaching the airfield. I had no idea what the hell was coming. Better to be prepared."

Matt nodded. He looked back at the driver, who was still sitting still. "Hey, let's gather up a few baht for this guy. I doubt he can go back to his day job after helping us."

The three men dug into their pockets and coughed up enough baht to make the driver's day. Matt turned back to the van, and that's when he noticed Erik was still sitting inside. "Something is wrong with Erik!" he said as he raced to the back door of the van.

Erik was sitting with his right leg hanging out and his head tilted back. His breathing was labored and his eyes were shut. "Erik!" Matt shouted. He placed his fingers on Erik's wrist. "He has a weak pulse!"

Steve and Seamus were at his side in a flash. The three men maneuvered Erik out of the van and onto the ground. Steve searched his torso and extremities for a wound. "Nothing on this side."

Matt looked back into the van and that's when he spotted the large blood stain. "He's hit in the lower left back! There's blood all over the seat!"

Steve and Seamus slowly rolled Erik onto his right side. Steve lifted the soaked camouflaged shirt near the wounded man's left hip. "I've got an entry wound!"

Matt and Seamus held Erik steady as Steve explored Erik's back. A few moments later he'd found what he was looking for. "The exit is just under his left armpit. Probably hit bone in his hip and that sent it straight up. Likely bypassed the kidney back here, but he's lost a lot of blood."

"He never said a fucking thing. That whole ride here," Matt mumbled.

"Not his style, boss. He may be younger than us, but this guy thinks old school. Let's get him on the plane and patch this shit up. We need to get him to Phuket fast or he'll bleed out."

Steve was right. They'd put intravenous fluid on the gear list, but that wasn't in the cards. All they had was a supply of combat bandages and coagulant powder. It would have to do. Matt helped the other two men lift Erik off the ground and into the CASA. There was plenty of seat space, so they placed him on his right side and belted him into position. Steve began pulling bandages out.

"I can have us in the air in less than five minutes. Pull the last wheel block and tell me when you have a full head count in the plane!" Seamus moved past Matt and climbed into the cockpit.

Matt left the plane and kicked the block of wood free of the right-side landing gear. Then he jogged over to driver's side door of the van. He handed him the pile of cash and reached out his hand. The driver took the money and then slowly gripped Matt's outstretched hand.

They shook hands without sharing words. The man had probably saved their lives, and Matt didn't even know his name. He released his hand and ran back to the CASA. They needed to get going and fast!

Seamus pushed the limits of the cargo plane, and they made excellent time. As the CASA circled the main airport, preparing for final approach, Matt ran the operation through his mind for the hundredth time since getting airborne. Someone in Seamus's intelligence network had passed the bogus information to the team, and he knew Seamus could ferret out who that person was.

Seamus's people likely were innocent of the deception, but they would know their source. Matt would follow that trail until they found out who was responsible for the setup at the camp. The gloves were off. An eye for an eye was the new rule of engagement. He would cauterize this threat with extreme prejudice and then go to where Vicky was being kept against her will. He knew now in his heart exactly where she was and who she was with.

The CASA rolled to a stop, and the ambulance waited for Seamus to wave them forward. The tail ramp lowered and the Thai emergency personnel rushed inside the plane. They were in the cargo bay for five minutes as Matt, Seamus, and Steve waited outside. Once they'd placed an intravenous drip in place and stabilized Erik on a carry board, they gingerly walked out of the plane and over to the ambulance.

"I'll ride with him," Steve said.

Seamus raised his hand. "No, let me go. I can make this little event go away if I can speak with a few people at the hospital. We don't need the police investigating our operation. Besides …" Seamus looked Steve up and down. "You look like an extra in a Vietnam movie!"

Steve started to argue, but realized Seamus was the right one to go. Matt watched the vehicle speed away and felt a tightness in his gut when they cranked up the siren. "He's right about one thing: we don't fit in. Let's get back in the plane and get into our civvies. Then we can figure out our next move. Besides, I want to check in with Jackson, see how he made out."

Steve shot Matt a thumbs-up and walked up the ramp. Matt took a step and then staggered a little. He steadied himself by grasping the ramp hydraulic arm and waited until the feeling passed. He'd been running on empty for at least the last twelve hours. He checked his watch and saw it was nearly three in the afternoon. They'd been moving continuously for over 24 hours.

Matt finished changing clothes and then went forward to figure out how to close the tail ramp. He found the auxiliary power switch, then thumbed through the aircraft manual Seamus kept in a pocket below the co-pilot seat. He found the toggle and moved it. The tail ramp eased up a foot and then stopped. Matt continued to tap the toggle gingerly, raising the ramp until a green light flashed on, signifying a locked ramp.

Seamus had left the keys in the starter, so Matt took those and waved Steve over to the side door. They kept their handguns tucked safely under their shirts, but left the rest of the mission gear and firepower in the CASA. Matt locked the side door and put the keys in his pocket.

"Where now?" Steve asked.

"We need sleep. We'll go back to the hotel. Seamus seemed to have pull there. I'll call him when we get there and tell him we need to meet up in the morning after some shut eye. I'll also ask him to run this lead to ground, find out who set us up."

Steve stretched. "I don't know about you, but I'm getting way too old for this shit."

Matt smiled. "Really? I feel pretty damn good!"

Steve punched Matt in the shoulder and laughed. "Sir, you are so full of shit!"

Seamus linked up with the two former SEALs around ten in the morning. He'd spent most of the night at the hospital, first greasing palms to keep the wounded patient confidential, and then making sure one of his personal security professionals was placed in Erik's room. Erik was stable and would be fine once time and treatment allowed the short-term effects of the blood loss to fade. The doctors said he was lucky the bullet ricocheted up instead of inward, where it could have destroyed his vital organs.

He'd also sent out an alert to his network in Bangkok. He wanted the name of whoever it was that fed his people the false information. He was confident he'd know soon. In the meantime, he needed to tell Matt and Steve about Erik's status and, of course, plan their next move.

Matt and Steve sat down at Seamus's table with their backs to the wall. Seamus wasted no time updating them on their friend's condition and the armed guard he'd placed in the room. Matt listened and became angry all over again.

He'd slept like the dead the night before and was mentally fresh, but his body was screaming at him. It felt like he'd played contact football for ten hours without pads. "This must be what getting old feels like," he'd told Steve on the elevator ride down. Steve for his part hadn't argued. Getting old sucked, but it sucked more for the superhero class, he explained. Matt vaguely understood the point. For a long time, he hadn't resembled a superhero at all.

Matt calmed his heart rate and waited for Seamus to finish his report. The waitress came over, and they all scrambled to look at the menus. The three men hadn't eaten in over a day. Once the food was ordered, Matt settled down to business. "We locked up the CASA." He fished in his pocket and pulled out the key to the plane. Seamus took them and placed them on the table next to his glass of water.

"Thanks for that. I expect I'll hear something soon regarding the source of the bad intelligence."

Steve snorted. "Bad intelligence is when the target isn't there or the map coordinates are wrong. This wasn't bad intelligence. Whoever set us up engaged a hit team armed with automatic weapons. It was a kill order, and we were the targets!"

Matt gave Steve a stern look. Seamus was an ally; he wasn't responsible for the operation going sideways. "Seamus, after we eat, we need to buy some more clothes. We'll only be out for a few hours; then we'll wait here in the hotel for your folks to give us a target."

Seamus shrugged and looked at Steve. "I get it. You're pissed. But I'm pissed, too. Blue is dead and Gold was wounded, just like Erik. We're all taking hits here, and we all want payback."

Steve's head dropped and he paused before responding. "Sorry, Seamus. I'm frustrated. It's been a little over a month now and we still haven't found Vicky. All this other shit isn't helping."

Matt remembered something. "Hey, I do have some good news. I spoke to Jackson early this morning. His FBI friends in Bangkok were able to get the three girls onto a plane, and they are safe in Guam on a US military base. It should be a matter of days before they are reunited with their families."

Seamus smiled. "So, it hasn't all been a waste." Just then his cell phone buzzed. Seamus took the call and listened intently. After three minutes, he said goodbye and hung up.

Matt and Steve waited for the punch line, and Seamus didn't disappoint them. "It was A-wut, Roger Maddox's man here in Thailand. I have two confirmed links to him. He was the one who set us up."

Matt's hands curled into fists. "Seamus, I need an address."

Chapter Twenty-Six

The footsteps. Vicky's life now consisted of footsteps. She'd lost track again of time; time was becoming an old habit. Here, time stretched on and on, punctuated every so often with a plate of food and a water bottle shoved through an open door. She never saw the person putting the food down and was afraid to try. No one had hurt her, and that was enough to hold onto.

Vicky remembered watching old adventure movies, even war movies, with her dad from an early age. In those movies, the hero or heroine rarely lost faith. They trusted in their skills and their raw determination to win, and that was enough to overcome in the movies. Was life really like that? Could she will herself to survive?

She wasn't much of an athlete, but she'd watched her dad exercise relentlessly during the dark days after his injury. He acted as if he could reverse the effects of a roadside bomb by becoming more powerful in other ways. She'd cried after watching him.

He'd always been such a happy person, quick to make a joke or spontaneously decide to throw everyone in the car and go find something fun to eat. He hadn't been home much, and her mom began to resent that deeply; but when he was home, life was wonderful. They were a family living life with Mr. Large-and-in-charge leading the way.

One thing she did pick up was that the effects of exercise on the brain were positive. Her dad always seemed more normal after a workout, that was until he slowly dropped back into self-loathing and sadness. So, she began to exercise. At first it was a few knee push-ups, then a few sit-ups. It was exhausting. Her diet wasn't sufficient to provide a high level of energy stores, but she did it anyway.

For many days now, she'd used exercising to push away the fear and the growing realization that she was never going home. Her choice of exercises had expanded as she struggled to remember everything her dad did in the garage gym he'd put together back home. Body weight exercises mostly: push-ups, sit-ups, planks, squats, and lunges. Even tricep push-ups--her dad said the teams called them triangle pushups because of the triangle you made with your index fingers and thumbs.

Fight training was also on her daily schedule. She knew a few self-defense moves and how to throw a right cross. She put the various pieces together to create a dance of sorts. Punch, punch, elbow. Punch, punch, knee. She stood up and stretched. It took a few days to get used to the regimen physically, but she felt the benefits. She was getting firmer, stronger. She was also planning to fight back.

Footsteps. This time they were different. Not flip-flops flapping past her door or heavy shoes, the ones presumably worn by her guards; these were softer, placed with deliberation. Not sneaky, but calm, purposeful. They stopped outside her door. Vicky went from curious to concerned. Different after all this time wasn't a good thing. She steadied herself and mentally ran through the punch, elbow, knee sequence.

The doorknob turned and the door swung open a quarter of the way. "Vicky?"

Her heart leaped into her throat. Was it a rescue? No one had used her name since her kidnapping. No one! She relaxed her stance and bit her lip. "Yes, it's Vicky. Who are you?"

A tall man with a pockmarked face stepped around the door and into the room. He was smiling, but his eyes were weary, sad even. Vicky didn't feel threatened, more curious. Who was this man?

"Vicky, may I come in?" Again, the sadness. Vicky also felt a wave of warm humidity. The air flowing into the room was heavy, not like the climate-controlled room. Where was she?

Vicky's left leg began to twitch. She didn't know what to say. If he was bad, then this might be the time to fight. Could he be good? Her brain heard her respond automatically. What was she doing?

"Yes, I'd like that."

Roger Maddox stepped into the room and closed the door. "They don't like it when I move around," he said. "I've been here so long they don't care about my walks, but they'd be mad if they knew I was speaking with you."

Vicky's eyebrows rose up and she tilted her head slightly. He was a prisoner? A prisoner like her? "Please sit down. They don't check the room, ever. The only time the door opens, it's only wide enough to shove a plate of food through. "Please," Vicky said as she pointed to a chair.

"Thank you," Maddox replied. He walked slowly to the chair and lowered himself down using his arms. "How long have you been here?"

Vicky shrugged. "I don't know. I tried to mark the time as it went by, first on the large ship, then on the smaller one, the one with the other girls." Vicky paused as a thought came to her. "Do you think they are here somewhere?"

Maddox shook his head. “I wouldn’t know. I’ve been held in a small containment area. I saw the light from your door and took a chance someone might be in here.”

Vicky realized the man was taking a risk. The guards didn’t check the room, but they would investigate hearing a conversation. She moved around the bed and sat across from the man. “We should try to be quiet. I don’t know if they’d hurt us, but I don’t want to find out. What’s your name?”

Maddox smiled. “My name? It’s Henry. Just call me Henry.” Vicky smiled and relaxed even more.

“Hello, Henry. My name is Vicky.” She stood up and took a few steps toward Maddox, reaching out with her hand. “Pleased to meet you!”

Maddox took her hand into both of his and looked down. “It’s been so long since anyone’s been nice to me, so long.”

Vicky felt a tinge of intuition, but brushed it aside. They were both victims of whoever controlled this place. She realized the touch of his soft hands gave her comfort. “Yes, I’m lonely, too.” She gently pulled her hand back and Maddox let her. “Henry, do you have an escape plan?” she asked excitedly.

Maddox shook his head. “Escape? From this place? No, I never thought to consider escape.”

Vicky smiled. “That’s okay. My dad taught me to always be prepared, situational awareness and all that. He went to a special school in the navy where they taught him how to escape from prison camps.”

“Your father seems like an extraordinary man, Vicky. I’d like to meet him someday.”

Vicky nodded. "He is, he is, Henry. He was a Navy SEAL."

Maddox's eye twitched slightly. The daughter of a special operator. Why did that hit a nerve? The feeling passed quickly, and he focused again on the exquisite young form standing in front of him. He knew from experience that it took time. Time to gain confidence and then, hopefully, affection. He also knew the longer he waited the better it was in the end.

"So, what would your father do?"

Vicky smiled broadly. "He'd plan to escape. That's what he'd do. You want to hear my plan?"

Maddox smiled back. "Yes, Vicky, I would very much like to hear about your escape plan."

A-wut tried to shake his head, but the doughnut restricted his movement. He always took a massage when he suffered a setback, and this setback was a big one. The battle at the hunting camp was a disaster. Besides not eliminating the Americans, he'd lost six good men. Correction. Six of Maddox's good men.

Borrowing the boss's Bangkok crew to kill the American rescuers seemed like a no-brainer at the time. Get the job done and get it done right. The misinformation campaign had been brilliant, and the idiot superheroes had taken the bait and ran with it, straight into the perfect trap. Except it hadn't been so perfect.

A-wut grunted in pain as the masseuse placed a sharp elbow on a particularly tight back muscle near his right scapula. She was a pro, a real sports trainer. Ugly as sin and as strong as a weight lifter, she wasn't going to give him a happy ending afterward. That was why he had a girl staged in his bedroom. She was his happy ending.

He'd had a thing for Lucila for six months. Taken off the boat in the harbor, she'd caught his eye and he'd snatched her out of the pipeline. A California girl with a head full of crazy ideas. A-wut had a thing for redheads, especially fifteen-year-old redheads. She would be fun for another six months at most; then he'd sell her to the local boys. She'd be fully trained by that time.

A-wut groaned and turned back to look at the stocky Thai woman. "Take it easy! I'm going to feel worse that I felt before you came in here. A massage, get it? Not torture!"

The masseuse smiled a mean smile, her lids half covering her cold black eyes. "Not torture," she purred in Thai. "Not torture."

"That's right, you ugly bitch!" He rolled back onto his front and dutifully placed his face in the doughnut ring.

The time flew by, and A-wut listened as the woman quietly let herself out of the penthouse apartment. He lay on his back for a while contemplating how Maddox would react to his bungling a hit on so large a scale. It seemed like every time he did something to cauterize the mess made by the Americans, it just got worse instead of better.

He heard the door behind him open slowly. "What did you forget, you ugly bitch? The money was on the table next to the door!"

"Thanks!" A deep voice answered behind him.

A-wut attempted to jump off the massage table, but was prevented by a strong hand gripping his hair and jerking him back down. Another man walked around the table and looked down. He held up a piece of paper and looked back and forth a few times before folding it and placing it into a pocket.

"It's him, alright. The sketch was spot on." Matt lifted his shirt and pulled out the silenced 9mm. "I'm going to look around a bit. Keep this asshole in check!"

Steve nodded. A-wut watched the second American move into the bedroom and began to shout a warning, but a hand was clamped over his mouth. "That wasn't smart, asshole." Steve took his thumb and lower index finger and adjusted their position slightly. A-wut's air supply was suddenly cut off.

Steve watched as A-wut's eyes grew large in panic, and he began to thrash around, struggling to breathe. Steve waited a few seconds then shifted his hand again. The intake of air through A-wut's uncovered nostrils was violent. He stopped jerking and regained his composure.

These were Americans. He was unarmed. Americans were the good guys. As long as he didn't fight, they wouldn't kill him. He needed time to figure this out. He always figured this shit out.

Matt came back into the open concept great room, towing a young redhead wearing a blanket. Steve's eyes widened. "What the hell?"

Matt's face was dark. "She's a sex slave. She won't tell me much except she's from California. Thinks she's in love with this skinny fuck." Matt pointed toward A-wut with his chin.

"She going to come with us on her own?" Steve asked.

“I doubt it,” Matt replied, pushing the girl down into a handy wing back chair. “She won’t tell me her name or anything about how long she’s been away from home.”

Steve nodded. “Stockholm syndrome. Happens to a lot of kidnap victims. She’s probably aligned herself with these assholes. They work on them, you know. Takes time, but eventually the kids break down and begin to see the bad guys as their family and everyone else as the bad guys.”

Matt shrugged. “Or she’s truly in love with this guy. Who cares? We need to take care of him and get her to Jackson’s friends here in the city.”

Steve nodded. “Why don’t you call Jackson now? Maybe his guy can take her off our hands, meet us at the hotel’s service entrance.”

Matt nodded and shoved his pistol back into his waistband. He left the shirt tail tucked behind the grip so the girl could see it clearly. Matt wasn’t taking any chances. In Iraq, cute little kids were used by the enemy to kill Americans, Americans too naïve to anticipate and react to the threat. Too many Disney movies and restrictive rules of engagement usually resulted in American casualties.

He dialed the cell phone and waited until Jackson answered. He gave the ex-FBI man the name of the swanky high rise and hung up. “He’ll call me back with a pickup time and a name.”

Steve reached over and pulled a white towel from the rack on the side of the massage table. He shoved A-wut forward then wrapped the towel around the man’s neck. A-wut began to speak, but his words were choked off. Steve took a turn on the towel in back and A-wut’s eyes bulged out.

"You going to towel him to death?" Matt asked.

"Not sure. Feels cleaner this way. My skin crawls just touching this guy."

Five minutes went by with Steve alternately loosening and then tightening the towel. A-wut was subdued; even his eyes had lost their ability to communicate. He was in survival mode.

The cell phone rang and Matt answered. He checked his watch and nodded. "We'll be down there."

Hanging up, Matt looked down at the girl. "We've got five minutes to get down to the garage receiving area. Jackson's contact is going to be there in a blue Subaru. I need to get this kid dressed. Did you remember to bring the syringe?"

Steve nodded. "Seamus gave me the stuff that only calms you down. It was the best he could do. It will keep her controllable, but immobile enough that you will have to carry her."

Matt reached down and lifted the redhead up. He steered her back into the bedroom and looked around. *She must have come here in street clothes of some kind.* A moment later he found her shorts and T-shirt. She refused to put them on so Matt had to dress her. Once the negligee was off and she was dressed, she looked like a typical American teenager.

Steve lifted A-wut up and off the table. "Do you know what a static position is my friend? A static position is when you extend your arms and legs out away from your body. You need to keep your head up and arch your back."

Steve continued to walk A-wut across the room. The Thai's feet barely touched the floor. "A good static position is balanced, no leg or arm is extended further than the other. The main reason you want to employ this technique is simple."

Steve opened the sliding glass door to the veranda. "Terminal velocity is around 120 miles an hour. That's really fast! A good static body position will slow that down to as much as 70 miles an hour, that is if you are wearing a baggy jumpsuit. Naked, it doesn't much matter what position you use. You're still going to die."

Steve threw the smaller man out over the glass balcony and watched him make a swimming motion with his arms before he disappeared. Steve didn't watch A-wut fall; sixty floors was pretty damn high, gravity was a killer.

Matt stepped into the main room just as Steve closed the sliding glass doors. "Where's A-wut?"

"The man is untrainable. Worst exit I've ever seen a jumper make, and that was after I gave him a class! You just can't train some people."

Matt smiled. "Okay then. We need to get down to the garage. Once Jackson's man takes the girl off our hands, we have some planning to do!"

"Roger that, sir. Roger that!"

Chapter Twenty-Seven

The pickup went off without a hitch, allowing Matt and Steve a generous window for their escape from the towering hotel. Matt knew it was only a matter of time before hotel security began running through their surveillance footage and spot the two of them transferring the girl in the loading area.

He also knew that didn't connect them with the fall, which would be presumed to be a suicide, at least for a while. Eventually a witness might place the girl in the penthouse and that would lead the security people and probably the police to the video showing how she left the building.

The team wasn't taking any chances. They'd driven from Phuket to Bangkok in a "stolen" car that one of Seamus's associates allowed them to borrow for a few days. The car was parked five blocks away. Once they were on the road, Matt would check in with Seamus to see what their buddy Gary had come up with since they'd left Phuket to find A-wut.

The walk went quickly, and they soon were working their way southwest out of the big city, looking for the main artery south to Phuket. Matt let Steve drive so he could speak with Seamus. He dialed the number and waited. If Gary came up short, the trail was dead. Trying to find Maddox as he moved around the world was a fool's game. He needed a single location, a high probability location. Anything else was mush.

The cell phone rang and rang. Matt waited too long then hung up. "He could be busy. Give it a few minutes and try again."

Matt looked at Steve and knew he was right. "Watched pot, right?"

Steve nodded as he evaded a taxi. "Yep, a watched pot never boils. Chill out. We did a good thing back there."

"Two good things. I sure hope that girl can get her head right again. I can't imagine …"

"I'm sure it's worse than what we could imagine. A mental and physical violation like that changes people forever. With the right kind of help …"

Matt knew Steve was right. He wasn't in a position to truly appreciate the horror of what it must be like for a young girl, enduring a total loss of control over her body and her destiny. A daily dose of evil. He was glad they'd saved four so far, even if they'd failed to find Vicky. At least four girls had a fighting chance at a normal life again.

Matt jerked. He'd had the cell phone volume up to the highest output, and in the small car it sounded like an air raid siren. "What the fuck!" Steve exclaimed.

"Sorry!" Matt answered the call. "I'm here."

Seamus's gravelly voice was clear and loud. "We have a target. He's in position, but we have no idea when he might move again. And we're in luck, he's not that far away."

Matt smiled. "We're just clearing the city. Can you make the logistics arrangements? Oh, by the way, we need to get Erik transported out of Thailand by tonight. Someone might connect the dots, and it's time for all of us to unass this country!"

"Affirmative on both counts. I'm way ahead of you on the evac deal. Erik is slated to be flown out by an Australian medical evacuation company in three hours. He'll finish his rest and recuperation at Gary's place in New Zealand. As for the logistics, Gary had an idea, sort of double oh seven stuff. But considering where the high value target is right now, it might be the best way to get there fast."

Steve continued to drive and Matt tried to calm his mind. He wanted to plan, to create a timeline for the operation, but he didn't know shit. He was left trusting an ex-pilot, who he'd only known for a week, and a reclusive ex-team guy he'd known for a few days. The odds of catching Maddox were slim to none. He was a mover and a shaker and reportedly always hopping from continent to continent. Gary's intel might be accurate, but every passing hour made that information more useless.

Matt and his fellow SEAL operators were used to high-value target missions. The called them HVTs. The missions came in two flavors: kill or capture. HVT missions always were dependent on real-time knowledge of the moving parts.

Bodyguards, weaponry, the specific building and exact room where the HVT would be found, and other key target data points. Often there was an unmanned aerial surveillance vehicle that watched the target and updated the inbound SEAL strike team on a minute-by-minute basis. That wouldn't be happening this time.

Matt had heard the old-time SEALs tell stories about the days before high-tech data feeds, real-time command and control, and satellite imagery down to the square foot. Those guys relied on patience and intuition. They missed more often than not; but they kept at it, night after night, silently retreating to reload for the next opportunity. Then, when everything lined up just right …

Matt and Steve weren't a strike force. They didn't have time to be patient. Vicky's life, or at a minimum, her sanity, relied on Gary's information being spot on. They'd only get one chance. The phone jerked him back to reality.

"God damn it! Turn that fucking thing down!" Steve looked at Matt and grimaced.

"Shit! Sorry, man." Matt answered the phone.

"Matt, Seamus. Change in flight plan. I need you guys to continue south, but head over to a port town called Surat Thani. It's on the Gulf of Thailand, just north of Phuket but across the peninsula. I'll meet you there."

Matt frowned. "What's in Surat Thani? Our weapons and other gear are in the plane."

"No sweat. I'm flying the CASA from Bangkok, just as soon as I see Erik leave on that Aussie bird. I'll meet you at the port. I can explain more once you're there. Meet me at pier 19. It's near the port control tower. I'll get your stuff over there one way or another."

Matt looked at Steve. "We need to drive to a place called Surat Thani." He placed the cell phone back to his ear as Steve attempted to pull up the map application on his smart phone.

"Okay, flyboy. We'll meet you there. Can't wait to hear the game plan."

Matt hung up and looked out of the window. "Seamus has a plan, and he'll get all our shit to this port city on the gulf. Seems confident. I'm not so sure."

"That's because deep inside you're a control freak, sir." Steve grinned. "I can still remember you as a wet fart at SDV Team Two. You sucked in the minisub and you sucked at everything else, too. That asshole Sandoval stuck you in the Reconnaissance and Surveillance task element because you sucked so much."

Matt grunted. "Yeah, how'd that turn out?"

"Well, if I remember right, I got a bullet and you got the Navy fucking Cross. That's how that turned out!"

Matt chuckled. "The way I remember it, I got a bullet and you got the Silver Star."

Steve turned onto the highway, leading them east toward the gulf coast. "Yeah, same difference. The real loser was Sandoval. That fucker had to kiss your ass every day after that, even if he was a lieutenant commander. Tried to claim credit for planning the mission and all that bullshit. Commodore at Group Two yanked a knot in his ass to shut him down. So long, Mr. Sandoval!"

Matt turned. "I never heard that part. He actually tried to claim credit for the airport op in Egypt? He was still back in Virginia Beach!"

"Yep. That's how most officers behave, though. You, now, you're different. Had something to prove, your daddy a war hero and all. How could you not end up a daredevil, the son of a Medal of Honor Marine?"

Matt looked down. He'd grown up under that shadow. It was open knowledge in the teams that his dad was a national hero, but he'd never set out to become one himself. The thing in Egypt just happened.

"Well, I'm happy everybody made it out alive," Matt mumbled. Then he perked up. "Of course, I was all about the hero shit when I saved your ass in Colombia!"

Steve howled. "WHAT? You didn't save my ass; I was just about to execute my escape plan when you and your ugly band of desperadoes showed up and spoiled it for me. Another few minutes …"

"Maybe another few years …" Matt retorted, laughing.

The two former SEALs went quiet and spent the rest of their drive together remembering the past. All the faces and all the sacrifices. All the broken marriages, broken heroes, and all the heroes, many lost forever. Teams and shit.

Pier 19 wasn't easy to find. Surat Thani was a complicated tangle of roads, ruts, alleys, and paths that defied navigation. Steve's map application failed immediately upon entry into the confusing port city. After a few false positives, Steve found what appeared to be a main street through to the gulf.

"Hey, there it is. I see water!" Matt's shout caught Steve's attention, and he slammed on the brakes. He backed up twenty feet and looked down the narrow street to his left.

"Yep, there it is!" Steve turned down toward the port, and once there stopped the car to survey his options. "You see any signs?"

Matt looked to his left and then to his right. He was just about to answer when he spotted the port control tower. "There! The tower. Seamus said it was near that tower."

Steve turned right and drove as close as he could get to the three-story building. The port tower wasn't impressive, but it was tall enough to allow the port manager a clear view of the waterways and the pier system.

"Where's Skid Mark?" Steve stretched out the first word in the call sign, affecting a southern drawl.

Matt shrugged. "I have no idea. I'll give him a call, just on the outside chance he's on deck already."

Matt made the call and waited while his phone ringed several times. He hung up and faced Steve. "No joy, I'm afraid. We'll have to sit tight and wait for him to link up with us here."

Steve smiled and pointed. "I think he's ahead of schedule."

Seamus stood and waved at the car until he caught Steve's attention. He watched the two men exit the vehicle and waited until they joined him on the quay wall. "Well, glad to see you two finally made it!"

Steve crossed his arms and scowled. "Next time let us steal a halfway decent car. This bucket of bolts barely made it this far."

"Nice to see you again, too, Steve," Seamus responded with a smug look.

Matt was anxious and checked his watch. "So, what's the plan? Did Gary come through for us?"

Seamus nodded. "Oh, I guess you could say that. Follow me." He turned and started walking toward the port control tower.

"Hey where the fuck is pier 19? We couldn't find it," Steve barked out, sidestepping a pile of dog shit.

Seamus pointed ahead. "Just follow me. It's on the other side of the tower."

The three men maneuvered around piles of cabling, cargo containers, and broken-down machinery, following Seamus as he wound his way to, and then beyond the control tower. Matt was last in their file formation, and he watched as Steve banged his shin on a piece of metal jutting out from a pile of trash. His partner swore and muttered something about Thailand and moved forward. Matt avoided the obstacle.

At last Seamus stopped walking and the three of them stood together. “Now what, super genius?” Steve was quickly losing his sense of humor.

Seamus nodded to the left. “That’s pier 19. It’s a covered pier. Nice to have when you need it, right?” Seamus stepped off and lowered himself down a short ladder to the next level of the pier platform. Matt and Steve climbed down behind him. As soon as they were with him, Seamus walked briskly into the long structure that covered pier 19 from the quay wall to the pier tip.

Matt’s eyes took a few seconds to adjust to the darkness. As he began to see details, his eyes opened wider. “What the fuck?”

Steve whistled. “Tell me that’s for us.”

Seamus beamed and nodded. “Courtesy of Gary. Gentlemen, our chariot awaits!”

Matt and Steve walked farther down the walkway that ran along the port side of the gleaming vessel resting against the pier. “It looks like a fucking space ship!” Steve exclaimed.

Seamus agreed. “Damn near. It’s Thunder Child XSV 17 built by Safehaven Marine. Seventeen meters in length, it’s designed for speed and the ability to pierce waves rather than ride over them. It’s a self-righting boat, damn near unsinkable. A pair of turbo-charged diesel engines drive this baby at speeds up to 54 knots!”

Matt was impressed. “What kind of legs?”

Seamus scratched his chin. “It has fuel capacity at cruising speed to cover 700 nautical miles. Sleeps ten and has shock mitigation seats for six passengers. The vessel is designed for law enforcement or military intercept. It’s our ride to Cambodia.”

Both Steve and Matt twisted around to look at Seamus. “Cambodia? Is that …?”

Seamus nodded in the affirmative. “Yes. Maddox has a private island approximately 290 miles from here. That’s a seven-hour trip at forty knots cruising speed. The place is called Bamboo Island; it’s about a mile west of the island of Koh Ta Kiev. The Cambodian government turns a blind eye to his activities, so he’s free to do anything he wants there.”

Matt’s hands curled into fists. “Anything? That’s where she is, I know it. Where’s our gear?”

Seamus gestured toward the point. “I’ve already had your equipment and weapons loaded. Gold is onboard. I outfitted him for the job, figured since you were one man short ...”

Matt nodded and smiled. “I love working with Navy men!”

Steve slapped Seamus on the back. “Too bad you didn’t bring more gear; you could join us!”

Seamus smiled. “Well, it just so happens that I did. I thought you’d never ask!”

Matt laughed. The more the merrier. They needed all the help they could get. Without detailed schematics of Maddox’s estate, they’d be forced to split up and cover more ground. “Do we have anything information at all on this place?”

"Nope, the compound has always been private property. Sorry, we'll just have to figure it out as we go." Seamus waved his hand. "All aboard, gentlemen."

Chapter Twenty-Eight

The XSV seventeen wasn't glamorous on the inside. The sleek lines, narrow hull, and commitment to space for the oversized power plant left little room for guests. Seamus indicated where to strap into the shock mitigation seats, then went forward to speak with the skipper of the craft.

Matt watched him leave. "Seamus said Gary keeps this boat in Singapore. He bought it direct from the manufacturer as a prototype two years ago. They're selling them commercially now. I wonder how much one of these beasts goes for?"

"Who cares? We can't afford it. Hey, you ever take a ride in our Mark five boat?" Steve asked. "Badass to say the least."

Matt nodded. "Only a few times. We were so focused on the sandbox, we rarely conducted legacy training, you know. Combat ship attacks, arctic warfare, insertions other than by aircraft."

Steve finished making his adjustments and lay his head back into the plush headrest. "You hear the teams are going back to those old missions and insertion methods. The young guys are grumbling about it, of course, but there's fewer and fewer ops going down for frog inland these days."

Matt wasn't really listening. He'd been off the team guy net for quite a while anyway. He looked at the digital clock across the compartment from his seat. They had seven hours to travel. Despite the cushy, scientifically-designed seats, the ride was going to be brutal. Seven hours is a long time, enough time for their target to leave the island. Enough time for Vicky to suffer more.

“Hey, Seamus! When the fuck are we rolling out of here?” Matt shouted.

A few seconds later, Gold stepped into the passenger compartment. “We leave now. Skipper teaching my boss how to fly boat.” His big toothy grin told them all he wasn’t expecting Seamus to do well.

Gold climbed into one of the shock seats and buckled up. He yelled a word in Thai, then closed his eyes. Matt felt the twin turbo charged diesels even before he heard them fire up. It felt like an earthquake, a wave of power coursing through the light vessel from back to front.

The powerboat backed up until it cleared the tip of the pier, then slowly rotated. The keel was long and the beam so narrow that, riding in the seats mounted on the centerline, it felt to Matt that they were moving the boat by leaning their body weight instead of being pushed that way by the swing of the vessel.

“Like a skateboard,” Steve muttered, feeling the same thing as Matt. “Think there’s a chance we’ll get any sleep on this rocket?”

Before Matt could reply he was pressed back forcefully into the seat. The XSV accelerated rapidly as it departed the small port. In a few seconds, the press was so significant that Matt knew the answer to Steve’s question. There wouldn’t be any sleeping on this trip.

Vicky felt the hand on her shoulder and knew it was Henry. She smiled. Over the last few days she’d grown to like and trust this sad man. He seemed to have figured out a way to dodge the guards and make time to visit her more with each passing day. She rolled over and looked up at his smiling face.

"Good morning."

Maddox's smile faded. "Yes, of course it is. How did you sleep?"

Vicky stretched her arms up over her head. "Better than usual. No bad dreams this time."

Maddox nodded. "I guess we have nothing to talk about today, then." He began to rise but Vicky's hand shot out and grabbed his wrist. He looked down at her hand and struggled to contain his excitement.

"Please, stay here with me. We can talk about something else. My dad. You like to talk about him, don't you?"

Maddox sighed and sat back down on the edge of the bed. "Why don't we try a different topic for a change. I lost my wife to illness a few years ago. We were soul mates, the perfect match. Do you have a boyfriend?"

Vicky's eyes teared up. This man's life was one tragedy after another. "I've had a couple of, well I guess they were boyfriends. I know they weren't my soul mates, not like you and your wife."

Maddox noticed Vicky's hand was still on his arm, but now she was unconsciously rubbing it to give him comfort. He didn't have much time left. He was scheduled to leave the next day and he had to make a decision: continue the slow process and revisit this young beauty at a later date or take her any way he could, regardless of the violence needed to experience her this early.

"My wife and I had something very special, so special I doubt I'll ever marry again. I'm still filled with the desire to love, to give my love to another human being, but …"

Vicky sighed. Henry was fascinating. Sad yet open to his emotions, unlike her dad in so many ways. She felt a pull toward him that surprised her. The love her dad showed for her and toward her was rougher, a crude sort of exchange of words and looks that she was sure mimicked his interactions with fellow SEALs. Her dad wasn't a hugger; he was a warrior. Henry was different in a nice way.

Matt woke up. He'd lost count of the number of times he'd dozed off so far. Looking at his watch only depressed him, so he sucked it up. The ride felt like a trip to the moon in a cramped space capsule. The shock mitigation chair was as comfortable as it could be; but to protect the user, one had to be immobilized, and that was uncomfortable all on its own.

He'd been dreaming this last time. An odd dream. He and his sort of pet lizard, Steve, were all alone on a pristine white sand beach. The water was a crazy light blue, like advertisements for Bora Bora. There were no people, no buildings, no evidence of mankind in any direction. Just he and Steve staring out into the blue, still water.

He shook his head. Dreams were supposed to mean something, but he didn't have a clue what message this one represented. Had Steve died alone in his apartment in the Keys? He felt a pang of guilt at the thought. Maybe when this was all over, he'd call back and check in on his friend, his only friend.

Steve and Gold seemed to be having no problem sleeping. Every time Matt woke up, the other two were blissfully passed out. He looked at the digital clock he'd ignored for so long. It read 11:43. They were six hours into the trip. He only had to endure another sixty minutes, and they'd be at their destination, the tiny Cambodian island called Bamboo.

He began flashing back to his childhood. Why not? What else did he have to do? When he was young, he saw everything his father did as a threat or a nuisance, all negative. Matt grew up under the shadow of the great Arthur Barrett; but as a child, the full weight of that circumstance had yet to haunt him as it would in later years.

As he tracked his life through high school and then college, he noted that the specter of his father had morphed into a firm resentment. The old man had passed away before Matt began his university studies, but he certainly would have disapproved. The only path for Matt that was acceptable was the Corps, enlisted preferably.

So, it was ironic that Matt had ended up in an even more elite combat unit. A shame Arthur Barrett didn't live to see that bright golden eagle pinned on Matt's chest. Matt knew his father would have figured out a way to deride the achievement; it was his nature to be negative. Matt knew this, but also realized his father had a lot to do with his succeeding at BUD/S.

His mind-set and discipline were in part the product of a strict and unforgiving upbringing. No excuses accepted, no failure to execute left uncritiqued. The mental stress and psychotic chaos of SEAL training didn't faze Matt much; he just didn't possess good judgement. That shortfall almost got him dropped from BUD/S and was absolutely his problem in dealing with minisub operations.

Steve was right; Lieutenant Commander Sandoval was too. Matthew Barrett should never have been in a fight to the death in Egypt or anyplace else; but it happened anyway and made all the difference from that point of his career onward. The Navy Cross was over the top, a political award more than a true reflection of his valor. It sat on his chest for the next thirteen years, drawing stares and comments. He knew he wasn't worthy, yet it didn't seem to matter to anyone else. The medal was a symbol, and he'd become a symbol also.

Steve jerked awake and snorted loud enough for Matt to hear it over the sound of the twin diesels. Matt glanced at the time display and was rewarded with the realization that he'd daydreamed through forty more minutes. A few minutes later, he felt the XSV throttle back. The sound was reduced considerably and the G-forces pressing him back into the seat were cut in half.

Steve looked over and shouted, "Hey there, sleepy eyes, time to ruck up!"

Matt shook his head and didn't respond. They had intelligence on the estate, but hadn't had time to study whatever it was Gary sent them. The boat throttled down again, and it was clear they didn't need to be strapped into the shake chairs. Matt unbuckled first, followed by Steve and then Gold. Seamus popped his head into the compartment and smiled.

"I trust everyone enjoyed the ride?" he said. "We're on the east side of the island of Koh Ta Kiev. Maddox's place is a few minutes' cruise to the west. I figured this was a good spot to study the information we have and make a plan. We still have about six hours of darkness to plan, insert, execute the rescue, and extract."

Matt grinned. "You sound more like a squadron commander every day, sir!"

Steve chimed in, "Maybe, but I kind of miss the Captain Ron character we met that first day in Phuket. Now that was a leader of men if I ever saw one!"

Gold burst out laughing, and Seamus shot him a stern look. "*Captain Ron* is his favorite movie," Gold said. "You aren't the first person to make that comparison."

Matt stepped out of the chair and flexed his stiff muscles. "Where's the material?"

Seamus disappeared and then stepped back into the passenger compartment. "Here's what Gary sent and a few charts I was able to procure before I left Bangkok. Bamboo Island has a narrow beach all around the perimeter. The rub is it's also very shallow, only a few feet of depth until you get out a few hundred yards from the beach. There's not an allowance for a boat landing, especially this particular boat."

Steve blew his nose loudly. "No shit? Can Gold swim?"

Seamus nodded. "We both can. You'll need the two of us to help you. Gary's sources indicate the island has a few day workers at Maddox's estate full-time, whether he's in residence or not. They clean, maintain the place, and act as a mild security deterrent. When he does visit, he brings at least three professional bodyguards with him. They are with him wherever he travels."

"Any insight as to their backgrounds? Nice to know who we're up against," Steve added.

Seamus shook his head. "No. Gary's take is to assume the worst, tier one special ops types. European or even former South African commandoes. Maddox doesn't take risks; he mitigates them. Whoever he has watching over him is bound to be top notch."

Matt was listening, but focusing more on the island, looking for a reasonable infiltration point. "This little notch here, at the tip of my finger. The depth is five feet greater than the rest of the shoreline. We can infiltrate there."

Steve leaned over and looked at where Matt was pointing. "Yeah, that makes sense. Might be an old channel used to bring supplies to the island. Looks dredged. We'd have enough water so we can swim instead of crawling in across the shallows."

Seamus nodded. "All I need for the skipper is the drop-off point and the pickup point. I told him we'd signal we're leaving the island for the extraction point by using a flashlight. Three long flashes followed by one short flash."

Steve smirked. Seamus was really getting into the maritime operations shit. "What if the sun's up when we need an extract?"

Matt stood back from the charts. "Tell him to wait three hundred meters due south of the tip of Bamboo Island. If the sun's up, we'll just swim to that point. Make sure he understands: three hundred meters."

Seamus spun around and disappeared into the cockpit of the high-speed boat. A few minutes later he returned, flashing a thumbs-up. "He's good to go. Wants to know when you will be ready to leave."

Matt thought for a second. "We need twenty minutes to get our shit together. How long from here to the drop point?"

"He said ten to fifteen minutes. The boat has GPS navigation, so he's already plugged in the point three hundred meters south of the island."

Matt rotated his head, stretching his sore neck. "Okay, here's the deal. Steve and I will be a pair and the two of you will follow us in the water, across the beach, and then to the estate. We have silenced pistols, so we'll handle whatever needs to be handled. Got it so far?"

Seamus nodded and Gold just smiled. "Does he speak English well enough to understand what I'm saying to him?" Matt asked.

"Sure. Gold is solid. He just doesn't like to speak English, makes him feel stupid. I guarantee he is fully capable of following your instructions."

Matt looked at the young man, and Gold only raised his thumb up high. "Good to go!"

Steve laughed. "Now that's communicating!"

Matt checked the time. "Once we enter the estate, we stay together. We don't have the layout, so we'll start a search from the point of entry until we find Vicky."

"Rules of engagement?" Seamus asked, a serious look on his face.

"Anyone carrying a weapon gets shot. Maddox gets a round, *after* we find out where Vicky is being kept, not before!"

Steve cracked his knuckles. "Simple enough for even a frogman to understand. I suggest we hurry and get jocked up. Time's a wastin'!"

Matt nodded and moved to where his gear was staged and strapped down. They didn't know if Maddox was still on the island. And even if he was, what if Vicky wasn't here either? As he pulled the tiger stripe cammies over his head, he realized it didn't matter. It was what it was. They'd get in, find her, and get out. That was the mission. His gut told him they were going to win this time.

Chapter Twenty-Nine

Seamus went forward to check the time remaining before reaching the insertion point as Matt finished arranging his magazine carrier. Luckily Seamus brought the large plastic bin from the plane that held extra AK magazines, bottled water, and extra radio batteries. Steve also was replenishing his war load.

"Looks like I shot more rounds than I thought back in that fucking boy scout camp," Steve grumbled.

Matt nodded. "Me too! Canteens were damn near empty."

Seamus came back and pulled his nylon bag out of a cubbyhole. "I'm sticking with a pistol, guys. Not familiar with the AK."

Matt shrugged. "That's still one more gun than we would have had. Are you sure you still want to do this?"

Seamus didn't answer, just continued getting ready. He was committed. All in. Steve finished his preparations and saw that Gold had been ready before he was. The young Thai was sitting on the edge of a shake chair with a Mona Lisa smile on his face. He lifted his hand and gave Steve a thumbs-up.

Steve grunted and returned the gesture. "Time to drop?"

Seamus looked up from his bag. "Shit, sorry. The skipper said five minutes, so my guess is we're essentially there by now."

On cue, the boat, which had been cruising at a slow but steady speed, noticeably slowed down. As it did so, the gentle swells in the Gulf of Thailand began to rock the shallow draft vessel left and right on its narrow axis. Matt took a deep breath and slowly let it out. From Gary's description of the estate and its security measures, they were in for a fight, unless they were lucky and found Vicky quickly.

He knew each man on the four-man rescue team was focused and ready to do what had to be done. It wasn't wartime, and killing anybody, even human traffickers, was a crime. Matt knew all their lives were at risk now and later. The best way to execute this job was old-school. Sneak and peak, kill, and then slide out before anyone knew what happened.

"Hey, Seamus, does your skipper up there speak English?"

Seamus had finished dressing out and was leaning against the bulkhead, trying to steady himself. "Already wrote me off, did ya?"

Matt nodded. "Just thinking ahead. Contingencies and shit."

Seamus laughed. "Yes, his name is Casper. Don't ask. He's a Kiwi. If things go bad, we can call him on the tactical VHF radios and he'll do whatever we need him to."

Steve slapped Matt on his shoulder and squeezed. "Okay, sir. Let's get this shit show started."

It was sketchier getting into the water than Matt had anticipated. There was little to no deck topside. Each man edged close to the water and then clumsily slid, making a scraping noise as the weapons edged scratches into the sleek paint job. Matt waited last. As he slid, he knocked on the hull hard, two knocks. His signal to Casper that they were off the vessel.

The water was soothing and the salt water provided a comfortable buoyancy that relieved Matt's sore muscles and aching bones. The waves rolled past them toward the beach in a regular set of seven. They weren't high enough to interfere with his view of Bamboo Island.

The intelligence provided by Gary noted that Bamboo Island was frequented during the day by scuba tours, sailboats, and random shuttles filled with beach goers from the nearby mainland; but at night the island became a ghost town. Except for the one resident with a home on the tiny land mass: Roger Maddox.

The three-hundred-yard swim was relaxing after the seven-hour bone-shaking ride in the XSV. Steve led the pack, with Seamus and Gold swimming side-by-side behind him and Matt bringing up the rear. Matt was confident in his and Steve's abilities as far at stealth, patrolling, and accurate shooting. They also would gel nicely in close-quarter combat, should they be forced to fight inside any of the estate buildings. He was concerned about the two strap hangers.

Strap hangers were non-operators attached to the team for some purpose, usually a finite skill set the special operators didn't possess. Matt and Steve had conducted plenty of missions with this technical baggage embedded in their team, but it slowed things down and often caused control problems.

SEAL, Army Special Forces, and other elite operators trained to their craft and performed at the highest level of execution. The repetition was arduous, thousands of hours and thousands of rounds; but in the end, operators began to think and act as one brain. The closest analogy in civilian life was watching a group of kids playing pickup basketball.

Kids who played together as they grew up, for years, instinctively knew what their friends were going to do, anywhere on the court. No verbal direction, no hand signals, just instinct honed from playing together. SEALs performed like that. *But not this time. Not this mission.*

At the midway point in the swim, Steve angled right at forty-five degrees. Matt wondered why until his knee banged on the compact sand beneath him. They were heading into the shallows. Steve was looking for the deeper channel, which should exist to the right somewhere.

Matt paused to check his watch; it was 1:14 in the morning. He hoped the search for the channel didn't take too long. They only had four and a half hours before it became light enough to be seen swimming back to the XSV. He turned and followed the pack for another four minutes before Steve changed course again, this time headed back to the beach. A second later, Matt felt his feet swing clear; they were in the channel.

The ambient light from the stars and partial moon illuminated the white sand beach, making it easier to gauge progress. Another ten minutes passed, and Matt felt the group's pace slow. Then his knees hit the sand. It was time to crawl the final twenty yards.

Steve crawled up onto and over the white sand, disappearing into the tree line beyond. Seamus and Gold crawled up to the trees and halted, waiting for Matt. Matt joined them and slid in between the two men. A few moments later, Steve slid back out of the trees and joined his teammates.

"Clear ahead. I can see lights, so we can use them to find the estate."

Matt listened and then nodded in acknowledgement. This was the point of no return. He knew they were going to kill people tonight; he and Steve knew what that meant.

"Last chance to stay out of this, guys," Matt said, whispering and turning his head to look Seamus and Gold. "Once we leave this beach, there's no going back. We will be murdering people; that's a crime anywhere in the world. This isn't combat. Take a minute to think about that."

Seamus smiled and nudged Gold with a sand-covered elbow. "We knew that before we left the boat. Don't worry about us, Matt. We'll stay out of your way, but we're doing this."

Gold nodded as if to confirm his feelings on the subject. Steve was impatient. "Hey, sir! Are we done with the legal briefing? We need to get our asses in gear!"

Matt was satisfied. "Yeah, yeah, I hear ya. One last thing. If we get separated or we get blown off this target, make it back to this spot. The sand is undisturbed everywhere except where we came ashore, so look until you find this spot and wait. Wait only until the sunrise starts to glow over the horizon. When that happens, swim. Get to the XVS."

Matt held up a thumb and everybody responded with a thumbs-up. They were ready. Matt tapped Steve twice, and the former SEAL senior chief smiled before turning and retracing his path into the trees. Seamus and Gold waited until Steve was out of the way and then followed him, single file. Matt looked back toward the XVS; it was invisible out there in the night.

The distance to the estate was only 75 to 100 yards. Steve and Matt had discussed the pace of their patrol as it approached the buildings and had split the difference. Steve would move as fast as he could until in his judgement they were too close. Then they would move slower.

The four men reached the manicured lawn and stood there surveying the property. Maddox's compound consisted of six buildings. A boat house, a large storage shed, a pump house for fresh water from the mainland, a block house which likely held the power plant for the estate, and two residence buildings. One was smaller, and in Matt's estimation might house five to six people. Maybe Maddox's support and service staff, maybe a few security personnel as well.

The larger residence building was perhaps six thousand square feet in size, single story. Matt pulled Steve close and whispered into his ear. "Well, it's clear to me; big guy is in the big house. Agree?"

Steve nodded. "Vicky might be kept in the large shed or the smaller residence structure. Just saying. Maybe we should quietly check those before going big." Steve pointed to the larger residence building. "Once we enter that place, we know we'll make contact with his executive protection guys."

Matt hated wasting the time it would take to clear the other structures first. He wanted to get to the end of this odyssey, but Steve's tactical insight made perfect sense. Matt grudgingly acquiesced.

"Okay. I don't like it, but you're right." Matt grabbed Seamus and pulled him closer. Gold leaned in. "Steve and I will lead shoulder-to-shoulder. Do not fire your weapons if you see somebody. Let us decide and, if needed, take them out with the pistols. Only use those AKs if we start getting our asses handed to us."

Seamus whispered, "How are we going to know when that happens?"

Matt grinned. "Trust me, you will know!"

The back side of the compound wasn't as well-lit as the main residence, and that allowed Steve and Matt to shave off distance by cutting across the lawn to reach the large shed quickly. Matt indicated he wanted Seamus and Gold to wait in the shadows while the two frogmen cleared and searched the structure.

Four minutes later, Matt and Steve exited the shed and shook their heads. Matt motioned for Seamus and Gold to join them as they moved directly to the small residence. Most of the windows were open to allow the sea breeze in, and that gave Matt an idea. He conferred with Steve and again told the straphangers to wait in the shadow at one corner of the building.

Matt followed Steve as he moved from window to window, listening and looking inside. At two windows they heard the distinct sound of snoring. The front entrance door was open, and a small lamp illuminated a parlor-sized room beyond. Staying on their hands and knees, they moved past the light source and continued the window checks around the perimeter until they at last rejoined Seamus and Gold.

"All the windows are open and the front door, too. I can't believe they are keeping hostages in this building."

Steve was right. Matt was happy the two searches were behind them. He checked his watch; it was five minutes after two. Steve saw him check the time and waited for Matt's next decision. Matt didn't hesitate. He pointed to the large residence and tapped Steve on the shoulder. It was time to find out if Vicky and Roger Maddox were still on the island. It was also time for Matt to discover if he still had the skills he thought he'd left behind long ago.

Steve led the four men to the side door of the main residence and paused to allow them to catch up. He reached his hand out to check the doorknob, turning it slowly. The mechanism rotated, and the door swung open freely. The house wasn't locked!

Matt started on the right side of the hallway and Steve on the left. On a nod they began moving, pistols at the ready, waiting for a threat to pop up. At each door they stopped and gingerly tested the knob. They'd agreed back on the boat that Vicky would be in a locked room, so they would bypass everything until a locked room was discovered.

They reached a cross hallway, and Steve waited at the intersection for Matt to pick a branch to search. Matt didn't have a clue; but something was pulling him to the right, so he moved that way. Steve slid up and loaded on the left wall and they began the search process all over again. Seamus and Gold stayed four steps back and lined up behind Matt. Every few steps, Matt looked back to make sure they were in tow. *Straphangers!*

Laughter echoed suddenly through the house, coming from behind them. It was clear enough to distinguish two, possibly three, voices. Matt and Steve froze and listened. Two minutes went by and the voices faded. They were somewhere else in the large house, but not moving toward them. Matt waved to get Steve's attention, then pointed down the hall. There were four more rooms to go.

Vicky was happy to have Henry's friendship and especially happy he decided to visit her tonight. He'd explained that the guards stayed in the main part of the house after nine o'clock, allowing him to sneak out and roam a bit. Vicky didn't know how her newfound friend was able to unlock the door so easily, but she saw him lock it behind him when he came in. He was always paranoid the guards would find them together.

Tonight, Henry was carrying a small athletic bag with him. He put it on the floor next to the bed and sat down. Vicky sat cross-legged in the center of the bed; she was curious about the bag.

"What is that?" she asked, pointing down toward the floor.

Maddox smiled a friendly smile, a warm smile. The smile of a friend and confidant. He was making progress. He'd been able to coax this girl to discuss her physical relationships with two boyfriends. She warmed up to hearing his advice on the subject: his warnings and his veiled description of the joys of physical intimacy. Given a few more days, he knew she'd allow him to become her mentor in more ways than one. He didn't have that time.

"A surprise. A few games, ideas really, to help pass the time. But first I have a treat for you!"

Vicky's eyes expanded. "A treat? What is it?"

Maddox reached into his pocket and brought out a small bottle. "I stole it. It's like a soft drink, tasty and wonderful. I'm sorry I only have one left; I drank all the rest. Here, see if you like it as much as I did!"

Vicky eagerly snatched the small bottle from Maddox's hand. "I can't wait. Anything is better than the gruel they feed me every day."

Maddox waited. He was already beginning to stir in anticipation of experiencing this young spirit. Vicky was a stronger soul than most of the girls he'd had in the past. It was a shame she'd never feel most of what he was about to do to her.

Vicky unscrewed the cap and froze. Maddox saw the hesitation. “What’s wrong?”

Vicky lowered the bottle and pointed to the door. “The knob! It just turned by itself!”

Chapter Thirty

Maddox glanced over his shoulder. He watched the doorknob for a moment, then looked back at Vicky. "I didn't see it move. The guards would just unlock and open the door if it was them. There's nothing to worry about. Drink."

Vicky heard the words, but she knew what she saw. Her concern wasn't for herself; it was for Henry. If he was caught with her, then they would find a way to make sure they never saw each other again. Until she met him, she hadn't realized how lonely she was.

"I know what I saw!" Vicky's right hand still held the small bottle, but now it was down by her side, irritating Maddox.

"Okay, I'll go to the door and listen. I assure you there's nobody out there." Maddox stood up and stepped over the athletic bag. He walked to the door and made a show of placing his ear against the cool wood. That's when he heard something.

"What the fuck!" Maddox's voice shocked Vicky. It was deeper and loud.

"Be quiet! They'll hear you and take you away!"

Maddox looked back at Vicky, a different expression on his face. She was taken aback a little by his transformation, but still focused on his safety. "No! Don't open the door!"

Matt was stacked behind Steve, his weapon at the ready as Steve worked the lock. Many SEALs went through locksmith training to assist in doing this very same thing, silent entry during a building takedown. Crowbars, shotguns, and demolitions were all great breeching options, but they made noise.

“Got it!” Steve held up a thumb.

The door swung open so fast that Steve almost tumbled into the room. Matt was startled, but recovered quickly by shoving the silencer attached to the barrel of his 9mm automatic into the forehead of the man standing in the doorway, a look of bewilderment on his face.

Vicky saw the whole thing and realized the guards had finally caught them together. She had to protect Henry! “Stop!” Her shout caused everyone in the door to hesitate, but only for a second. Matt couldn’t get around Steve, and the man in the doorway took advantage of this by stepping back into the bedroom.

Steve crawled into the room, going right. Matt moved to the right once Steve was out of the way. “Vicky?” Matt asked.

Vicky looked at the armed men dressed in military clothing and panicked. She hurled the small bottle in her hand at the man standing up near the open door; and as she did so, she threw herself off the bed and grabbed Maddox. She forcefully pushed him behind her and defiantly glared at Matt and Steve. Seamus and Gold crouched outside the room and waited. The sound of voices carried down the long hallway.

Matt raised his weapon and tried to smile. “We are friends. We’ve been sent by your dad to find and bring you home. You are Victoria Burnell, correct? Daughter of Tom and Barbara Burnell?”

Vicky’s resolve faltered. Maddox sensed this and whispered in her ear. “They are lying, Vicky. All the guards know the history and names associated with the people they guard. They are not your rescuers. Don’t let them fool you; don’t let them keep us apart!”

Matt picked up on some of the conversation, and he took a step forward. They didn't have time to hang around here; any minute the guards could come looking for their boss. If he had to, he'd knock Vicky out and carry her home. This bullshit had to stop.

"Vicky, don't listen to him. His name is Roger Maddox. He's a human trafficker of the worst kind. He buys and sells girls like you for men who want sex. He's not your friend or your protector. He's a piece of human shit!"

Vicky listened, but wasn't convinced. "Are you a SEAL?"

Matt nodded. "We both are, I mean were. Your dad asked us to help, and we've been searching for over a month, ever since you were abducted in Honolulu."

Seamus peeked around the doorway and saw what was unfolding inside the bedroom. He was concerned. They were wasting time! Matt took another step toward Vicky, and she backed into Maddox as a reflexive action. Maddox placed his hands on her shoulders, only inches from her neck.

Steve moved a few steps into the room on his side and looked at Matt. "I have a shot. Let's kill this fucker, grab her, and get off this island!"

Matt knew Steve was right. But Maddox might be quick enough to move Vicky into the path of a bullet, so they couldn't take the chance. He needed her to separate from the pedophile millionaire. But how?

Vicky's mind was racing. There was something familiar about the intruders speech pattern, the way they stood. The way they communicated through a simple glance. It reminded her of her dad. Could they be telling the truth? Could Henry be a monster?

Vicky started to push away a little, but Maddox held her firmly in place. "I have a question," she said, looking back and forth at the two armed men. "Can you finish the sentence, *the only easy day ... ?"*

In unison Matt and Steve completed the phrase famous throughout the SEAL teams, "*... was yesterday."*

Vicky shook her head even as she slid her right hip out and dropped her torso eight inches. Maddox was unprepared for the left elbow strike to his groin, and he doubled up, releasing his grip on Vicky at the same time. She broke free and ran to the other side of the room, joining Matt and Steve.

Maddox recovered quickly but the sight of two leveled barrels checked his advance. Matt gently pushed Vicky behind him and moved toward Maddox. "You're in deep shit, asshole." Matt growled.

"I say we drop him right now and get the fuck out of here!" Steve hissed.

Matt shook his head. "I want to know everything he knows about his supply chain. Names, locations, methods. There are girls out there somewhere, waiting in some dark hole for the horror this piece of shit promotes. It all ends right here, tonight."

Maddox stood up straight and smiled. He was a business man and what he was listening to sounded like the start of a negotiation. "I don't know who you are or who send you but I can help. I have what you're looking for but first, lower those weapons. The last thing we all need is an accident. Your both excited, stressed out. I suggest we all just relax and work something out that's mutually beneficial."

Matt's lip curled as he listened. Maddox was a human being, not an enemy of the United States and not a convicted criminal. Yet, it was taking all the control he could muster to not put a bullet in the scumbag's tiny brain.

Matt lowered his weapon and pulled out his smart phone. "I want you to tell me everything. If I believe you're feeding me bull shit, you die. If you try to alert your guards, you die. If you so much as twitch and I don't approve, you die. Do we understand each other?"

Maddox eased back a step and sat up against the night stand. He grinned and slowly crossed his arms across his chest. This was a game he knew well. He'd survived the assault, survived the first round of negotiations, and now he was in the driver's seat. These paid thugs were all brawn and no brain. He relaxed.

"I can give you details you seek but I'm not stupid. You'll have to remember the information; I'm not going to give you my recorded confession. Those are my terms take it or leave it."

Matt stepped to his left and pointed at Maddox. "Put one in his right leg."

The popping sound from Steve's pistol caused Vicky to jump. Even a suppressed bullet makes a sound, especially when it's fired right next to you. She watched Maddox clutch his leg just above the knee and grimace in pain, conflicted emotions racing through her mind. He'd never harmed her. Never tried to even touch her. Her instincts told her he wasn't the monster these men claimed. But he'd never denied who he was to these men.

Matt took two steps closer to Maddox. "No yelling, no crying. If you alert the guards my friend here will aim a little higher up your leg next time, if you understand my meaning." Matt held out the smart phone and pressed record. "I want it all. Start talking."

Maddox wasn't listening. The pain was excruciating and his leg throbbed and shook with the trauma of taking the round at near pointblank range. To make things worse the bullet had gone through his leg's soft tissue, passing into the nightstand behind him. Upon impact the wood had exploded sending sharp slinters the size of toothpicks into the back of his other leg. Maddox was angry and scared. Things were getting out of control.

His face told the story. Anguish followed by arrogance. He would tell him anything that came to mind. Old safe houses, old information that no longer mattered. These idiots wouldn't know the difference and it would buy him the time he needed to figure a way out of this dilemma.

Matt watched the change in the other man's face and read the meaning. He closed the distance between them rapidly and swung his right leg in a short but powerful Muay Thai kick that struck Maddox just to the right of the bullet wound. Maddox gasped and doubled over as pain washed over him.

"We are working with powerful people. The FBI is aware of our presence here in Asia and waiting for any information we can provide. Once you provide the details you'll be placed in our protective custody until the FBI and Interpol confirm what you've told us. Fuck around and you end up dead. Play by the rules and, well, at least you won't be dead."

Maddox gritted his teeth. He had to play the long game. If what this thug said was true, he had to give up his network. He needed time. Once in police hands he could bribe his way out of any jail. He just needed time. Besides, he could always rebuild a new supply chain of girls. There were always buyers.

Maddox began to talk. It was all over in ten minutes, Names, places, dates, and details of how the girls were moved around prior to auctioning them off. Matt was pleased. Now, more girls could be saved. Steve moved Vicky away from the door and waited for Matt to signal the interrogation was over. Matt backed up, placing the smart phone back in it's water proof bag.

"We need an exit plan. He can't walk fast so one of us will have to drag him to the beach. Once there, we can swim him out to the boat."

Steve nodded and looked at Vicky. "You ready to leave this place?"

As Vicky began to answer an explosion erupted from the door. Maddox jerked upright, a look of uncomprehending surprise on his face. A red stain started to spread down his shirt, starting just above the collar. Seamus's shot had entered the pedophile's neck, just below the trachea. Not an immediate kill shot, but respectable for a former pilot.

Matt swiveled his weapon around, expecting to engage a guard, but what he saw was Seamus standing in the doorway holding a pistol.

"What the …? Why?"

Seamus stared at Maddox, a subtle smile on his face. "For Blue. You didn't think I came all this way to let you kill him, did you?"

A series of three pops interrupted their conversation as Steve pumped three well-placed bullets into Roger Maddox's diseased and evil brain. Maddox flipped backward and hit the bedroom wall before slowly sliding down into a pile next to the nightstand. He twitched, but there was no doubt he was dead.

"What the hell did you do that for?" Matt demanded.

“It was time for us to haul ass. He was going to die anyway.” Steve responded.

Matt sighed. Steve was right. It was the right tactical call. Maddox had been as good as dead already. He extended his hand to Vicky. “Come on! We need to get the hell out of here!”

The sound of footsteps coming down the hallway indicated to Matt that time was up. It was going to be a gunfight, and they were outnumbered. Gold charged down the hallway and opened up with the AK, dropping two surprised bodyguards. The report of the heavy caliber assault rifle was deafening. Steve jumped past Seamus and sprinted after Gold, taking out a third bodyguard who’d stumbled into the hallway and the scene of carnage it was becoming.

“Go, Go, GO!” Matt yelled, holding Vicky’s hand but keeping her behind him. Steve and Gold arrived at the intersection and Matt yelled again, “LEFT!”

Steve and Gold burst out onto the porch and waited for the rest of the team to catch up. Seamus now was acting as rear security, his AK up and ready. Steve surveyed the grounds and made a command decision. The shortest distance between two points was a straight line. They were heading straight for the beach extract site.

The group sprinted across the large grassy area; and as they reached the trees, a shot rang out from the house. “Everybody okay? No one hit?” Matt whispered.

The group huddled in the first few feet of foliage and waited. Matt watched the estate and looked for pursuit, but after sixty seconds he realized there wasn’t any pursuit. “Move fast, Steve. We need to get in the water!”

“Don’t have to say it twice, boss. Let’s move!”

The long series of flights were debilitating, but the feeling of personal satisfaction was welcome. He'd been a mess when Tom first asked for his help. A loser and almost a PTSD statistic. The rescue had been difficult, but it also had been enlightening. He wasn't sure he could return to his old existence in Key West. A few weeks earlier, on a whim, he'd asked Jackson if he could find someone given just a name. Jackson had laughed. That's what the Bollinger Group did, he had said. Matt gave him a name and then forgot about the request.

Vicky sat quietly next to him, sleeping off the effects of a long and terrible adventure. Miraculously she'd survived untouched. She'd likely require counseling for the mental trauma, but she was strong. Matt knew she would recover. He returned to thoughts of his future. What would he do now?

He checked his watch. They would be landing in Detroit in less than thirty minutes. Barbara and Tom emailed Matt and said they would be there to get Vicky. Tom had extended an invitation to stay with them for a while, but Matt had declined.

He was catching a connecting flight, Virginia Beach. Jackson had found Sherry, divorced and living in the same neighborhood she'd lived in all those years ago when Matt was a young officer in search of glory.

He knew there had been a deeper connection between them, and he hoped that feeling was still there for her, too. He'd keep his act clean and see how it went. One thing was for sure, he was back on the road to sanity and he owed it all to a request to help a fellow SEAL in need. He owed it to the legacy and power of the brotherhood.

THE END

Made in the USA
Columbia, SC
02 October 2021